WITCH HUNT

By

Leanne Karella
Vivienne King

Paranormal Romance

New Concepts Georgia

Be sure to check out our website for the very best in fiction at fantastic prices!

When you visit our webpage, you can:
* Read excerpts of currently available books
* View cover art of upcoming books and current releases
* Find out more about the talented artists who capture the magic of the writer's imagination on the covers
* Order books from our backlist
* Find out the latest NCP and author news--including any upcoming book signings by your favorite NCP author
* Read author bios and reviews of our books
* Get NCP submission guidelines
* And so much more!

We offer a 20% discount on all new Trade Paperback releases ordered from our website!

Be sure to visit our webpage to find the best deals in e-books and paperbacks! To find out about our new releases as soon as they are available, please be sure to sign up for our newsletter (http://www.newconceptspublishing.com/newsletter.htm) or join our reader group (http://groups.yahoo.com/group/new_concepts_pub/join)!

The newsletter is available by double opt in only and our customer information is *never* shared!

Visit our webpage at:
www.newconceptspublishing.com

Witch Hunt is an original publication of NCP. This work has never before appeared in book form. This work is a novel. Any similarity to actual persons or events is purely coincidental.

New Concepts Publishing, Inc.
5202 Humphreys Rd.
Lake Park, GA 31636

ISBN 1-58608-879-3
© 2006 Leanne Karella & Vivienne King
Cover art (c) copyright 2006 Dan Skinner

All rights reserved, which includes the right to reproduce this book or portions thereof in any form whatsoever except as provided by the U.S. Copyright Law.

If you purchased this book without a cover you should be aware this book is stolen property.

NCP books are available at special quantity discounts for bulk purchases for sales promotions, premiums, fund raising, or educational use. For details, write, email, or phone New Concepts Publishing, Inc., 5202 Humphreys Rd., Lake Park, GA 31636; Ph. 229-257-0367, Fax 229-219-1097; orders@newconceptspublishing.com.

First NCP Trade Paperback Printing: September 2006

Prologue

From the Journal of Lina Brennen:
When I was a child, all I dreamed about was being normal. And now that I'm adult? Yeah, that's still my biggest dream.

* * * *

"Well, Granna, it's time to move on again. The villagers are getting restless. If I don't leave now, they'll be coming after me with pitchforks and sickles."

"Oh, sweetling, this is the twenty-first century. You know they don't do that kind of thing anymore."

After laying another neatly folded pair of slacks into her suitcase, Lina turned toward the chair in the corner of the bedroom to send a good old-fashioned glare at her great-great-grandmother, Merona. Granna's ghostly aura was extra bright today; she was happy they'd be moving on. They'd stayed in Chicago for nearly a year, and Merona had been getting restless. She'd said there was nothing to accomplish in this "barbarous city." She'd used that very term for nearly every big city they'd stayed in.

"How many towns were you chased out of that way?" Lina asked as she went to the closet. She scooped up all the hangers at once and dumped them on the bed to start folding.

"Only a few. Most of the time I left before anyone caught on." Her aura seemed to brighten even more as her sweet round face broke into a cherub-like grin. "You're just so determined to help everyone. When you do that, it's easier to get caught."

Lina wanted to throw all the clothing into the bag without folding it. She hated packing. She hated moving. She just wanted some place to call her own. She'd been on the move for the past fifteen years, and it was getting old. "Jane said I should do what I need to do. Do you think I should have let that little girl suffer when I could help her?"

"Jane was a do-gooder, and you know it." Though Merona's words seemed harsh, Lina knew better. Merona had been proud of her granddaughter, Jane. Just as Lina knew that Merona was proud of her.

The phone rang. It had been ringing non-stop for three days now. Newspaper reporters, television reporters, curiosity seekers. It had happened before. Lina was sure it would happen again in the future.

She felt like crying. She felt like raging against this ... this thing she had.

"You are upset."

Well, duh. Why wouldn't she be upset? She'd made it almost a full year without the attention, without the shocked gasps, without the fearful glances thrown at her. She'd found a job in a private school, working in the office. It had been a dream fulfilled. She could be around the children but not have close contact with them. She could watch them from afar, dream her dreams. Oh, how she longed for a child of her own!

But that was not to be.

To have a child of her own, she needed a man of her own. The man. Like she'd ever find him.

Merona's pale face wrinkled into a frown as she rose from her post in the corner of the room and came toward the bed. "What is floating around in that head of yours, child?"

Lina scowled at Merona as she stuffed the corners of her suitcase haphazardly with T-shirts to fill in the space. "Oh, Granna." Lina sighed as she threw down the shirt she'd wadded into a ball and turned toward the window, folding her arms around herself for comfort. She so wanted someone else's arms around her. Anyone's. Someone to make her feel ... "I want a home, Granna. A home and a husband and a child of my very own. Why can't I have one? You did. Granna Jane did. Why am I so different?"

Lina felt the cool brush of air on her hair and knew Merona was trying to comfort her. "You will have all your wishes fulfilled, my darling child. In your own time. You cannot rush true love. It must find you. And then, my sweet Lina, all your dreams will come true."

Granna Merona had been saying those same words to her all of her adult life. At thirty-two, she was beginning to doubt them.

"Now, sweetling, it is time to dig out that great map of yours and let us find a new place." Merona sat down on the edge of the bed. "A small town this time. This place is ridiculously cold and windy. The weather makes the inhabitants bitchy."

"Small town," Lina mumbled. They'd tried that before. The townsfolk had almost come after her with the pitchforks and sickles. She gave a sigh, pulled the atlas from the top shelf of the closet, and flung it carelessly on the bed next to Merona. "You pick this time, Granna."

With a glittering chuckle, Merona waved her fingers at the atlas and the pages fluttered open. "We've never been to Arizona before."

Arizona it is.

Chapter One

From the journal of Lina Brennen:
My life has been an unending journey of beginnings. Over and over I've started from scratch. New town, new place to live, new job, new life. Just for once, would it be possible find something permanent? Happily ever after can't only be in the storybooks. I want mine.

A home of my own. Two point three kids. White picket fence. And a man with sparkling eyes, a charming smile, and a voice to make a woman melt.

* * * *

Lina clicked on the stereo in her '91 Ford Escort, about the only thing in the car that still ran with no problems. Saguaro cacti and red rock flashed by her windshield in a kaleidoscope of desert scenery. A mirage of water shimmered just above the melting blacktop road.

The closer she got to the borders of Mexico, the more Tejano music she was forced to listen to. The romantic melodies of the Spanish guitar filled the car. She wrinkled her nose and switched the station. Tejano music was something she could only take in spurts.

A grin spread across her face and her hand stilled when the sultry sound of Marvin Gaye crooned in her ear. She shifted in her seat, singing along to Sexual Healing.

"I want sexual heal ... ing." Throaty laughter spilled from her lips at the sound of her voice breaking. "Oh, jeez, maybe I need to think about not singing."

"Yes, child. I think that might be a good idea." Merona stuck a finger in her ear and grimaced.

Lina narrowed her eyes and stuck out her tongue. "Always a critic."

"No, I just believe in brutal honesty." Her wide blue eyes sparkled with mischief.

"Gee, thanks, Granna." She smiled and shook her head. "So, you suggested Arizona. We're here. What now?" Lina ran her hand across her forehead, wiping away the beads of sweat prickling uncomfortably on her brow. The soft sound of her tinkling golden bracelets jangled with the movement.

"I'm glad I'm a spirit. You look like you're suffering." Merona's words came out half sympathetic, half teasing.

"Thanks for stating the obvious." She rolled her eyes.

The air conditioning had stopped working. Again. Forcing Lina to roll down the windows. The hot, dry air punched her in the nostrils. She exhaled forcibly.

Lina squirmed to the left, but her thighs didn't follow. She might as well have been super glued to the seat. Her brows scrunched together, and her mouth twisted with disgust.

"Pick a place, Gran. I can't take the heat. I can't take driving in this any longer."

Merona turned and stared out the window. Lina flashed her grandmother a look. She could practically hear the woman's mind clicking with thought. A green highway sign came into view.

Merona cocked her head, her golden aura pulsed brightly, and a grin spread like butter across her gentle features.

"Unegi, Arizona. Ten miles. I like that. My soul likes that." She nodded and shot Lina a look. "That's it. That's our stop."

"Unegi? What kind of name is that? Are you sure, Granna?" Lina honked her horn at a passing SUV.

Merona's eyes widened. "Why did you honk?"

She shrugged. "His bumper sticker said, 'Honk if you love whales.' So, I honked. Boredom made me do it. Anyhow, why Unegi?"

The turnoff ramp was rapidly approaching, and she wanted Merona's answer before she took that leap of faith.

Her stomach twisted in knots, wondering for the millionth time if maybe, just maybe, this would be her last move. Ever. She'd always dreamed it would happen someday, that she'd never have to pack up again, but that was a fading hope. This made her fifteenth move in seventeen years. And she was only thirty-two. At age seven, she'd come into her powers. That's when her life had become one big move after another.

She cringed at the thought. Powers. I'd give them all up in a heartbeat if I could.

All she'd gained for these so called powers was an inability to trust people, and a loss of her innocence. Damn it all to hell, why? She ground her jaw. Why? Why couldn't she just be normal? She should have three kids by now, a husband and that white picket fence, instead of having to run from state to state like a felon.

Lost in her daydreams, Lina took the turn, finally realizing her grandmother had yet to answer.

"Granna, why haven't you answered me?"

Merona studied her nails and whispered, "It means ugly in one of the many Native American languages."

"What?" Lina slammed on the breaks. The luggage in the back seat and a half eaten bag of chips went flying through the air. "No! No way. You know how I am about signs."

Her grandmother threw her arms up in the air. "Exactly! That's why I didn't tell you. You and your silly signs. Lina," Merona pointed to her chest, "you're going to have to trust me on this. Sometimes the heart knows what the mind does not."

Lina lifted a brow and shook her head. She spotted a gas station to the left. "Absolutely not. I didn't leave Chicago for a town called Ugly. We're going to fill up with gas, and you're going to choose a different place to stop."

Merona pressed her lips tight.

Lina rubbed her temple, a rising throb of a pain building behind her eyes. She turned on her blinker and headed toward the Chevron.

What was her grandmother thinking?

A bright red pickup and a police cruiser were parked in front of the otherwise deserted gas station and mini-mart.

She snorted, imagining an overweight, doughnut-eating, coffee-drinking cop making his morning rounds. Lina glanced at her watch. Although, it was way past noon. Maybe they ate doughnuts all day. She shrugged. Didn't matter to her. She'd be out of this town, pronto!

Lina sighed and took off her seatbelt. "Granna, don't do anything, oh, I don't know,"--she waved her hands through the air dramatically--"ghostly."

Merona lifted a white brow, her smooth skin tightening into a fierce scowl. "Such as?"

"Don't scare the humans. I'm just going to fill the gas and come back. I love you, Granna. Don't be mad at me." She lifted the corner of her lips into a semi-smile.

"I love you too, sweetling. But we're not leaving."

Lina shook her head. "Whatever you say, Granna." Better to keep Merona happy than to argue a moot point. Lina, after all, was the driver.

She opened the door as dust devils twirled and danced in the distance. The arid landscape was foreboding and unappealing. How could she possibly be happy here? No. Best to move on.

Lina started to stand when her grandmother's cold fingers flitted across her neck in a gentle caress. She turned around.

"Your destiny awaits you. Mind that first step."

Lina's brows drew together and she blinked. "What?"

Merona just smiled.

She shook her head and exited the vehicle. The wind shrieked around her, and her hair whipped against her cheeks, stinging her eyes. Lina frowned, thinking of Merona's words. Her grandmother was wise, very wise. Usually there was some meaning behind her cryptic remarks if Lina took the time to consider them. But she wasn't in the mood right now, and she wanted out of the wailing wind.

She opened her tank and placed the pump in. The price of gas was astronomical. "Friggin' gas prices. What do they think, we're rich or something?" Thank goodness she drove a little car or she'd be completely broke before she found a place to live.

Once it finished pumping, she grabbed her purse from the back seat and ran toward the building, her head bent low to keep the flying dirt out of her eyes. As she pushed on the door, she tripped over the half step and threw out her arms to prevent her fall.

"Oh!" She braced herself for the impact but fell, instead, into the rock-hard arms of a rescuer.

She grabbed a hold of blue sleeves to steady herself, bunching the fabric. Gradually her eyes traveled the length of the arms. They were big. Really big, and muscular. She gulped.

"You okay?" A deep-timbred voice resonated through her veins. She shivered and gave a tiny nod. Her mouth suddenly dry.

She stared at his chest. The shirt stretched across well-formed pecs. Her skin prickled. Lina licked her lips and gazed up into the bluest eyes she'd ever seen. They were royal blue, like the sky at sunrise. Black as pitch hair framed his chiseled, heart-stopping face.

That face broke into a grin, his straight white teeth flashing brilliantly against the deep, natural tan of his Native American skin, and she gave a tiny start.

"You gonna just stare at me all day?" He chuckled.

She blinked, heat crept up her neck, and she backed out of his arms. "Oh jeez." She laid her hand against her forehead, her bracelets jangling loudly. "I'm so sorry. I'm such a klutz."

"Hi, Klutz. I'm Sheriff Trent Godfrey. I don't recall ever seeing you around." He stuck out a large, tanned hand. A well-formed hand. Oh hell, she thought, what isn't well formed about this one?

She grinned, the tight knot of nerves slowly unwinding in her gut, and she took his hand in hers. A shock of awareness slid up her arm like an arc of electricity.

His eyes widened a bit. Had he felt it, too? And what was it, exactly, that she'd just felt? This couldn't be normal.

"Stop botherin' that pretty little thing and let her pay for her gas."

Lina forced her gaze from the Sheriff to study the woman behind the counter. Her gray hair was pulled back in a fluffy bun, and she wore loads of sparkly blue eye shadow. Her lips were a deep coral.

Trent leaned down and whispered, "She's one of the town's busybodies. Good ol' gal." Lina inhaled his spicy scent of sage, wood, and leather. Then he winked at her, and her heart nearly stopped altogether.

He turned away. "All right, Louise, she's coming. Just keep those britches on."

What the hell was happening to her? Lina looked for an escape, but the only way out was through the front door, and she still had to pay for her gas. Her emotions were out of control. She hated being out of control. That's what kept her one step ahead of the pitchforks and sickles. That instinct had saved her hide more than once.

"Well, thanks for the timely rescue," Lina said as she dug in her purse for money.

Trent turned, his blue eyes blazing with ... something. Something she'd never seen in a man's eyes before. Heat. Humor. Maybe a little lust? Her skin tightened as flashes of his naked form sliding along her slick skin exploded in her mind.

"I've yet to hear your name, klutz." He grinned, his square jaw begging for a kiss.

"Le ... Lina." She stammered, unable to get the image of his body out of her mind.

He took the hand she held against her cheek into his. His thumb slid along her knuckles. "That's a beautiful name, LeLina."

She let out a breathy chuckle, only too aware of his flesh against hers.

"You just passing through?"

"Staying," she whispered. Then her eyes widened and she wondered what she'd just done. This wasn't good. Every brain cell she possessed had gone on vacation the moment she stumbled into the sheriff's arms.

He stroked the inside of her wrist, and she shivered.

"Do you know where you're gonna stay?" His peppermint breath caressed her cheek.

"No."

"Perfect." His smile widened. "I've got the perfect place." Two large strides took him to the counter. She stared after him in bewilderment.

"Louise, can I borrow a piece of paper and a pen?"

Louise rolled her eyes. "Do you know how much you look like an excited puppy?" She directed her warm brown gaze to Lina. "Watch this one here, he's a heartbreaker." She handed Trent a pad and pencil.

Lina shifted from foot to foot. Why was she doing this? She could still turn around and leave. So why was the thought too painful to even contemplate? This wasn't normal. Granna's words rang in her ears. Your destiny awaits you ... That wily woman knew something, Lina was sure of it.

The scratching sound of the pencil stopped and Trent turned, a white sheet of paper in his hand. Damn, he was one fine looking man. Lina Brennen was not a woman who fell at men's feet. But she could easily see herself at this one's feet.

"I've got a wonderful place for you...." His smile dissolved and one black eyebrow arched, "...and your husband?"

She snorted. "Nope, don't have one of those."

"Child?"

"Nu-uh, that either." That all too common twinge of sadness bit into her.

His grin returned, the wattage of the smile nearly blinding. Nice straight teeth, she noticed once again.

Louise's big belly laugh broke the silence. "Why don't you just ask her out, son?"

"Give me time." Trent shoved a hand through his hair and gave her a crooked grin. He spoke the words as if for her ears alone.

A warm glow flowed through her.

"Anyhow." He shrugged and handed her the sheet of paper. "Give me an hour so I can fix it up a little, and I'll show you the apartment."

She took the paper and shoved it into her shorts pocket.

He bit his bottom lip, an endearing trait she found charming. His warm hand trailed down her bare arm. "Okay, see you then."

"Yeah."

He exited and that's when it dawned on her how easily she'd given into him. Perplexed and dazed, she went to the counter.

Louise looked out the window. "Don't worry about him, honey. He has that effect on all the girls. He's been trying to rent that apartment for ages."

Lina knew she'd meant the words as consolation, but her heart twisted in response. That was even worse. Was she so hard up to meet a man that the first one she ran into turned her into a blathering idiot? She gritted her teeth. No way! She had a mind of her own and wasn't going to capitulate to him so easily next time.

She grabbed a candy bar and thwacked it down on the counter.

"Give me that, too."

Louise chuckled. "Oh, yeah. You fell under the Godfrey charm."

Lina paid and left. She tore open the wrapping of her Butterfinger and slid into the car.

Merona grinned. "Fine looking man, that one." She fanned herself and leered suggestively as Trent drove away in the police cruiser. "Get that tickle down in your, um, spine, did you?"

She shot her grandmother a droll look and took a big bite of her candy bar. "What the heck happened to me in there?"

"It was meant to be. I told you we were staying."

"Yeah, yeah." Merona was hiding something, and Lina aimed to find out what it was.

* * * *

Trent pulled away from the gas station and wondered what had come over him. He'd just made a colossal fool of himself in front of a slip of a girl with the coordination of a hatchling. What was she doing in Unegi? And why would she want to stay?

He ran a nervous hand through his hair. He needed a haircut. What had come over him? The instant her compact body had tumbled into his, a strong yearning had set up residence in the pit of his stomach. When she'd looked so shocked at her clumsiness, he'd wanted to wrap his arms around her and hug her. Hug her. For crying out loud!

She kinda looked like a flake, with the jangling gold bracelets and that silky next-to-nothing blouse of an odd shade of purple. And the earrings. They looked like small hubcaps. He shook his head. And now he'd offered her the apartment above the sheriff's office. Just what he needed. A gray-eyed blonde that made his blood heat to an unbearable pitch.

Maybe she had family in the area. He gave a snort as he pulled his car into the back parking lot at the sheriff's office. He knew everyone in this tiny backwater town. He'd grown up here and had only been gone for a few short years when he lived in Phoenix. No one he knew was related to anyone like her.

* * * *

"No way, Granna!" Lina yelped as they drove into the town--and that was using the word lightly--of Unegi. There was Main Street, the road they were on that ran through the center of what looked like a set for a B-rated western movie. The buildings were weathered and the signs faded. There were a few off-shooting roads, all dirt, that led to some rather less than auspicious looking houses.

"It's not so bad," Merona commented. Her head turned from side to side as she took in the dilapidated buildings. "Kind of charming, really. Look, there's the sheriff's office. And look at that quirky little café. How cute. The Tumbleweed Diner." Merona pointed.

"Yeah. Cute." Lina pulled up in front of the sheriff's office and shut off the car. The number on the door of the building matched the one on the paper Trent had given her. What? Was he renting out a jail cell as an apartment?

"Don't look so down. This is the place for you. Trust me." Merona waited until Lina had exited the car before floating out after her. At least Granna didn't open her door anymore. A few times of getting very strange looks and Lina had put a stop to that.

"Granna, how many times have you said those words to me? You always want me to trust you, and look where it's gotten me." Her gaze roamed over the shops along Main Street. "I'm waiting for John Wayne to come riding up on a horse and draw his side iron."

"Silly," Merona chided. "I told you the Duke is living happily in the body of a twenty-two year old computer whiz in Silicon Valley."

A bubble of laughter broke through, disintegrating Lina's anger at being stuck in this place. "Really, Granna. And where is Clark Gable?"

"I suppose he's still buried right where they put him."

Lina yelped and swung around to bump right into Sheriff Trent.

Trent laughed and took Lina's hand in his. Why does he keep touching me? She tried to pull away, but he held her in a seductively firm grip. "You always stand on the sidewalk talking to yourself?"

"Yes," she said a bit more forcefully than she'd meant. "It's my favorite pastime." She glanced up and down the empty street. "Besides, I don't think there's anything else to do here."

Trent raised a raven's wing eyebrow at her. "I thought you said you were staying."

"Yes. Well. I, uh ... that is...." She tugged on her hand, and he finally released her. "I might have made a mistake."

Trent nibbled at his full lower lip and squinted up at the sky. "I guess there's not much here for someone like yourself. I noticed your Illinois plates. City girl, aren't'cha?" He rubbed his long, blunt fingers over his darkly stubbled jaw. "We don't get many people around these parts that stay more than a short spell."

"There'd really be no point. I need a job, and it doesn't look like there's much in the offering."

That sparkling grin split Trent's face, and Lina's heart went to thumping. "Well, a job I can help you with. The Tumbleweed's looking for a full-time waitress."

"That's very kind of you, but unless you're doing the hiring, I probably wouldn't get the job. I've never waited tables in my life."

"Come on." Trent grabbed her hand again and all but dragged her down the sidewalk. "My mom owns the place. She's hard up for help. If you can lift a tray and keep from dumping it on the floor, she'll hire you."

Chapter Two

From the Journal of Lina Brennen:
Granna said life takes some strange twists and turns. What you have to do is listen to your heart. My heart hasn't spoken to me in more years than I can remember. If it did speak now, I don't think I'd even know what it was saying.

* * * *

Trent pulled open the glass door of The Tumbleweed Diner and breathed in the air-conditioned coolness spiked with the scent of the deep-fat fryer and sizzling burgers. A warm hum of low-current electricity rode up his arm from the hand holding onto LeLina. Damn if he didn't like the feeling. Damn if he didn't want to know if there was more to it than an awareness he hadn't felt in more years than he could remember.

"Hey, Mom," he called as he pulled LeLina up next to him. "I found you a new waitress."

Abigail Godfrey turned around from where she'd been filling a cup of coffee. "You did, did you?" She smiled. He loved his mother's smile, always so warm and loving. He never had to question her loyalties. "You know, you can't just drag some poor woman off the street and force her to work here, Trent."

He chuckled. "Mom, meet LeLina ... uh...." Jeez, he'd totally lost it. He wanted to rent this woman an apartment and set her up working for his mother, and he didn't even know her last name. LeLina pulled her hand from his grip--he probably shouldn't have still been clinging to her, anyway--and stepped forward. "Actually it's just Lina," she said, reaching over the low counter, holding her hand out to his mother. Her voice was cool, smooth, and sexy as sin. "Lina Brennen."

He shivered and swung around at the touch of icy fingers tickling the back of his neck. No one was behind him.

"Nice to meet you, Lina. I'm Abigail Godfrey." His mother shook hands with Lina as Trent rubbed the back of his neck to dispel the disturbing sensation prickling his skin.

"Mrs. Godfrey," Lina said and smiled. God, she had a pretty smile, Trent thought. Her teeth weren't quite straight, and her eyes tended to crinkle a bit. She was as cute as anything he'd ever seen in his forty-two years.

"Call me Abby," she said as she set a cup of coffee in front of the one man at the counter. "So, where did the boy find you?"

* * * *

Lina cast a glance back at Trent to see his strained expression. Granna stood just behind him, blowing on his neck, of all stupid things! Damn it, Gran, leave him alone!

"He can feel me." Granna chuckled. "Not often can they actually feel me. This is fun."

Lina ground her teeth and glared as hard as she could. Merona could hear her telepathically, she just refused to listen. She moved next to Trent, stepping between him and Merona.

"Lina?"

The heat of a blush started to rise up her neck, and she cursed her fair skin. She cleared her throat. "I'm sorry. What was it you asked?"

Abby sent her son a worried glance then zeroed her gaze back to Lina. "I asked where Trent picked you up. He's always trying to find help for me,"--she laughed--"but they don't stick around very long."

The woman was strikingly beautiful, and didn't look anywhere old enough to be Trent's mother. Trent had to be close to forty, but this woman looked more like a sister, not a mother. Her sun-kissed, Native American skin was flawless. Her black hair, just like Trent's, hadn't one bit of gray in it. And the blue eyes....

Lina shook her head. "I kinda bumped into him at the gas station."

Trent sucked in his breath and took a step to the side. When Lina looked, he was rubbing his big, dark hand over his ribs.

I'm warning you Granna!

Merona cackled. "He's so cute, isn't he?"

"Order up."

Abby turned toward the order window and lifted a huge plate, mounded with sizzling fries and a big, juicy burger. Lina's stomach growled.

Trent's lips quirked as he glanced down at her. "Hungry?"

Blasted blushes. Lina just nodded. How embarrassing. She wanted to turn around, run out the door, get into her ancient little car, and get the hell out of Dodge. But she didn't ... She glanced up at Trent's smiling mouth. Wow. What sexy lips he has. She didn't want to leave yet. There was something about this guy--

"There sure is something about this guy," Merona said, cutting into her thoughts. "He's sexy."

"Granna...."

"Pardon me?" Trent said, that one eyebrow lifting.

Shit!

"Uh ... Yeah ... Hungry." Lina slipped onto one of the eight stools lining the counter. "That burger looks good," she said to Abby when she moved in front of her. "I think I'll take one. And a diet cola."

"Sure thing, honey," Abby said with a grin, but sent Trent another worried glance.

"She thinks you're loony," Merona said as she floated onto the stool next to her.

Shut up.

"I think it's funny. You have the studman there who can feel me, and his mother thinks you're the one who's short a few screws."

Shut up. Lina buried her face in her hand. Sometimes she wished Granna was visible to others. How many times had people given her "that look" when she spoke aloud to her?

"Mind if I join you?"

Lina glanced up at Trent standing over her. Every time she laid eyes on the guy, he just seemed better and better. Jeez.

She shook her head and Trent sat down. Right on Merona. Lina clasped her hand over her mouth to hide her smile. Goose bumps visibly popped out on Trent's dark arms. He shivered.

Merona huffed and glided to the next stool. "That was rude of him."

Lina turned her face away from Trent who was rubbing his arms and looking cutely confused.

"Mom," he said. "I think you've got the air conditioning a bit high, don't you?"

Lina snorted and nearly fell off her stool. Okay, so it was funny how he reacted to Merona. Rarely did this happen. Most people were too emotionally closed off to experience a spirit. Trent was ... special.

* * * *

Trent narrowed his eyes at Lina. Her cheeks were flushed and her shoulders shook with suppressed laughter. And those gorgeous dove-gray eyes sparkled with humor. What was wrong with her?

He gave her a crooked smile, wondering if she were sane at all. "Anything you'd like to share with me, Lina?" Trent whispered in her ear, not wanting to give his mother any more fuel for the fire.

Lina arched a golden brow and gave him a sideways glance. "Not really." She bit her bottom lip between her teeth, wrinkled her nose, and shook her head. "Sorry, this heat's making me a little on the silly side today."

She leaned back and pulled her fall-wheat-colored hair into a haphazard ponytail, tiny tendrils curled around her cheeks. She reminded him of a cheerleader he once dated in high school.

"So," she said, "how about we start over?"

He nodded, more than a little intrigued by this mysterious woman.

Lina stuck out her hand. "I'm Lina and new in town. Tell me a little about yourself."

Eccentric. Vivacious. Perfect.

The pluckings of a long-dead emotion centered itself in his chest.

"Trent Godfrey, town sheriff."

* * * *

"So are you and your mother both Native American?" Lina asked around a bite of burger. Ketchup dribbled onto the white porcelain plate.

"Hmm," Trent nodded. Grabbing the last curly fry off his plate, he dipped it into her ketchup then shoved the fry in his mouth, chewing quickly. He sighed and leaned back in his chair, not making eye contact with her. "Most everyone in this town has roots, one way or another. Why do you ask?"

Lina swallowed, took a sip of her cola, and leaned back. Her stomach bulged a bit painfully, but at least she was satiated. "Your hair and skin. Dead giveaway. I used to live in South Dakota at one time. Lots of Sioux up that way. Became friendly with a few and went to several powwows."

Intrigued by his native roots, she wondered what he would think of her grandmother. After all, a huge part of Native faith centered on spirits and the afterlife.

"Do you practice the old ways?"

Trent's jaw flexed. "Old ways?"

Lina frowned. Had she said something wrong? A nervous stammer crept into her voice. "You know, the ... the old Indian ways. Praying to the ... spirits of your ancestors." With each of her words, she noticed his shoulders tensing, his back going ramrod stiff.

Merona's eyes widened, her aura dimmed to a distinct pewter color and flickered rapidly with her distress. Something Lina had rarely seen.

Trent took a slow sip of his root beer. The tension in the air was suddenly very palpable, like a taut string on a fiddle before it snaps. Lina swallowed and drummed her fingers on the countertop, her bracelets tinkling with the movement.

"Spirits," he began, "and the old ways, died a long time ago." His voice was low and methodical, though his words conveyed a depth of emotion she couldn't begin to comprehend. He was angry, of that she had no doubt.

Lina shivered. Then Trent inhaled and gave her a tight, grim smile. "Anyhow, let's talk about something else." His black mood lifted as quickly as it had come.

She could tell he wanted to put this particular conversation behind them, so she went along with it for the time being. But in the back of her mind, she wondered, and feared that she'd never meet a man able to understand and accept her for what she really was.

"So, you move a lot?" he asked.

What in the world would make him ask such a question? Lina licked her lips. Now they were treading on dangerous territory for her. She shrugged and affected a nonchalant attitude and gave the same answer she always gave to this question. "Not really. This is only my third move." Yeah, and cows can fly. She nearly snorted aloud. If only he knew.

Abby wiped down the counter as the lone diner shuffled up to the register. He shoved his hand into the back pocket of his grease-stained coveralls and withdrew his wallet. "Same time again tomorrow, Ms. Abby?" The accent seemed strangely out of place, twangy, with a Southern drawl.

Trent leaned in, his warm breath caressing her earlobe just moments before he spoke, sending a wave of tingles arcing down her arms. "That's Willy."

She turned to stare at him, entranced by his full, firm lips. His presence was electrifying. Even the hairs on her arms stood on end. Though Mr. Sheriff may not believe in magic, there was something very magical about him. She would ask Merona later. Granna would know the mystery of this riddle, or at least she hoped so. She rubbed her arms.

"He's the local mechanic in town and comes in like clockwork everyday...." His deep voice surrounded her. Lina heard him speaking, but it seemed so far away. And she couldn't make out much of what he was saying.

Trent's tanned hand brushed down the front of his blue button-up shirt. Lina's gaze was riveted by the movement. An image of those hands sliding up her skirt and pushing down her shirt made her nearly groan. She ground her teeth.

Why couldn't she resist him? She'd never reacted this way with any other man. The fact that she was thinking this way about a total stranger was both appalling and frustrating, and ever so slightly intriguing.

"...I'm sure of it. Wouldn't you agree?"

Her eyes widened and she jumped, only now realizing he'd asked her a question. What was she supposed to agree to?

Merona covered her mouth with her hand and let out a soft giggle. "Just go with the flow, sweetling. Let this happen naturally, the way it's supposed to, and stop fighting it."

Oh, hush, Granna. And stop reading my mind. I've told you before how much I hate that.

Trent shifted in his seat and glanced around the nearly empty diner.

"Did he hear me?" Merona asked, her eyes widening with speculation.

Trent frowned and turned his head, then shrugged.

Lina's heart skipped a beat. Was it possible? No way. Only a handful of people had the ability to commune with the dead.

Trent waved a hand in front of her face, breaking her eye contact with Merona. "Are you okay, Lina? This makes about the third time you've spaced out on me." His intense blue eyes studied her, a frown marring his hard features.

She forked a hand through her hair and expelled a long breath. "Truth is, I'm a little tired. It was a long drive and I probably need to see that apartment of yours before I collapse from utter exhaustion."

And before you make me look any more foolish to these people, Granna.

Bah! Merona waved a hand through the air and then glided toward Abby and Willy who were talking to one another.

Trent stood. "I left the keys in the car. I'll get them. You stay here in the air conditioning a bit longer." He patted her arm in a friendly manner, but the touch sizzled, branding her and imprinting him deeper into her heart. This was a man a girl couldn't easily forget with a few vodkas and Bob Dylan tunes.

Trent walked out of the diner, the bell above the door jangling with his departure.

Her blood roared in her ears, drowning out all other noises. Something was about to happen. Something bad. She always sensed it right before her skills would be needed. Lina's gaze roamed frantically around the room, searching for a clue, anything to indicate what was going to happen. Her heart rate spiked, chills raced down her back, and she broke out in a cold sweat.

Merona zipped from listening in on Abby and Willy's conversation to her side and laid a chilling hand on her forehead. "Sweetling, what's wrong?"

Lina grabbed her chest. "I dunno...."

Abby turned her head. "You say something, Lina?" Her gentle voice was soothing but didn't help to alleviate the pressure building in Lina's skull.

She jumped to her feet and walked toward the wall of windows facing the street. Whatever it was that was going to happen, was going to happen soon. Very soon.

Then she heard it. The dull roar of a souped up motor, speeding down the road. Lina narrowed her eyes, her heart pounding painfully against her chest. A black cat licked its paw, its bright pink tongue sliding along its shiny fur in a rhythmic motion. The cat stretched and sat up, and that's when Lina noticed that its belly was unnaturally large. She was pregnant.

She bit her lip, watching it all happen. The cat jumped off the sidewalk. The tan truck, kicking up dust, never wavered and ran headlong into the sleek feline, crushing it.

The driver of the truck never even slowed.

Lina let out a yelp and flung open the door. Hot tears streamed down her face.

"Wait, honey," Abby yelled, but she was mindless to get to the cat.

Lina knelt on the scorching blacktop and cradled the broken body of the bleeding cat in her lap. Its legs were flattened, and a huge laceration had ripped open one of the haunches. The cat's mouth hung open. It panted shallowly for air.

Merona settled by Lina and bowed her head. Her golden aura flared brightly. A tingle shot through Lina's veins, her fingertips became warm, then hot, until they glowed with a soft white light.

Lina's tears dripped into the feline's wounds. She touched the cat, trailing her fingertips over the breaks and abrasions. The pink tissue gathered, reforming. The bones popped and snapped back into place, the cat let out a piercing scream. Then gray flesh covered the pink, and a bald patch of skin lay exposed.

"Lina, stop," Merona whispered. "The sheriff is headed our way."

She glanced up to see Trent stalking toward them, a scowl on his face. Indecision warred within her. She could heal the cat fully, but it wouldn't be realistic. After all, she hadn't been the only one to see it get run over. The best thing would be to let the cat have a minor limp, though it went against her moral code to do so.

"Are you all right?" Trent reached her side and knelt.

She nodded and wiped the tears from her eyes, unable to speak.

Trent shoved his fingers through his hair. "Dumb bastards," he hissed. "Idiots love to run over stray cats and dogs. It's become a sort of game with the locals. I try to stop them the best I can, but it's near impossible." His burning blue eyes narrowed as he ran his hand over the cat's fur. "I thought I'd seen that thing get completely smashed."

Lina's heart skipped a beat and she set the cat down and got to her feet. Oh god, not now. She hated to lie but was forced to, once again. "It nearly did. Some of its fur came off," she pointed to the limping cat that meowed pitifully, "and it has a tiny limp. But thankfully no serious damage done."

Abby walked up next to Lina and Trent and bent down to examine the feline. "I could have sworn...."

Lina rubbed the bridge of her nose, her lips quirked into a semi-smile. "It must have seemed worse from inside."

"Must have," Abby whispered. She glanced at Lina and frowned.

"Nana!" A female voice called. All three heads turned.

"Jessica." Trent's smile returned, and his eyes sparkled with delight as he walked toward the girl. He grabbed her into a fierce bear hug and asked, "How was school today?"

"Good," Jessica said as she carefully extracted herself from Trent's arms.

The child was a smaller, female version of Trent, with raven-black hair and sun-kissed skin. The only difference was the eyes; the child's were green instead of sapphire, moss green, brilliant, with tiny flecks of gold. Lina's heart increased in speed. About twelve years in age, Lina guessed. And so beautiful.

"Who's she?" Jessica gave a small nod toward Lina.

"Sweetie, meet Lina." Trent's voice was warm and deep. His gaze shifted to her face. "Lina, meet my daughter, Jessica, or Jess, as she prefers to be called."

Daughter? Lina swallowed. Her visions of white picket fences and sexual romps under the stars faded fast. A lonely bitterness filled the cave of her soul. If this was his daughter, then where was his wife? And did she really want to know?

Chapter Three

From the Journal of Lina Brennen:
There are three kinds of people in the world. Those who believe, those who don't, and those that are scared of me.

* * * *

Trent didn't understand the strange look on Lina's face. She didn't like kids? He gave Jess a squeeze around the shoulders and glanced down at the keys in his hand. "Lina's going to look at the apartment," he told his daughter. "And Nana is going to give her a job." He glanced at his mother. "Right, Mom?"

Abby cleared her throat. "Yes, well...."

Lina stepped back onto the sidewalk and ran the back of her hand over her forehead, damp tendrils of hair clinging to her cheeks. "I understand, Mrs. Godfrey. I don't really have any experience waiting tables. Maybe it'd be better if--"

"Of course Mom'll hire you," Trent cut in. Then cursed himself for being so stupid. Lina didn't look like she wanted to be here, and his mother kept giving him the oddest look. They'd all be better off if she just got back into that rattletrap car of hers and got the heck out of town.

But he didn't want her to leave. There was something about her-- and damned if he didn't want to see if that something was as special as he thought it might be. Then again, if she didn't like kids.... Jess was his life. After Nancy walked out on them nearly ten years ago, Jess was the only thing that kept him going sometimes. His daughter, his mother, and his job. He'd thought he was content.

"Don't let her go."

He spun around so fast, Jess nearly tumbled to the ground. He kept hearing things. A voice. Another shiver arced up his spine and he slapped at the back of his neck. It was at least one hundred-five in the shade, but he kept getting the chills. Maybe he was coming down with something. But he felt fine.

"Dad, you all right?" Jess asked, her green eyes clouded with concern.

"Fine, honey." He backed up against the wall of the diner. Cop instincts? He hadn't worked the Phoenix beat in many years, and little Unegi sure didn't have any hardened criminals he had to look out for.

Trent knew everyone in the town of five hundred and twenty-three souls. Even the trouble-making animal killers were familiar to him.

"Trent," Abby said. He brought his gaze back to his mother. "Why don't you take Lina to see the apartment? It might not be what she's looking for, you know."

He nodded, leaned down, and kissed Jess on the cheek. "Why don't you go grab a bite with Nana and I'll be back in a bit?"

Jess nodded. Frowned. "Dad, you gettin' sick? You don't look so good."

Trent turned his attention back to Lina when he heard her ... growl? She was staring at the front of the diner, a fierce scowl on her porcelain face. Oh boy. Maybe she wasn't right in the head. Then she shook her head, squeezed her eyes shut, and pinched the bridge of her nose.

Heat. The heat was getting to her. To him, too. "Go on inside," he said to Jess and his mother. "I'll be back in a little while." He placed his hand on Lina's arm, and she jerked as if he'd bitten her. "Sorry," he said quietly. "I think we need to get you inside."

Lina cast another glance at the diner then shrugged. "Yeah. It's hot out here."

Jess and Abby went inside, leaving them alone on the quite street. "Most of the townsfolk go into the bigger towns for work during the days," he said to Lina, trying for any little bit of conversation to expel the tension. "Other than the shop owners, the place is like a ghost town on the weekdays."

Lina just nodded and stared across the street at the mercantile.

"Come on." He headed down the sidewalk next to Lina, wanting to put his arm around her, pull her close to his side. That thought alone sent another chill through him. He rubbed his arms.

It's not like he'd been celibate for ten years. There were a few women he dated occasionally, a few he'd spent a night or two with, but none of them made him want to ... cuddle. He shook his head at the thought. It was simply because she was new, unique, and gorgeous. There really wasn't any other explanation. Perhaps it was time he got out more. Out of Unegi. Maybe he'd go into Phoenix this Friday night and check out the clubs. It'd been a long, long time since he'd done that.

He rounded the side of the sheriff's office and climbed the long wooden staircase to the second floor. "It's pretty small," he warned. When he unlocked the door, the knob was sizzling hot. "But it's fully furnished." He pushed the door open and stepped aside to let Lina in.

Meow.

They both looked down. The cat that'd so recently been run over stood on the tiny landing, wrapping its furry little body around Lina's legs.

"Looks like you've got your first visitor," Trent commented with a slow grin.

Lina bent down and picked the cat up. "Do you allow pets?"

He rubbed his chin. "Never thought about it. I suppose, as long as it doesn't tear up the furniture or make the place smell, it would be all right." Like he'd deny her a pet. Just watching her snuggle the ragged feline against her chin and run her fingers through its fur made him wish he were small and fluffy.

He nearly laughed aloud. He was anything but small, but he wouldn't mind her petting him like that. Not one bit.

When Lina smiled up at him and stepped through the door, her arm lightly brushed his chest. And a deep ache set up inside him. He shook it off and shut the door to keep some of the heat out.

"I turned on the air conditioner a while ago, but I'll turn it up," he said as he headed for the window, which held an ancient air conditioner. "If you keep the drapes drawn during the day, the heat'll stay down."

"I don't know...." Lina made a slow circuit of the living room/kitchen/dining area, inspecting the counter tops and plush blue sofa. "I don't think your mom really wants me working for her. And without a job, I could never pay the rent."

Trent clamped his bottom lip between his teeth and shoved his hands into the back pockets of his jeans. Lina walked around the apartment again, the cat still tucked against her as she lovingly ran her hand over its head and back. The thing had started purring. Loudly. He guessed he wasn't the only one taken by the woman. She peeked into the bedroom and the bathroom.

He wondered what she saw, if she liked it. Her face was devoid of any sign of emotion. She shook her head a couple of times. Maybe she had a tick or something.

* * * *

"Just look at that lovely painting above the bed. And, oh my, what a nice big bed that is. You've never had a king-sized bed before. Wouldn't that be fun?"

Knock it off, Granna. I can't stay here. He thinks I'm a nutcase, and so does his mother. And you--you're not helping anything. So just shut up for a few minutes.

Merona chuckled and floated onto the bed and sprawled out. "Oh yes. Lots of room for two."

Yeah, me and Lucky here. Lina kissed the kitty's head. If I stay, I could keep her. Make sure her babies are all right when they're born. I've never had a pet before. And most animals don't like you either, but Lucky here doesn't seem to mind.

Merona propped her head on her hand as she lay on the bed. "A black cat for the witch. How fitting."

Lina shook her head. I swear, if I didn't love you so much—"

"Mom will give you the job. She's just cautious. She's had a lot of waitresses come and go. This isn't a town many people move to, just away from. Why are you here, anyway?"

Damn it! She'd just spaced out in front of him again and missed whatever the heck he'd asked her. Lina refrained from rolling her eyes at her grandmother and placed her attention squarely on Trent's inquisitive face. Frustration at her inability to focus was mounting within her. "I'm sorry, Trent, the heat is really getting to me." Lina made a show of fanning her face. "Could you please repeat that last bit?"

He shoved his long, lean fingers through his hair and squinted at her. As if intensely studying her for some sign of brain damage.

God, he must think I'm really crazy. I'm not making a good impression right now. Focus, Lina, focus!

"You know, on second thought, you do look exhausted. We'll make small talk later," he finally said.

Lina ground her molars, hating her lack of attention, especially when her grandmother was around. If she didn't want to be run out of this town, too, she needed to act as normal as possible. And today she'd acted anything but. She pasted on a fake smile and nodded.

His lips quirked and he lifted his hand. "So, um...."--he cleared his throat--"anyhow, what do you think? Will it do?" His royal blue eyes studied her.

Again, she turned and took in her drab and rather Spartan surroundings. With a few touch-ups here and there, she could make this place look more than presentable. Lina laid a finger against her chin, imaging how she would style it. Add a few potted plants, some festive colors and her knick-knacks, and the place would be downright homey. The beige shag carpet was an eyesore, but with a few throw rugs, nothing she couldn't overcome. The place had a certain seventies motif that she found rather appealing.

She turned and nodded. His eyes lit with ... excitement? She couldn't be sure, but it lifted her spirits. Even if his excitement only stemmed from money in his pockets, it still made her feel better.

"You'll take it?" His smile was devastating in its effect; her knees weakened and she nearly melted.

"Yes."

He shook his head as if clearing his thoughts, and the smile faded. "Will you need help bringing in any of your stuff?" Trent looked at his watch.

Lina wrinkled her nose. Not that the idea wasn't tempting, it was. It really was. But she wanted to talk to her grandmother without fear of looking like an idiot. That, and the fact that she didn't even know if Trent was a married man. He wore no wedding ring, but in today's day and age, that didn't amount to a whole hill of beans. Thinking about it stung, so she pushed it to the back of her mind.

"You know, Trent. Not that I don't appreciate the offer, but I'm better at doing this by myself and well, I've already taken up too much of your valuable time."

"If you're sure."

"No, for crying out loud, Lina! What are you doing letting him walk away like that? Jeez, girl, do you ever want to get a man or not?" Merona wagged her finger under Lina's nose.

Trent's eyes widened and he whipped his head to the side. If she weren't such a nervous wreck right now, she'd laugh her butt off at his display. And he thought she was an odd bird.

He rubbed his hand over his head and headed toward the door. "Yeah, okay, just give me a holler if you need anything." And with that, he shot out her door like he'd seen a ghost.

Well, he'd heard one, that was for sure.

Lina clenched her jaw and leveled her gaze at her meddling grandmother.

"How dare you? You know he can hear you. Why in the world would you frighten him like that?" All the tension and anger of the last few moments, months, years, felt as though it was coming to a head. "Granna, if you want this place to be our last move, then you've got to stop with these juvenile pranks!"

Merona sighed and glided toward a wooden rocking chair in the corner of the room. "Sweetling, you're probably right. But believe me, when you get to this state, pranks are the only enjoyment you get out of life." She shrugged a white shoulder. "Or semi-life, in this case."

Lina blew out a breath and rolled her eyes. She sank down onto the rather comfy sofa. Her stomach was twisted in knots, her head ached, and she was sweaty. But she knew she shouldn't take out her anger on her grandmother. "I'm sorry, Granna. You're right, I suppose. But, please, let's try to keep it to a minimum. When you're around me, at least. The less crazy I look, the better for the both of us, believe me. I don't want to move again. I don't think I have the energy for another one."

Merona trailed her hand along the cat's spine. "This will be the last move, sweetling."

Lina's heart thudded in her chest. In all the years, she'd never heard her grandmother utter or even think those words. "What?"

Just then, the feline let out a yowl and ran for Lina, landing with a proprietary plop on her lap. Lucky lifted her back paw, the one that had been crushed, and licked at it, reminding Lina that she still needed to heal her entirely.

She flexed her fingers, beckoning the fire to enter her once more. Then she grazed her fingers along the cat's leg. A bright, white light encompassed the feline, black fur sprouted on the gray patch of skin, and Lucky was as good as new once more.

Merona chuckled and stared at her hand. "Guess my touch is a tad too cold for the kitty."

Her grandmother had become close-mouthed again, but her words rang as loud as a bell in Lina's ears. Was it possible? Her last move? She trembled at the thought.

"What did you name this thing again?" Merona asked.

"Lucky," Lina replied automatically.

Merona wrinkled her nose and patted her perfectly coifed hair. "You sure you like that name? Why do people always have to name their pets such silly names? I prefer Elvira or Petunia."

"Ugh." Lina stuck out her tongue. "That's dreadful, Granna. It's Lucky and it will stay that way."

Merona's mouth set into a prim line. "Whatever." Her hand waved through the air. "But, I never would have thought I'd see the day when you would take in a black cat. You and your silly signs. Don't you know black cats are bad luck?"

"She's pregnant, so that's null and void." But maybe her grandmother had a point. Lina hadn't thought about it in all the excitement. Could the color of a cat's fur really determine the cards fate would hand her?

No, she shook her head. Now she was really letting her imagination run wild. Unegi was a new start and new beginning for her and Merona.

"Anyhow, Granna...." Lina switched topics; she really didn't feel like discussing her newly acquired pet. "I want to ask you something."

Merona raised a white brow and smiled. "Why you get tingles racing through you whenever Trent touches you?"

Lina nodded.

"It's the magic of your destiny." Merona glided from the rocking chair toward the large window facing the street. "The sun's setting, sweetling. Don't you think you ought to unpack the car?"

It unsettled and disappointed Lina that her grandmother refused to tell her more. But spirits were notorious for speaking at their own pace. She mulled over Merona's words. The magic of your destiny. It sounded lovely, but foreboding at the same time.

Lina winced as a pressure built behind her skull. A major headache was brewing. She needed her Tylenol fast, before it got too out of hand. And that meant she needed to unload her car. "I suppose I oughta." She stood and headed for the door.

"Oh, and sweetling, you'll probably want to go and ask Trent to finalize the apartment transaction. He ran out of here rather fast, wouldn't you say?"

Oh jeez. She closed her eyes. She was sure the last thing Trent wanted was another visit from the crazy lady. However, she realized the wisdom of her grandmother's words.

She only hoped this next visit would run a little more smooth than the last one.

* * * *

Trent slid onto the stool at the counter and waited for his mother to finish wiping down the tables. Jess sat in the corner booth, her schoolbooks spread over the table. She didn't like being disturbed when she was doing her homework. She wouldn't speak to him until she was done. Good thing school was almost out for summer vacation.

He sighed. His little girl was growing up. In just a few months, she'd be an official teenager. "Great," he muttered and scrubbed his hand down his face. There were times she was the sweetest, most loving little thing in the world. And there were other times that she reminded him of ... He sighed. Of a miniature version of her mother.

She had Nancy's mossy green eyes and killer smile that wound his chest up so tight, sometimes he thought it might choke the life right out of him. But where Nancy had killed something inside him, Jess kept him warm. He loved his little girl. Though she hated for him to call her that now, he thought with a smile as he watched her nibble on the end of her pen. You'll always be my little girl, baby Jess. No matter how old you get.

"You really want me to hire her?" Abby asked as she slipped onto the stool next to Trent and pulled a pack of smokes out of her apron pocket.

Trent dutifully removed the cigarette from his mother's fingers, broke it into thirds, and dropped the leavings in the ashtray. "You don't like her?" he asked, ignoring her scowl as she pulled out another cigarette.

"What's not to like? She has the concentration of a fruit fly. Her clothes leave a bit to be desired and she's...." She flicked her lighter, and Trent grabbed the cigarette right out of her mouth.

"Damn it, Mom. These are going to kill you."

"Damn it, son, when did you get so bossy?" She moved around the counter, leaned back against the cabinets, and lit her smoke.

Trent rolled his eyes. "To serve and protect. That's the motto of the sheriff's department." He stood up, reached over the counter, snagging the cigarette from her, and grabbed the pack from her front apron pocket while he was at it. "So consider it my civic duty to save you from yourself," he said, slipping it into his shirt pocket.

Abby narrowed her eyes at him and planted her hands on her hips. "Damn liberals always think they know what's best."

Trent chuckled. "I did vote for the republicans, you know." Then he sighed. "Back to Lina. You don't want to hire her?"

Abby folded her arms and tilted her head to the side. A sign she was considering every angle of the situation. "You want her to stay, don't you?"

Trent raised an eyebrow, neither confirming, nor denying her suspicions.

Abby leaned her elbows on the counter, glanced at Jess in the far corner of the diner and whispered, "I haven't seen you look at a woman that way since...." She cast another glance at Jess.

Trent's gut clenched and he leaned back. "Whoa." He shook his head. "She's cute, all right." He leaned back toward Abby. "Okay, so she's really cute, but that doesn't--"

"Two weeks. If she breaks more dishes than her pay, she's outta here."

Trent let out a slow breath. That's what he wanted, right? Damned if he knew. The little woman definitely stirred his blood. But at this point in his life, was that a good thing? He cast another glance at Jess. This time in a girl's life, she needed a woman around. A woman who wasn't her grandmother. Then he remembered the look on Lina's face when he'd introduced her to Jess. That wasn't a good sign at all.

Trent buried his face in his hands. Lord help him, his brain was fried.

The bell jingled over the door. "Excuse me?"

Chapter Four

From the Journal of Lina Brennen:
A new home, a new hearth, that's what Granna says.
And she says, home is where the heart is. Maybe she's confused. I've never had a home. No hearth, and no heart there, either.

* * * *

Trent almost chuckled at the softly spoken words, from none other than the woman he'd known less than four hours who was making him insane. He turned around. "Yes?" he asked, raising his brow and smiling at her.

Lina glanced behind her and then her shoulders relaxed and an honest to God, genuine smile tilted her full pink lips. "You ran out so fast, you forgot to leave me the keys."

Idiot. Feeling sheepish, he dug into his jeans pocket and pulled out a set of keys. "Sorry." But hearing that woman's voice ... Workings of an overactive imagination, that's all. He'd stayed up half the night last night keeping an eye on the Thornton farm. It still amazed Trent that cattle rustling was such a popular sport round these parts. Exhaustion, that's all that was wrong with him.

Lina slipped the keys from his hand, carefully, as if making sure not to touch him. "One other thing," she said as she pocketed the keys, "um...." She glanced at Abby who was making busywork behind the counter, acting like she wasn't listening.

"You got the job," Abby said. "You're on a two-week trial. If you can carry a tray without dumping it on someone's lap, and can handle the dinner rush, you can stay on as long as you like."

Lina smiled and her shoulders relaxed even more. "Thank you, Mrs. Godfrey. I'll do my best."

Damn, the woman was beautiful. Especially when her eyes flashed pleasure and those full lips parted in that incredible smile, showing off her slightly crooked, perfectly wonderful smile.

"Told you to call me Abby. You be here at six a.m. when I open tomorrow. Diner's open from six a.m. to seven p.m. You get the afternoon off. And we're closed Monday and Tuesday. Think you can handle that?"

"Yes." Lina's smile was about a million watts of brilliance, and Trent's stomach clenched again. Along with other parts he needed to keep under control. She turned back to him. "So, is there some kind of rental agreement I have to sign? A deposit, or something?"

A one year lease. No, two, if I can convince you to allow conjugal visits. He chuckled at himself. "No. I know where you work. You don't pay the rent, I'll just have Mom garnish your wages." He gave her a wink and was pleased to see a slight blush crawling up her neck. He thought about following that blush with his tongue. Wondered if she tasted half as good as she smelled. Like cinnamon incense and sand verbena, natural, musky and sweet.

Lina cleared her throat. "Okay. Well. Um." She backed toward the door. "I better get settled in, then. Goodnight." She turned and walked smack into the door. Trent was halfway off the stool when she grabbed the door and gave it a hard shove as she mumbled a few choice words.

"Flake," Abby said, her lips quirked into a grin.

"That she is," Trent mumbled, as he swiveled toward the counter. "But she's a cute flake."

Abby set a tall, frothy root beer down in front of him. "Don't know if she'll last the two weeks, though."

"You gonna date her, Dad?"

Trent closed his eyes for a moment and sighed. The two women he'd brought home over the years, the only semi-serious relationships he'd established, had not gone over well with Jess. She didn't want anyone usurping her position as head female in the house. She tended to make life a living hell for him. Another reason he spent most Friday nights at home. And now that he had a child going through puberty who was as smart as a damn whip, he couldn't just go out for a night on the town anymore. The girl would know what he was doing.

"Well?" Jess persisted as she walked across the diner.

And because she was nearly a teenager, it was time to stop hiding behind being a dad, and be honest. "And what if I do?" he asked, turning toward her as she sat down on the stool next to him.

Jess shrugged one shoulder in that teen speak he couldn't quite decipher any more. God, he was getting old. He spiked his hand through his hair. "Would that be a problem for you?" he asked.

Another one-shoulder shrug as she toyed with a napkin. "She seems nice."

Trent's eyebrows shot up. This was the first time Jess had ever said that about a woman. She hated any woman he even glanced at twice. Just a year ago, she told him that he'd done such a lousy job picking the first one he shouldn't bother trying again. Of course, that was during a rousing argument over her mother, one of the few times in the last ten years that Nancy had called and wanted to see her, and Jess didn't want to go.

"So," Trent said, carefully choosing his words, "if I wanted to take Lina out on a date, that would be cool with you?"

"Yeah. But you're not allowed to bring her home for the night."

He'd just taken a sip of root beer and he choked on it. "What?"

"I don't want no woman in the house after midnight."

"I don't want any," Trent automatically corrected, then shook his head. "Okay. Deal."

Jess turned her gorgeous smile on him and did something she didn't do very often anymore. She wrapped her arms around his neck and hugged him.

* * * *

Good Lord! Lina rolled her eyes heavenward, the heat of a blush still stinging her cheeks as she walked with a furious pace down the sidewalk toward her car. She couldn't believe she'd just done that. "Ugh," she groaned. Running into a door of all things. That was a serious dumb-blond moment, and she'd gotten enough of those jokes to last her a lifetime. While she wasn't as graceful as a swan, she had also never been that uncoordinated. The things that man did to her equilibrium.

Lina kept her eyes toward the ground and shoved her hands in her shorts pocket. How had she gone from this morning, thinking that Phoenix would be her next home, to suddenly being stuck in backwards Unegi?

"Hello, buttercup." The smooth male voice broke her from her unruly thoughts.

Lina dropped her keys and stiffened her spine. "What?" she snapped and turned, about to give the idiot a sound tongue-lashing for scaring her out of her wits.

But she lost her words as she stared into warm, cinnamon-colored eyes. Were all the men here Adonis look-alikes? He was tall, with a rugged face. Square jaw, chiseled cheekbones, and a mane of wavy blond hair framing a tanned face.

The stranger leaned against her car and hooked his thumbs into his belt loops. He screamed cowboy, what with his too-tight jeans, alligator-skin boots, and overly large, golden belt buckle. He made Lina wary, but curious.

A slow, lazy grin spread across his face. "How ya doin', buttercup?" he asked again.

Lina narrowed her eyes. Was this man hitting on her? In the city, it was easy to get lost amongst the many beautiful faces, so the attention was flattering. Especially from this gorgeous cowboy who sent her heart into a minor tailspin. At least he helped her not think about Trent, and that was a good thing. Or was it?

"What are you doing here, Ty?"

Lina's lashes fluttered. That voice, that gravelly, sexy as hell voice. She turned and saw Trent with his thick arms crossed against his massive chest. Her heart didn't just turn over, it dove into her stomach. Oh, God, who was she kidding? Trent was just too good looking for words.

"Hey, man." Ty lifted his hands in a submissive manner. "Just being friendly. You can't arrest a guy for that, now can you?"

Lina glanced at Ty. His gaze slowly traveled up the length of her body and then he gave her wink. She shivered, with excitement or repulsion, she wasn't sure which. But she did know that the male preening was a heady intoxicant.

Trent's gaze shifted to Lina's face, his look was possessive, feral. She licked her lips.

"Well, reckon I should head on out. Lovely meeting you, miss," Ty said. Before Lina could react, he'd grabbed her hand in his and lowered his head. "Hope to make your acquaintance again real soon, buttercup," he whispered, his hot breath fanning her wrist, seconds before he kissed it.

Trent inhaled deeply in the background.

"Um, sure." She snatched her hand out of his.

Ty's grin was brash, filled with masculine pride. Slowly, and as if he didn't have a care in the world, he sauntered down the sidewalk, whistling a tune to himself.

Her heart beat faster than normal, and her skin tingled with awareness. Not from Ty's kiss, but from the man standing mere inches behind her. Trent was so close she could feel his body heat. Lina turned and gazed at him. His jaw was clenched, his hands balled up into fists at his side.

"What were you doing talking to that idiot?"

Taking umbrage at his possessive tone, she squared her shoulders and glared at him. "That is none of your business."

His jaw flexed, his eyes narrowed at her. "That cocky bastard is my business," he spat. "Believe me, Lina, you don't want to go courting trouble with the likes of Ty Brock. He's left too many a broken heart in his wake."

"And that's your business, why? Don't forget, Trent Godfrey,"--she waved a finger through the air--"that I'm a grown woman and I can say hello to my new neighbors whenever I damn well please."

Trent shook his head, and a slow smile, like butter melting on warm bread, spread across his face. Then he chuckled, a deep, rolling, gravel on the bottom of the river noise that did crazy things to her insides. "Point taken."

And just like that, her fire was gone. She quirked her lips into a semblance of a smile, wondering how it was that Trent was capable of being a Neolithic caveman one second, and a pleasant individual the next. "You drive me crazy, Trent Godfrey."

"Welcome to the club, Lina...."

"Brennen," she said.

"Lina Brennen." He rolled her name like warm honey off his tongue. The effect was devastating, and she bit her lip to keep her composure.

"What did you come out here for, anyhow?" she asked with a raised eyebrow.

"I came to offer my help once more, and to see if you were okay from your crash into my mother's door."

Lina gave a sort of half laugh and rolled her eyes. "You would remind me of that, wouldn't you?"

"Of course." Trent shrugged. The breeze kicked up, lifting the locks of his black hair off his forehead in an unruly and all together boyish display. One she found mighty appealing.

Lina shoved her hand into her pockets to keep them from reaching out and patting his hair back into place. Or maybe just running her fingers through it, drawing him closer and kissing the stuffing out of him.

"I could use the help, I suppose." She unlocked her car door and trunk. "Help yourself," she said, and pulled a box from the back seat.

Trent sent her a tight smile and walked over.

Was she really ready to call this place home? she wondered, as she glanced at the front of the sheriff's office. The shifting winds picked up Trent's scent of cologne and leather. Lina's gaze floated away from the old building front to roam over the mountainous backdrop, all red from the light of the setting sun. The orange sky gave way to streaks of pinks, purples and a sea of royal blue. The lonely cry of a coyote in the distance sang a sad song.

And Lina's heart felt peace for the first time. She was home, she was finally home.

****

She's right. Damn it anyway. I have no claim over her. And pretty-boy Ty is what every woman wants. Cowboy from the word go, he looks like a cover model on those trashy romances Mom reads. Yeah, what every woman wants. A pain set up in the center of his chest. A pain he thought was long buried. He shook his head and grabbed a box out of the trunk of Lina's little car.

"Where's the rest of your stuff?"

Lina, hefting the box she held against her chest, sent him a confused look. "This is it."

Trent's footstep almost faltered. "This is it? You don't have more ... stuff?"

She shook her head as she headed up the steps to the apartment. "I don't need a lot to keep me happy. My books, my pretties, my clothes. What more could I possibly need?" She pushed the door open and stepped through.

Trent followed. "Pretties?" he asked, as he set the box he was carrying on the coffee table.

Lina sent him one of those dazzling grins as she reached into the box she'd carried up, and pulled out a handful of black votive candles and a few sparkling crystal thingies. "My pretties."

Her pretties. Trent shook his head. She'd moved across the country with a little car of boxes and suitcases. Jess packed more when she went off to summer camp.

"What?" Lina asked, as she headed back to the door.

"Nothing. You just keep surprising me, that's all. Never met a woman whose entire household fit in a beat up little car."

Lina laughed, that sweet, sexy sound that sent a shaft of hunger through him. Damn it had been a long time....

"Mind if I come in?"

Trent turned toward the door. Jess stood there with a battered soft-sided suitcase from Lina's car.

"Of course," Lina said with a warm smile. "Thanks." She took the suitcase from Jess and took it into the bedroom.

This was all too strange. Jess, offering help? She probably just wanted to check Lina out more. He suppressed a smile. The same thought he'd had.

"Thanks for helping, sweetpea. That's very nice of you."

Jess gave that pre-teen, one-shoulder shrug as she peered into the box Lina had set on the counter.

"Don't be nosy," he whispered as he walked toward Jess.

"Oh, that's okay," Lina said as she came back from the bedroom. "How about you start emptying the boxes, and your Dad and I will bring up the rest of the stuff? You can just set it all on the counter. I'll figure out where it goes later."

"Sure." Jess's smile was a bit mischievous, but Trent let it pass. Maybe Lina would be good for her. To have someone--a woman--around that wasn't "old as the hills" as Jess said about Abby.

* * * *

Jess waited until Lina and her dad went out the door and started pulling things from the box. Lots of little black candles and some crystals on hangers. She glanced around the room as she worked. There was something really off about Lina, but she wasn't sure what it was.

Meow.

Jess glanced over at the black cat perched on one of the two dining room chairs, cleaning its face with its paws. That cat should be dead. She'd been walking down the sidewalk when she saw it get hit. The thing had practically been flattened. But Lina had rushed out there, picked it up, and then something even stranger had happened. She could swear that she'd seen some weird glowy thing going on. Of course, with the heat waves dancing off the pavement, she couldn't be sure....

"Where you want this?" her dad asked, as he came in with another two boxes.

Lina, right behind Trent said, "The top one goes in the bedroom, the bottom one goes in the bathroom." She set another box on the counter next to the one Jess had just emptied. "These are the dishes. Just throw them anywhere. I'll rearrange later."

Meow.

Lina smiled at her, went to the cat, and rubbed its head. "I need to get a litter box for Lucky here. Do you know if anywhere in town sells them?"

"Bob's Mercantile, just a block down and across from the diner does. He's got supplies for house pets." Jess studied the cat as it leaned against Lina's leg and purred loudly. "Amazing that he's still alive, isn't it?"

"Mmmhmm," Lina agreed with a smile. "She. She's going to have babies soon."

Dad came back into the room, slammed the bedroom door, and rubbed his neck. He was acting awfully weird, too. He kept looking at Lina like she was a steak dinner, and he hadn't eaten in a week. But he also looked rather pale, his brow furrowed.

"Headache, Dad?" she asked.

"Hm? Oh, um, yeah, a bit of one." He dropped his hand from his neck and moved toward the door. "I'll get the last of the boxes."

"Excuse me a minute, would you?" Lina said. She went into the bedroom, shutting the door behind her.

Really weird stuff going on here. Jess picked up the cat, examined its legs. The bald spot was gone. Maybe this wasn't the same cat?

"Don't you do that to him anymore," she heard Lina say from inside the bedroom. Creeping closer, she put her ear to the door. "I don't give a damn how funny you think it is. You're creeping him out. Leave. Him. Alone."

Whoa. Jess stepped back from the door just as Dad came back with the last two boxes. He set them down on the living room floor.

"What are you doing?" he asked.

She set the cat back on its chair. "Nothin'." She knelt in front of the boxes Trent had just set down and opened one. An entire box of books. "Oh, cool. Look at these, Dad." She pulled out three hardbacks, all by Sylvia Brown. "Life on the Other Side, Contacting Your Spirit Guide, and The Other Side and Back: A Psychic's Guide to Our World and Beyond.

Her dad grabbed the books from her hand, frowned fiercely as he read the titles, and then put them none too gently onto the empty bookcase. "Let her unpack her own books. I don't want you reading that garbage."

Ignoring her father's gruff tone, she reached into the box and drew out three more books. Visits from the Afterlife, another Sylvia Brown, The Afterlife Experiments: Breakthrough Scientific Evidence of Life After Death by some guy named Schwartz, and The Shining, by Stephen King. "Wow, what a collection," Jess mused.

"I thought I told you to leave her books alone." Trent grabbed the books from her hand and shoved them onto the shelf next to the others, then closed the flaps to the book box.

Jess frowned up at him. "What is with you, Dad? Get a grip. They're books."

"Not the kind of books you need to be reading."

She huffed out a breath. "Fine. Whatever." She got to her feet, went to the next box, and started unloading more candles and incense. The incense holder was a black carved dragon. A few more crystals, a really pretty stone bowl, and a matching ... thing. She didn't know what it was.

"What do you think this is?" she asked her dad, as he busied himself putting dishes in the cupboard above the sink. He turned around and frowned. "That's a mortar and pestle."

Jess turned the colorful stone items over in her hands. Swirls of blue and purple and pink had been smoothed to a shine. "What's it for?"

Lina opened the door to the bedroom, came into the living room, and shut the door behind her. "I put potpourri in it. It's kinda pretty, don't you think?" she asked, taking it from Jess and placing it on the tiny shelf near the door. "I got it in this little store that sold supplies for aroma therapy stuff. You use it to grind up dried herbs." Lina turned back and sent her a bright smile. Jess had to give her that, the woman was very beautiful. No wonder her Dad was going loony around her.

"All very old fashioned," Lina went on. "I use a food processor to grind my herbs."

"You grind your own herbs?" Trent asked, and he dumped her silverware all willy-nilly in a drawer. Poor Lina was going to have a lot of rearranging to do.

"Mmhmm," Lina said. She pulled a beautiful, black, faux-fur throw from a box and laid it over the back of the sofa. "I make bath oils and stuff like that. Cheaper than buying the pre-bottled stuff, and I don't put any weird preservatives in it that take away from what its supposed to be." She ran her hand over the fluffy fur.

Trent put his fists on his hips and scowled. What the heck was wrong with him? "And what is it supposed to be?" he asked in that gruff voice he normally saved for when he was starting to get pissed.

Lina turned toward him and raised her eyebrows. "Well, all natural, of course."

Chapter Five

From the Journal of Lina Brennen:
Another new place to live. A new job. Another set of problems to deal with. Oh well, life must go on.

* * * *

After everyone had left, Lina set to work putting her new apartment together. Merona flitted through the air, her aura glittering around the room in bursts of green and gold, reminding Lina oddly of a June bug.

She sighed and grabbed her gauzy cream silk curtains and a curtain rod. Things had gone well between her and Trent at first. They'd unloaded the car amidst laughter and talking. He'd been kind, chivalrous, holding open the door for her, not allowing her to carry anything too heavy.

And then the damned herbs. It made absolutely no sense that someone could get so bent out of shape about her making her own soaps. But he sure as hell had. They were just friggin' herbs.

He'd clearly gotten uncomfortable around her books, but when he found out she ground her own herbs, he'd gone ape and practically dragged Jess from her apartment, with neither a backward glance or fare thee well.

"Want to talk about it?" Merona asked patiently, while she helped Lina hang the curtains in place.

"What the hell is so weird about me that every man I become interested in runs for the hills?" she ground out, her temper finally unleashing itself. "I mean, really, what did I do so wrong? I told him I ground herbs. Since when did that become immoral? God, you woulda thought I'd suddenly sprouted two heads the way he reacted."

Lina ground her jaw and walked over to the kitchen counter for her box of crystals and candles. Fire burned in her belly and she stomped her feet as loud as she could, hoping the brute would hear her downstairs.

"Some men, sweetling, are hard to figure out. Be patient with this one. He's got a story to tell."

She blew out a frustrated breath, lifting her bangs off her forehead. "Patience, Granna, I have in spades, but this man tries it. To the very limits." Lina stopped by the counter and dropped her chin to her chest. "He's wary of me," she muttered, her heart aching at the thought.

No matter how many times she moved, it was always the same. She could never hide who she really was. She wondered whether there were a man alive capable of accepting her for herself.

Merona glided toward Lina and laid a chilling hand against her back, rubbing in an up and down motion. "Don't worry, sweetling. And don't give up hope. He may be wary now, but soon he'll learn. He'll learn."

Lina pinched out a smile and walked toward the cedar coffee table. She laid down her box and began placing her black votive and white lilac-scented candles around the room.

"Granna, I love you for saying so, and you know I've never been a quitter at anything. But I'm weary," Lina finally admitted. "I'm tired of the constant moving, of the strange glances, and most especially of being run out of town."

Merona picked up a handful of white crystals and hung them from the windows. "Be patient, dear. It won't always be this way."

Lina snorted and threw a woven welcome mat on the floor by the door. Not that she didn't trust her grandmother, but she couldn't see things getting easier anytime soon.

* * * *

Trent drove home more than just tired; he was utterly exhausted and ready for bed. His mind was a foggy haze; the muscles of his neck were stiff and sore. He hadn't slept well last night, what with the stakeout for rustlers at Thornton's place. And all he'd been able to concentrate on today was the sultry newcomer.

Her long flaxen hair, smoky gray eyes ... He felt himself begin to harden. Groaning, he shifted in his seat and pushed on the gas. Why couldn't he stop thinking about her? Her verbena scent, her slightly crooked grin, even those gaudy bracelets she wore. She bothered him. Not in a bad way, exactly. But this incessant need to figure out who she was, what she was doing in this ragtag town, was starting to rankle. Trent pressed his lips together and sighed.

He turned left. His red adobe home three houses down beckoned him, heralding a promise of peace and sanctuary from these all-consuming thoughts. Quickly he pulled into his driveway and exited his car. The night smelled of desert, of sage and juniper. A tumbleweed rolled across his lawn in the gentle breeze, and a million stars shone down on him. The pregnant moon cast an eerie blue-white light around the darkened street.

Trent inhaled, allowing the tranquil desert scene to sooth his ragged nerves. He opened the front door and stepped through. He threw his wallet on the coffee table.

A voice blared from the television, "Are you serious? Twenty dollars for all this?"

"Yes! Just twenty dollars, and you could have this tea kettle set, liquid detergent...."

Trent turned toward his sleeping daughter. She was lying on the recliner, her legs propped up, her mouth slightly parted, the remote control held loosely in her grasp. He smiled, reached over, and shut off the television. A wave of tenderness washed through him at the sight of his child.

She wasn't his little baby anymore. When did she grow up? He still remembered her as a toddler, her diapers swishing back and forth with her jerky, erratic movements. "What would I do, Jess, if you ever remembered to shut the television off at night?"

Her only answer was a tiny snore.

Ah, who am I kidding? I love this nightly ritual. One they'd been doing now for nearly six years. He smirked, plopped onto the couch, took off his boots, then walked toward his daughter and scooped her into his arms.

"Hi, Dad," she said sleepily, snuggling her nose into his chest.

"Hi, honey," he whispered, and walked up the stairs toward her room. Her butterfly room, as he liked to call it. It was decorated from floor to ceiling with plexi-glass cases of butterflies from around the world. Pulling down the sheets, he laid her gently on the bed, kissed her forehead, and walked back out.

A quick shower and then he'd be off to bed. Trent stepped into the bathroom, turned on the showerhead, and began peeling his clothing off. Soon the room was rolling with steam. He smiled and stepped inside. The hot spray touching his skin felt like gentle fire and he groaned.

Trent laid his forehead against the cool tile and closed his eyes.

Images came unbidden to his mind of a time long ago, a time nearly forgotten. Of a ten-year-old boy sitting beneath a sea of stars. The lonely howl of a coyote in the distance and the croaks of horny toads surrounding him. The red glow of a fire cast eerie, dancing shadows around the barren landscape.

He'd journeyed to the sacred circle to commune with the spirits of his ancestors, to learn from them and grow wise in their ways. Finally, he'd felt ready to recite the chants and open up the portal to the dead.

He leaned his head back and opened his mouth, drinking deep of the briny fluid swirling in his mother's wooden bowl, then began the chants.

At first, nothing happened. The wind remained calm, the spirits dormant. Heat from the fire had pearls of sweat trickling down his forehead and neck, and still the boy pushed on. Squeezing his eyes shut ever tighter, he chanted louder, faster. His heart beat a hard, rapid tattoo in his chest.

"Come to me spirits of my people. Show me the way. Show me who you are. Teach me as you have been taught."

A great howling wind swept across the red clay earth. Tiny pebbles struck his cheek, ripping and gouging into his flesh from the intensity of the wind. A crimson streak of blood began a path down his neck. His heart picked up in speed. The spirits were heeding his call.

"Show me your will, revered ones."

Then the wind stopped, nothing stirred, no sound was made, and all the hairs on the back of his neck stood on end. He opened his eyes as the crying shriek of an eagle rent the air. Trent screamed and stood, but it was too late. These things were evil, soulless shades.

He gazed into the night as hollow, black shapes drifted toward him. Their moans and wails made his knees tremble and his heart stutter.

A cyclone of air surrounded him, and the eagle spirit drifted closer to his side, but the black amorphous shapes charged him. Leaping on him and ripping their talons down his sides, his face, reaching into his chest and squeezing the air from his lungs. Trent screamed and tried to run away, but they held him fast. The chill of their touch was like shards of ice singeing his blood.

They picked him up in their hands and lifted him into the air. His body began to seizure, foam escaping the sides of his lips as their mad chants filled his head, like the songs of a monk, except these were satanic, filling him with dread and death. He felt exposed and raw, his body in agony from the pain of their touch. Then a great white light enshrouded them and his body dropped to the ground, barely breathing, hardly stirring.

Trent's eyes snapped open and he shot away from the wall, nearly tripping over the rim of the bathtub where the water was now lukewarm. His breathing came in hard, heavy gasps. He blinked rapidly and shut the water off, waiting for his heart rate to slowly subside.

Would this nightmare never stop haunting him?

* * * *

Lina rolled over in bed the next morning and opened a bleary eye to stare, once again, at her clock. Five a.m. What with Merona's loud snoring in the corner and her fear of being late, Lina had hardly slept a wink. "Ah, hell with this," she muttered. Grouchy and sick of looking at the clock every ten minutes, she finally admitted defeat and threw her lavender sheet off.

Merona cracked open an eye. "You gonna get ready for work?"

"Mmm." Lina nodded and yawned.

"All right then," Merona said. "I'll see you at work, I'm gonna just catch a few more minutes of shut eye."

Lina rolled her eyes. Her grandmother didn't need to sleep, but Merona held fast to certain human customs, sleep being one of those. Lina just wished she understood why her grandmother always insisted on snoring.

"Fine," she ground out. "But, Granna, you have to swear to me, no funny business today. This is a really important day. If I fail to make a good impression, then I'll likely get fired, and with no source of income, we'll be moving on again."

"Honestly, Lina." Merona laid a hand against her heart. "As if you even needed to ask."

"Yeah, right." She shook her head and shuffled toward the bathroom, wondering what would be appropriate attire for waitressing.

* * * *

Trent ambled up the sidewalk toward the sheriff's office. It was still cool out, just barely in the seventies, and the sun was just beginning its rise over the mountains. A nice day for a walk.

Thinking back to last night and the way he'd yanked Jess from Lina's apartment, he groaned. He was such a fool. So she liked to make her own soap and grind her own herbs, nothing wrong with that. He was allowing the memories of his past to influence his idea of who Lina was. That wasn't fair to her. He scrubbed a hand down his face. He needed to make up with Lina and apologize. Why was it that he seemed to be doing a lot of that lately?

Trent knew she'd been upset. She'd practically stomped a hole through his roof, and rightly so, he figured. What was it about this slip of a woman that drove him to distraction?

A shadow caught his eye and he glanced up to see said woman running across the street toward the diner. She wore a tan overcoat, white sneakers, and nothing else. Her blond hair swayed gently behind her back.

A wicked smile turned up the corners of his mouth. The look reminded him of a flasher. He sure wouldn't mind being flashed by her, wouldn't even write her a ticket for it.

His heart stuttered in his chest at the thought. Blood rushed to his groin, his body tingled. Trent blew out a deep breath. He really needed to stop thinking about those things. It was dangerous to a man's sanity. He cleared his throat and crossed the street, glancing down at his wristwatch. "You're ten minutes early."

"Oh!" Lina startled and turned. Her eyes widened, then narrowed. They were the shade of a winter storm cloud this morning, tinged with flecks of violet. "Oh, you." Streaks of sunshine touched her pale blond hair, creating a halo-like effect around her head. She was stunning. Especially when she was all riled with him.

"What are you doing here?" she asked, then turned her head to the side.

She was mad. Damn, he hated this. "Listen, Lina, about last night."

Lina turned slowly, her face devoid of all emotion as she waited, arms crossed over her chest.

She drove him crazy, getting under his skin in a way he didn't want to study or even understand. All he knew was he liked it. Her spunk, her fire, her.

Trent scrubbed a hand down his face and smiled. "I had no right to make you feel that way, Lina. I'm sorry."

She sighed and gave him the sweet, crooked smile that set a fire ablaze in his gut.

"I want to ask you something," she said.

Trent guessed he'd been granted her forgiveness, and nodded.

Her hands fumbled with the belt of her coat and she opened her jacket, revealing her outfit underneath. "Do you think this is suitable waitress attire?"

Holy hell!

Trent swallowed the vile, sexually charged curse clawing up his throat. Her long, lean, sun-kissed legs peeked out from beneath a short denim skirt. A white tank top completed the ensemble. Her ever present bracelets jangled and she lifted a raised brow.

"Well?" She asked.

* * * *

"No. Hell no! You march your pretty little butt back up to your apartment and change into something respectable. There's no way on God's green earth you're going to flash that much skin in this town."

Lina didn't know if she should be irate at his reaction or not. His face had gone an odd shade of red-purple that she wouldn't have guessed was humanly possible, and his eyes flashed the color of blue fire. She bit the inside of her cheek as she listened to him bluster on and on about skin and legs and cowboys. She didn't understand half of what he ranted about. What she did hear was the "pretty little butt" remark. And since he couldn't seem to take his gaze off her legs, except to move to her breasts, she couldn't help but enjoy his reaction.

He finally stopped talking, fisted his hands on his hips, and glared at her. Damn, he looked good in his uniform. Black western boots, dark brown slacks and shirt that hugged every lovely muscle of his body. The gun belt really did something for him, and she could think of a few interesting things to use those handcuffs for. And the gold star over his heart.

She caught herself mid-sigh and straightened. But she couldn't help the smile that tilted her lips, no matter how hard she tried to hide it.

"You think this is funny? You wear that in there," he pointed at the front of the diner, "and it'll be the Alamo all over again."

"I thought the Alamo was in Texas, not Arizona." Oh, look, she thought, as she stifled a snigger. His face was getting even more purple. That couldn't be healthy. She stepped forward and laid her hand on his chest. His heart was beating a bit fast, but she couldn't feel any signs of a serious blood pressure problem.

"What. The hell. Are you doing?" Trent demanded, as he grabbed her hand and held it away from his chest.

She smiled up into his beautiful eyes. "Well, you looked like you were about to have a heart attack. I just didn't want it to happen on my watch." She slowly slipped her hand from his, this time letting herself enjoy the frisson of heat and electricity that flowed up her arm from his touch.

"My heart is fine," he ground out. "But there are men in there that are old. You cannot wear that ... outfit to work in."

Jealousy? Oh, that was way too much to hope for. She flashed him an evil little grin. "You don't like it? I thought it was rather cute. I've seen diner waitresses wearing much shorter skirts than this." She slipped the jacket off her shoulders, dropping it to the ground, turned her back on him, and peeked at him over her shoulder. Sure enough, his eyes zeroed in on her butt.

Trent let out a pitiful groan that made him sound as if he were in severe pain, and closed his eyes. "Lina, please."

She waited until he opened his eyes before she bent over to pick up her coat. Her skirt was short, but far from indecent. She really couldn't understand his reaction. He turned his back on her and stalked back across the street, never looking her way again.

Lina shrugged and went into the diner. It was exactly six a.m. Abby was behind the counter filling the coffee maker with water, and Jess sat in the corner booth, headphones on her ears as her head bopped to music, a paperback book held up in front of her face.

"Good morning," she said, heading for the counter. "Abby, could you tell me, is this okay to wear here? I've never done waitressing before, and I don't know...."

Abby turned around, gave her a good look up and down, then leaned over the counter and glanced at her feet. "Good shoes. That's all that matters. You'll do." She looked at the jacket in her hand. "Cold this morning?" She raised an eyebrow, just like Trent's.

Lina felt one of those stupid blushes crawling up her neck. Abby grinned. "Dump your jacket in the back, then I'll show you around. Mac, the cook, will be in any minute. First customer usually arrives around six-thirty. Then we're busy until nine. Have a couple hours to clean up, then the lunch crowd. You're off from two to five, then in for dinner until seven when we close. Clean up usually takes about a half hour after that."

Lina nodded and headed behind the counter. Her nerves jangled, her heart raced. She hated the first day on a new job.

* * * *

"Order up!" Mac called through the tiny pick-up window. Lina grabbed the order ticket, checked the table number, shoved a ketchup bottle, mustard bottle, and Tabasco sauce bottle into her apron. Picking up the plate of sunny-side-up eggs, home fries, corned-beef hash and toast, she headed over to the old man seated in booth three. The tables weren't officially numbered, but it was easier to remember who got what after she mentally numbered them and began writing the numbers on the order slips.

"Here you go, sir. Is there anything else I can get you?" she asked with a smile as she set the warm plate in front of him.

"Your phone number?" the old guy said with a gap-toothed grin.

She laughed good-naturedly and patted him on the shoulder. "Maybe next time, big boy."

He gave her a nod and such a cute, crinkle-skinned grin, she felt happier than she ever had at any job. She loved it here. The patrons were friendly, even when she'd mixed up a couple orders first thing that morning. Most were regulars, as she learned from Abby, and they'd taken her in stride.

"Order up!" Mac called again.

She unloaded the condiments on the table, sent the old guy a wink for good measure, and headed back to the pick-up window.

"So, how's it going?"

Not now, Granna, I'm a little busy. She loaded up the bottles in her apron again and picked up the order ticket, ignoring Merona's insistent chatter in her ear. Oh dear. The booth with four huge cowboys, who ordered four of the wrangler specials. She stared at the platters of food, wondering how she'd manage to get them across the diner without dropping anything.

Very carefully, she laid one on her arm, placed another in her hand and picked up a third. Oh well, the fourth guy would just have to wait a couple minutes. She headed across the room, watching the platter on her arm tremble a bit.

"Hey there, buttercup."

Oh brother, she thought as she raised her eyes and sent Ty Brock a quick smile. The plate on her arm tipped a bit and she rushed to the table, barely making it in time to drop one plate onto the table and grab the one that was about to take a nosedive.

"Sorry about that," she said to the men as she set the plates in front of three of them. "Back in a sec." She rushed back, grabbed the fourth platter, and hightailed it back to the booth. "There you go. Anything else I can get you?"

All four cowboys smiled at her and held out their still empty coffee mugs.

"Oh, sorry, jeez." She went back to the counter and grabbed the coffee pot.

"It's okay, darlin'," one of the four men said, his chocolate eyes sparkling with laughter. "You could make it up to me by letting me take you out this Friday."

That giddy little tumble in her tummy again. Man, she'd never been flirted with, hit on, and propositioned so many times in her entire life as she had in the last hour. "Thanks for the offer," she said politely, as she concentrated on filling all the coffee mugs without spilling one drop, "but I think I need to settle in a bit before I start dating anyone."

The third guy elbowed the second guy and number four gave a snort.

"Well, whenever you're ready to start, you let me know, okay, darlin'?"

Mugs filled, she lifted her gaze to him and smiled, trying to quell the blush that rode her cheeks. "You bet."

She headed to Ty's table. "Coffee?" she asked, holding the pot up.

He flipped the cup over in front of him and sent her that devil-may-care grin. He did have some amazing eyes. She'd never really seen that color before. Dark cinnamon, like something she'd put in one of her shampoos.

"How's the first day treating you, buttercup?"

Lina was careful not to spill the coffee as she filled his cup. "Just fine," she answered with a smile. That nickname was rather annoying. She much preferred the darlin's and sweethearts. Even the honeys were better than buttercup. She set the coffee pot on the table and reached for her order pad, and realized she still had the cowboys' condiments. "Back in a sec," she said as she dashed across the room, unloaded the bottles onto their table, and then rushed back to Ty's. She pulled out her order pad--ew, it had ketchup on it. She swiped in on her apron. "Okay. Now. What can I get you?"

Ty's grin was slow and lazy and he tilted his head to the side. She braced herself. That now very familiar look of his only heralded cockiness. Why did she have to go and ask him such a loaded question? Lina tapped her foot, all too aware of other customers that desperately needed her attention.

"Stupid jackass," Merona said with conviction. "I don't like this man, Lina."

He's fine, Granna. A little too sure of himself, but harmless.

"Well now, sugar pie," he drawled.

Lina grit her teeth. Okay, that was definitely worse than buttercup. Good lord that was lame.

"You really wanna know?"

No!

Merona glided toward Ty, her aura spiking with shades of black.

"Excuse me, miss." A customer called to her. Lina turned and gave him a weak smile. The bespectacled man held up his empty coffee mug with a jerk.

"Just a second please." Lina tried to keep her voice calm, though her body hummed with annoyance. The customer's mouth set in a straight line, and she turned once more toward Ty.

"Ty, really, I'm too busy for games. Give me your order."

Ty tilted his head. "So it's Ty is it? I see you've been talking about me behind my back."

Lina refrained from rolling her eyes. "No. Not really. Small town. You're bound to hear names pop up now and then."

"Well,"--he puffed out his chest--"did you know that I'm a champion bull rider? Won the belt three years in a row."

Oh merciful heavens! Now she was more than just annoyed at this man--who so obviously had a God complex--she was downright pissed off.

"Miss," the customer called again.

Lina turned and gave the gentleman a tight smile. "Be there in a second, sir."

"Worst service I've ever received," she heard him grumble.

Oh jeez, things were going from bad to worse. And the day had started out so good.

Out of the corner of her eye, she caught Abby staring at her. Jess stood next to her grandmother with a curious look on her face. Yeah, just what she needed. Abby was going to ream her for sure.

"Look, Ty. I'll come back when you're ready to order."

She turned. Hard fingers pinched her behind. Lina stiffened and gritted her teeth. Being flirted with was one thing, but it went way beyond the bounds of decency to touch. Aware of the fact that she was still being watched, she decided to just walk away. Her grandmother had no such inclination.

"You rotten little bastard," Merona shrieked.

Lina turned on her heel just in time to witness Granna grab the steaming cup of coffee and send it tumbling onto Ty's blue-jeaned crotch.

Her mouth dropped open and her heart threatened to jump out of her chest.

"Shit, this burns like a mother!" The café noise stilled at Ty's loud outburst. He grabbed the white table napkin and dabbed his pants with it.

All Lina could think to do was turn toward Abby. Abby's face was unreadable, not shocked, not upset, nothing. Jess's eyes were not looking at the dancing Ty, but rather at Merona's glowing aura.

Merona clapped her hands together and gave a swift nod of her head. "That will teach that louse to harass my granddaughter."

Granna! She silently screeched. What have you done? My job....

"Your job is fine and dandy, sweetling. But you can't expect me to sit idly by and watch this man treat you with such disrespect. Besides, you were nowhere near him. Nobody will even know what happened."

Lina's heart rate slowly returned too normal. The clatter of talking once more filled the diner with noise, and everyone went on about their business. Maybe her grandmother was right, and she'd be lying to herself if she didn't admit that it gave her a little thrill to see Ty get his just desserts.

Chapter Six

From the Journal of Lina Brennen:
Drama. Life is full of it. And maybe I'm being cynical, but I'd swear my life has seen more than its fair share.

* * * *

Lina sucked her lip between her teeth and casually strolled toward the counter where Abby sat with a lighted cigarette between her fingers.

Her pulse pounded erratically. The breakfast crowd had long since left. The diner had been cleaned and was now ready for the five o'clock swarm. If Abby was going to fire her, it would be now. She'd walked on pins and needles all morning wondering what would happen. Abby had barely uttered a word to her and that, more than anything, convinced Lina she'd lost yet another job.

"Ab ... Abby." She cleared her throat and tried again. "Abby, about this morning ... ."

Abby turned corn blue eyes on her and gave a gentle smile. "You were wonderful, Lina. Especially for this being your first time." She took a drag from the cigarette and exhaled. Gray curls of tobacco-scented smoke wafted through the air. "And don't even worry about the coffee incident. It could have happened to anyone. You weren't anywhere near Ty."

Lina refrained from snorting. No, it wouldn't have happened to anybody else, but she wasn't about to set Abby straight about that. The tight knot in her stomach slowly eased and she gave a swift smile. "Thanks."

Abby nodded and took another drag off the cigarette. "See you at five."

Before the woman could change her mind, Lina hightailed it out of there. She exhaled and rubbed her left temple, attempting to ease the rising throb of shooting pain. That had been close. Much, much too close.

"Oh, what are you worried about, Lina? You can't tell me the man didn't deserve it. Him and that cocky swagger. It was deplorable."

"Yeah, but, Granna,"--she turned and narrowed her eyes at her grandmother--"you should never have done that. I love you and your childish pranks, but you're really gonna have to curb those outbursts around me."

"Sweetling, I wasn't pulling a prank. That man got what he deserved."

"And then some," Lina said, and snorted. Remembering how Ty had cried out like a little girl made her lips quirk. All her pent-up emotions came rushing out and she threw her head back and let out a great peal of laughter. "Oh, God, Granna, that was hilarious." Lina wiped tears from the corner of her eyes.

"See, I told you." Merona grinned broadly, her warm blue eyes crinkling at the corners and she chucked Lina's chin. "Where are we going, anyway?"

Lina walked quickly down the sidewalk. "To the mercantile Jess was telling me about yesterday. I need to get Lucky a litter box and a bag of food."

"Ahh." Merona nodded and glided by her side. Her grandmother's face twisted and then laughter bubbled from her lips. Lina joined in, knowing she looked like an idiotic fool but not giving a rat's ass. She'd just survived her first day on the job from hell.

* * * *

Lina huffed and pushed strands of her blond hair out of her face. It was as hot as the devil outside and she'd just lugged ten pounds of cat food, ten pounds of cat litter, and a big ol' litter box from one end of town to the other. She needed to rest.

She plopped down on the couch and propped up her feet. Lucky jumped onto her stomach and curled into a ball, swiftly falling back asleep with a soothing, rumbling purr.

Her apartment was nice and cool after running the window unit all morning.

Merona glided to the rocker in the corner and sighed dramatically.

"I don't know what you're sighing for, Granna. It's not like you actually did anything to tire yourself out."

"Don't sass me, girl. And why do you have your feet all propped up like an invalid?"

Lina snorted. "I just so happened to carry a bunch of heavy things with me, and my feet are aching something fierce. I never knew being a waitress could be so tiring."

Just then, a solid knock landed on her door. Lina jumped. The shift caused Lucky to land with a thud on the floor. She gave a disapproving meow and padded off. Lina raised her brow and glanced at the clock on the wall next to the bookshelf. She wasn't due back at work for another hour.

A knock again, this time louder.

"Don't just sit there, sweetling, answer it."

Lina groaned when she placed her weight on her tender feet and walked toward the door. "Yes?" she called.

"It's Trent, Lina. Open up."

Her heart spiraled into her stomach and her mouth suddenly went dry. She opened the door and had to take a quick breath.

Trent's soulful blue eyes peered intently into her own. "I came to see how your morning shift went. Heard a rumor of you throwing coffee onto Ty's lap." He chuckled. "I just had to see if it was true."

Goose bumps trailed up her forearms. His grin was so disarming and much too breathtaking. She opened the door wider and welcomed him in.

"Well, I didn't throw the coffee on his lap. Though, I almost wished I had."

His long, blunt fingers shoved through his unruly obsidian hair, and he entered, sitting down on one end of the couch.

Lina closed the door and followed suit, kicking up her feet and groaning with relief.

"That bad, huh?"

She closed her eyes and nodded. "Worse. I'm so tired, Trent. There aren't enough words in the dictionary to explain how I feel right now."

He chuckled and patted his knee. "Give here."

Lina shot her eyes open and stared at him. "What?"

"Your feet. I'll massage them for you, and in return, I want you to tell me all about it. Start from the beginning." His lips tilted into a grin. "And don't leave out one little detail."

Nu-uh, no way was she putting her sweaty, tired feet in his lap. "Uh ... thanks, but no thanks." She got up off the couch and went into the kitchen. "I made some iced tea last night, want some?"

* * * *

A spike of disappointment went through him, but he pasted on a smile, anyway. "Sure." He'd just wanted to touch her. Even if all he could touch was her feet. He loved the way her skin felt, all smooth and rose-petal soft. She did look tired, but damn, she still looked good enough to eat.

He watched her pour two plastic tumblers of iced tea and carry them toward him. "Here you go. My own special blend." She plopped back down on the couch next to him after he took the cup from her.

He sipped, nearly choked. "What the hell is this?" He wiped his chin.

"Jamaican sarsaparilla and juniper berry." She gave him a look of concern, her forehead wrinkling ever so cutely. "You don't like it?"

Now, he didn't want to offend her, he'd done enough of that to last a lifetime, but it was god-awful. He set the glass on the coffee table and leaned back. "I'm used to tea that comes out of little bags with strings attached. Sorry."

Her smile was a little sad, and he hoped he hadn't ticked her off again.

"The combination cleans out all sorts of nasty toxins in your body. Juniper berry is very good for your kidneys." She set her glass next to his. "Not everyone has a taste for herbal tea." She folded her hands demurely in her lap and stared down at them.

He wanted to drag her into his arms and kiss her. Wanted it more than he would have ever imagined. Little tendrils of hair had slipped from the messy knot she'd pulled it into, and kissed her cheeks in a beguiling way. The denim skirt rode high on her thighs, showcasing a long expanse of beautifully toned, slightly tanned legs. He wanted to run his hands up them, under the skirt. To touch her, to hear her say his name on a breathy sigh as she--

"I really didn't dump the coffee on Ty. I don't know what happened. I'd turned away to help another customer, and the next thing I know, he's hopping around cursing a blue streak."

Ever so slowly, Trent brought his gaze up over her flat belly to the soft swells of her small breasts. His fingers itched to touch them, to run his thumb over her nipples and watch them harden.

"Even your mother said it wasn't my fault. I made almost fifty dollars in tips this morning. That's good, isn't it?"

He could see her heartbeat at the base of her throat. He wanted to dip his tongue into the slight hollow there, taste her. Taste all of her. To run his tongue, his lips, his teeth, from the top of her forehead to her toes.

"I really like the old men. They're so cute. The brothers, what were their names? Oh, yeah, Jake and Junior Barnes. They invited me to their place for a picnic on Sunday. But I told them I had to work. They said I could come out on my day off and go swimming in their pond."

Her ears, so delicate, so perfect. Her earrings were day-glow pink roses today, dangling from green vines. She had a little silver hoop in the top part of her ear. Even that seemed sexy. Her nose was cute, turned up slightly at the tip, delicate. And her lips. Dear Lord, her lips were the most erotic thing he'd ever seen. Full, perfectly formed, always glossy pink. So easily he could imagine them on his body, where he wanted them most.

Her tongue darted out over the bottom one and his body hardened in an instant.

"You gonna just stare at me all day?"

His brain went numb. Other parts of his body heated, throbbed. Blood coursed through his veins, sensitizing his fingertips. He reached up and brushed a long, silky curl away from her cheek, rubbed it between his fingertips. "I think I have to kiss you," he said, his voice unnaturally gravelly.

Her breath sucked in harshly, her lower lip trembled ever so slightly before she tucked it between those not so perfect teeth. Then her lips curved into a slight smile. "Please do," Lina whispered as she moved toward him.

She rested her small, elegant hand against his chest. The feel of her fingers curling into his shirt tugged at his heart. It had been so very long since a woman touched him so gently.

He finally looked into her eyes. His breath hitched. Passion. He saw it there in those deep pewter eyes. Passion and longing and ... He slowly lowered his head and brushed his lips over hers, softly, tenderly, breathing in her warm, musky, flowery scent.

She sighed against his mouth, her hot breath burning his skin, igniting a flame inside him he wasn't sure could ever be extinguished until he was inside her.

He cupped the back of her head in his palm. The loose knot slipped and a cool mass of downy hair slid over his hand, his arm, tickling his skin. His other hand slipped around her waist, down her back, and he pulled her closer, until her breasts pressed against his chest, her thigh touched his.

She lifted her arms around his neck and pulled him even closer. And then he moved in for the kill. She gave no resistance as he swept his tongue into her mouth. Oh God, she was sweet. Like a hot summer rain, sunflowers, and cotton candy. Her lips were damp and soft, so absolutely perfect.

Her fingers speared through his hair, tugging him even closer. He couldn't breathe. He could only feel. Her thigh slid over his as she practically crawled onto his lap. A sweet, erotic sound slipped from her throat, nearly pushing him over the edge of sanity.

Wrapping both arms around her, he laid her back on the couch, lowered himself over her, pressed against her, letting her feel how much he wanted her as his tongue delved deep into her mouth.

"Trent," she whispered when he raised his head to gulp in air. "Trent. Oh, Trent."

It was even sexier than he'd imagined. His name on her lips, her breath coming out in soft little puffs that brushed his overheated cheeks. Slipping his hand down her side, he tugged the hem of her shirt from the top of her skirt and his hand glided up her belly to the underside of her breast. Lace. He almost came on the spot just imagining what it looked like.

He skimmed his thumb over her breast, felt her nipple pucker, heard her quickly indrawn breath, saw her eyes darken with lust. For him.

Her fingers tugged on his hair and he brought his mouth back to hers. What a way to spend a hot, lazy afternoon.

* * * *

Oh yes! Lina thought as she arched her back against Trent's hard body and the hot hand that touched her so intimately. This was what she wanted. No, she wanted more. So much more. To feel him, all of him. Naked. Hot skin against hot skin. She reached for the buttons of his uniform shirt.

"Trouble's coming."

Her hands stilled on the third button. Get out, Granna!

Trent sucked on her neck and a moan slipped from deep inside her as she felt the pull of his lips all the way to her toes.

Merona floated over to the window by the door. "She's about to knock."

"No," Lina groaned. "Not now."

Trent's head popped up, his breathing harsh as he stared down at her, his brow furrowed into a fierce scowl. "Not now?" He pressed his hips against hers and there was no mistaking the fact that he wanted her. "Yes, now."

He lowered his head toward her just as the knock came.

"Get up," Lina whispered.

"Ignore it, whoever it is will go away." He nibbled on the corner of her mouth, ran his tongue along the curve of her top lip.

"It's Jess," Merona said. "And I think she's staring at me."

This was bad. Very, very bad. She needed to talk to Jess, find out if she really saw Merona earlier.

"Later, Trent," she whispered as she pushed against his shoulders.

"Now." He swept his tongue into her mouth again and she fought a battle with herself. Ignore Jess and enjoy Trent or hope that he came back later tonight, after she got off work.

The knock came again. "Lina? You home? Nana said you were here."

Trent shot off her like a stick of dynamite had gone off under him. "Oh, shit," he mumbled as he fumbled with his shirt, straightening it, tucking it into his pants. He glanced at his watch. "I better get back to work."

A giggle slipped out of her as she sat up. "You're on duty? Do the taxpayers know what you do while you're at work?"

He narrowed those sexy eyes at her as he did up his buttons. She laughed harder.

Jess knocked again. "Lina? I need to talk to you."

"Better answer the door," Merona said as she floated past Trent, touching his ear as she went.

Trent jumped and rubbed his hand over his ear. "What the hell?"

Stop that! Lina scolded as she got to her feet and headed for the door. And what the hell were you doing sneaking around watching me make out with him?

Merona laughed, a throaty laugh full of humor. "I've told you before, sweetling, I live vicariously through you."

That's just sick. Lina pulled open the door. "Hi, Jess, what's up?" She stepped aside to let the girl in.

"Dad? What are you doing here?"

"I ... um ... came by to see how Lina's first day of work went."

"Yeah, like he heard anything you said," Merona chuckled.

Not now! Lina silently yelled. Go to the bedroom, and stay out of trouble.

"Are you kidding? And miss this? Not on your life."

Jess tilted her head to the side and looked directly at Merona.

"Well. Trent. You've got to get back to work, right?" Lina asked, taking him by the arm and leading him toward the door.

"Yeah." He gave Jess a kiss on the cheek. "See you at the diner at six?"

Still staring at Merona, Jess gave a little nod. "Yeah. Sure. Whatever."

Trent looked behind him, as if trying to figure out what Jess was staring at.

"Gotta go," Lina urged. "Criminals are waiting to be arrested, or something, right?"

Trent gave her a crooked grin as he laid his hand on the doorknob. "Yeah, right. Can't really remember when the last time I actually arrested someone was."

"Kevin Jennson, drunk and disorderly," Jess said, sending her dad a big grin. "But you let him go the next morning."

A wide grin spread over Trent's gorgeous face. "That's right." He gave Jess an affectionate flick on the nose. "See you in a few hours. Stay out of trouble."

"I'm not the one getting into trouble," Jess mumbled as she reached up and smoothed down Trent's hair--the hair Lina had just had her fingers in, the hair she'd mussed up.

Trent's face did that strange reddish-purple color change again, and Lina had to suppress a little laugh.

"Right. Okay. Later." And then he was gone. He sure did have a thing with running out of her apartment, tail between his legs.

Lina shut the door and turned toward Jess. "So, what brings you here?"

"How'd you do it?" Her question was direct, her gaze steady.

Lina wanted to squirm. "Do what?" she asked innocently.

"The coffee on Brock. You were five feet away from him, but I know you did it. I want to know how." The girl didn't look twelve right now, she looked as suspicious as any adult ever had in every place she'd ever been caught in. And damn it, it was all Granna's fault.

"Don't you blame this on me, girl. That man got what he deserved. How could I stand by and let him touch you like that? No man has a right ... unless you want it."

Jess swung around. Her gaze locking onto Merona. "Who said that?"

She didn't look frightened, Lina realized. She looked ... intrigued.

"You heard something?" Lina asked.

"I see something, too. The same something I saw this morning. It looks like a big ball of glow-in-the-dark stuff over there." Jess pointed right at Merona where she sat in the corner on the rocking chair.

Lina didn't know what to do. Didn't have a clue. She'd never been in this situation before. No one, not one person in twenty-some-odd years had ever seen Merona.

"I'm Lina's great-great-grandmother Merona."

"A ghost," Jess whispered as she moved toward Granna. "How cool is that?"

"Not cool," Lina said with heart-felt disappointment rippling through her. Now Jess'll tell Trent, and if he had a problem with herbs--holy crap, what was he going to think about this?

"So, she like, lives with you?" Jess asked.

"Yeah, can't get rid of her. Look, Jess--"

"Why doesn't she look like a ghost ... or human ... or whatever? Is this like, just her soul? There's no body?"

Jess sighed, picked up the practically untouched glasses of tea off the coffee table, and took them into the kitchen.

"You have to let yourself see me," Merona answered. Lina knew she would. She was going to give Jess the same talk she'd given Lina when she was a child. Merona was loving this. She hated being ignored all the time. Little prima donna that she was, always wanting to be the center of attention. That's why she'd been bugging Trent every time he was around. She enjoyed feeling nearly human.

"What do you mean? I can see you. You look like a glow-in-the-dark cotton ball."

Lina dumped the tea down the drain and rinsed the glasses.

Merona chuckled. "Actually, I look like a twenty year old fashion model."

Lina couldn't help but laugh at that. "She's a liar, too. She looks like a wrinkled old lady in a calico dress with lace ruffles."

"Don't be rude, sweetling."

Jess's laugh was a little breathy, a little nervous, as she glanced from Merona to Lina and back. "So how do I let myself see you?"

"Wait, Granna," Lina said. "Jess, we need to talk about this first. If your father finds out--"

Jess fiercely shook her head. "No way would I tell the old man about this. Are you kidding? He freaked out about your books. Imagine if he knew you lived with a real live ghost!"

Merona chuckled. "Not exactly live."

Jess grinned, her bright green eyes sparkling. "You know what I mean."

"Promise?" Lina asked, though she hated to have a kid keep a secret from her own father.

"I swear it. He'd have a total farm."

Lina frowned. She hadn't heard that one before, must be teen-speak for having a lot of cows? She chuckled. "All right." She glanced up at the clock. It was ten minutes to five. "I've got to get to work. You can stay here for a while and talk to Granna if you want. Just don't be late meeting your dad."

"I'll make sure she gets to the diner," Merona promised, and gave Lina a brilliant grin. The old lady was really loving this. How could Lina not let her have her fun? She had so little to enjoy in life ... or death ... or whatever. Lina shook her head. "Lock the door before you leave, okay?"

"Okay." Jess smiled at her. "Hey, you know, it's okay with me if you and Dad ... you know ... get close and stuff."

"Thanks," Lina said as she headed for the door. *But if Dad finds out about this, there won't be any getting close.* Of that she was sure.

Chapter Seven

From the Journal of Lina Brennen:
Mischievous old bat! Granna won't leave the humans alone. And I get blamed for her little pranks. She's about two hundred years old. I really wish she'd grow up!

* * * *

Lina swung open the door of the diner and smiled. She was still exhausted, but she felt so ... alive. As she'd passed the big window in front of the sheriff's office, Trent had looked up, the phone to his ear, and sent her a little wave and a wink. He really was a yummy looking man. And he wanted her. Little tingles rushed through her at odd moments when she remembered the feel of his lips on hers, his hands on her body. No man had ever made her feel so ... electrified.

"Hi, Abby," she said as she headed to the back to get her apron.

"Hi. Jess find you?"

Her steps faltered a bit. She tied on the apron. "Yeah. She's still at my place."

Abby frowned a little.

"You know, that air conditioner in there is really good. She asked if she could hang out a while before she meets Trent for dinner."

Abby looked appeased with that answer as she picked up the coffee carafe and went to the only occupied table in the place. What did Trent say the man's name was? Walt? No, Willy. The town mechanic.

The man looked up at Abby and there was no mistaking the love shining in his soulful brown eyes. Lina shook her head and smiled. Must be something in the dry desert air. She could definitely see herself falling in love with Trent without much problem.

Or maybe one big problem. Namely, Merona. And if Jess opens her mouth and says anything ... Lina picked up a blank order tablet and tucked it in her apron pocket. She really had to think this through more. This time, if she was run out of town, it'd be by the sheriff. Talk about feeling like a criminal.

"Lina," Abby called, still standing at the table with Willy. "Come over here and meet a friend of mine."

Lina pasted a smile on her lips that she wasn't feeling right now, and headed across the diner.

"This is Willy Davis, Unegi's best mechanic."

Lina held out her hand to him. "Nice to meet you, Mr. Davis."

When his rough palm touched hers, her chest tightened. She met his eyes. They didn't look right. His skin was too pale. She had a difficult time catching her breath.

"Actually, I'm the town's only mechanic," he said with a playful grin. "That's why I can charge such outrageous prices."

"Mr. Davis," Lina said gently, as she laid her other hand on his shoulder. The tightness in her chest increased. "It's so nice to meet you."

"Well, now, darlin', I believe you've already said that." He grinned, but she could feel he was forcing the light-hearted attitude. Because his heart was pumping too hard. He was in pain. A vision of his arteries came to mind and she shut her eyes, letting herself see his problem. There it was. Her hands began to warm against him. If she could remove the clog, open it back up, then his pain would ease.

Willy sucked in his breath. Lina's eyes shot open. "Sorry," she whispered, and she jerked her hands away from him.

She turned and bumped into Abby. "Sorry," she said again.

"What was that all about?" Abby asked Willy as Lina made her way back to the counter.

Her hands shook. Willy needed help, but she couldn't do it right now. Not in front of Abby. Dear God, she thought as tears welled in her eyes, please let him hang in there until I can get him alone.

* * * *

Trent leaned back in his office chair, yawned, and stretched. He was late getting to the diner for supper but Jess was used to it. Bob Thornton spent a good hour and half chewing his ear off about those rustlers, wanted him to come back and stake out the ranch again tonight.

What he really needed was a good night's sleep. He hadn't slept well last night, thinking about Lina, thinking about that damned nightmare that came back to him at odd moments, like it had in the shower. And, well, he had a feeling he was going to be thinking about her again tonight. Especially after that rather incredible heavy petting session this afternoon.

Trent got up from his chair, took off his gun belt, and locked it in the bottom drawer of his desk. His snub-nosed .38 was tucked in his boot, so he only wore his "official" belt while he was "officially" on the clock. Not that he was ever officially "off" the clock, since he was the only law in this one-horse town.

He left the sheriff's office and locked the door behind him. Thinking about running out to the Thornton place after dinner didn't make him all that happy. He'd rather spend the evening with Lina.

And he wanted to find out why Jess had hung around Lina's apartment for an hour after Lina went to work. He seriously hoped she wasn't reading any of those idiotic books about communing with the dead.

Trent shivered. The last thing he wanted was Jess getting into any of that crap. Been there, done that, got the shit scared out of me.

The diner was packed when he went in. All the regulars, plus some. Abby even had Jess helping out, making rounds with the coffee pot.

"Hey, Dad," she said with a grin, as she walked past him.

"Sweetie," he said with a smile, knowing he couldn't break the rules and kiss her cheek in public.

"Hey, Sheriff."

Trent turned to see his friend, Stephen Webb, Unegi's very own Ph.D. Town family practitioner, shrink, pharmacist, and all around care giver. They'd gone to school together, been buddies since second grade.

Trent slipped into the booth opposite Stephen and grinned. "Thanks. Looks a little packed tonight."

Stephen gave a little smile and nodded toward Lina. "I think it has to do with the new waitress. She is one fine specimen of woman."

Trent had the sudden urge to smash his fist into his buddy's nose. "Really." His hands clenched around the menu, nearly crushing it. "I hadn't noticed."

Stephen cleared his throat, took a sip from his coffee cup, then grinned. "Funny. I thought I saw you talking to her this morning on the street." He propped his chin on his fist. "Seemed to me you were doing a lot of noticing. Especially when she turned around and bent over to pick up that coat she just happened to have dropped."

Trent glared at his friend. "Watch it, Webb."

Stephen chuckled. "Oh, I have been." His gaze slid off to the side, watching Lina as she approached with a platter of food.

Trent wanted to kill. She was still wearing the sinfully short skirt, that tight white tank top. And he remembered how every inch of her body had felt against his.

"Hey, Trent," Lina said as she set Stephen's plate on the table. "Hungry?"

"Oh yeah," he said before he could stop himself. Stephen chuckled. Trent ignored him. "I'd like the T-bone steak with fries. And a coffee. Please?" he added with a wink.

That pretty blush started moving up from her chest. Her eyes sparkled. Her lips tilted into a sexy grin. "Sure."

Lina returned to the counter for the coffee pot and he got lost in the sexy sway of her hips. He licked his lips, forgetting for a moment where he was, and who he was with.

"Mmmhmm." Stephen cleared his throat, bringing Trent's brain sharply back to focus. "Didn't notice, my ass."

Trent blew out a breath and shrugged. "All right, so she's hot."

Stephen raised a brow, a knowing smirk on his face.

"Okay, really hot. Better?" Trent asked sarcastically.

The bell jangled above the door, and Trent turned his head to see cocky Ty Brock swaggering through the entranceway. His temper, still hovering too close to the surface, flared up once more. He clenched his fists and flexed his jaw.

Ty tipped his hat to Lina and strutted to a corner booth.

That no good, rotten, low-down....

"Oohwee, Trent." Stephen shook his head. "You're jealous to boot. What is up with you and Ty? I swear, since the day that wife of yours left you, you've been up in arms when you see that man. We used to all hang out together. I miss those days."

Trent turned and nailed the good doctor with a glare. "Don't think my personal affairs are any of your concern, Webb. You ain't my shrink."

"Hey, just teasing. Sorry 'bout that."

"It's all right," Trent said off-handedly. He blew out a frustrated breath and focused on Lina's smiling face, his temper once more sliding into submission. He closed his eyes for a split second and inhaled her verbena-tinged perfume.

"Here you go, hot stuff," she said with a saucy wink as she filled his mug with steaming black coffee.

Stephen held out his mug and she filled it. "Hey, how about calling me hot stuff?" Stephen asked, his blue-green eyes crinkling with mirth.

Lina turned and stared at Trent's face. The look she sent him was passionate and sexy as sin. "I only say that when I mean it." Then she turned and flounced off.

Trent's chest tightened and a groan spilled from his lips. That woman was going to be the death of him.

* * * *

"Hey there, buttercup."

Here we go again, Lina thought, as she poured Ty's coffee. Granna, behave please, she pleaded.

"Hello, Ty," she said coolly, as set down the coffee pot and extracted her order pad. "What would you like to eat?" she asked, carefully choosing her words this time.

"You."

"Oh for goodness sake," she hissed. "Knock it off." She sent him her fiercest scowl.

"You asked, sugar pie. And I bet you're just as sweet as one."

Lina ground her teeth. "Burger? Steak? Fries?"

He gave her a cocky grin. "Burger. Nice and juicy. And a load of fries."

Lina scribbled the order and turned away. But she wasn't fast enough. He didn't pinch her butt this time, it was more of a caress.

"Oh, he's gonna get it," Merona ground out.

No, Granna. Please. There's too many people around. Lina slapped the ticket on the pickup window ledge.

"Why did you let him do that to you?" Jess whispered as she sidled up next to her. "He's a creep."

"No kidding he's a creep." Merona hovered next to them, her gaze fixed on Ty, a mean frown marring her normally gentle features.

"Is he like this with all women?" Lina asked as she poured cola from the fountain into two tall glasses.

"Yeah. I've heard rumors about him, too. About him and my mother."

Lina closed her eyes for a second. No wonder Trent couldn't stand the guy.

"My mother was...." Jess shrugged. "I once heard Nana refer to her as the town tramp."

"Oh, sweetheart," Merona said gently.

"It's okay," Jess said with another negligent shrug. "She didn't want me. I don't want her. I don't care how many men she's screwed."

"Jess," Lina said, taking her by the shoulders.

"Order up!" Mac called.

"We'll talk about this later, okay, honey?" Lina said. She'd lost her mother when she was young. She couldn't imagine never having one. Jess must be hurting something awful.

Jess bit her lip and nodded.

Returning to Ty's table with the plate of food, she was careful to stay out of his arm's reach. "Anything else? That's on the menu?"

"The diner's closed on Monday, right? Why don't you come out to my place? I'll show you how a rodeo pro does it."

Lina didn't even want to know what "it" he spoke of. "I'm going to be busy." She slapped the bill on the table.

"Busy doing what? You just moved here, don't know nobody yet."

"Washing my cat," she said as she took two steps backwards, away from the table, before turning her back on him.

"Oh, I do love a nice soft-- What the hell?"

Lina turned back in time to see him holding the ketchup bottle with two hands as it squirted the entire front of his face, shirt and lap.

And Merona was sitting on the table, her hands fisted around the bottle, holding Ty's hands in place, squeezing. Her eyes dancing with merriment.

Granna! Stop! Lina slapped her hand over her mouth, trying desperately to hold her laughter. From across the diner, Jess broke out in a peal of hysterical giggles. Heads turned.

Merona released Ty's hands and he dropped the bottle onto his plate. Curse words flew from his lips so fast, they were nearly indistinguishable from one another.

Lina heard Trent's deep, rumbling laughter, then others joined in. Abby walked up to Ty's table, plopped a towel down on it, and said, "Watch your mouth, sonny. There's younguns present."

Ty grabbed the towel and swiped it over his face. "What the hell kind of fu--"

Abby flicked Ty's ear. "You want to get kicked out of here? Keep it up. No fightin', no drinkin' and no damn cussin' in my diner. You know the rules. And keep your paws off my waitress."

Lina turned around and headed to Trent's table. Jess was sitting there, next to Doctor Webb. Trent had twisted around to see Ty. She slid into the seat next to him and buried her face in her hands.

Trent's big, callused hand settled on her bare thigh and he gave it a little squeeze. "That's two for two, from what I hear. Gonna tell me how you keep riggin' his food to explode on him?"

Lina giggled. Jess joined her.

Trent leaned over and whispered in her ear. "Can I walk you home when you get off work?"

Lina's heart gave a little tumble and tingles skittered down her arms as his breath brushed her neck. Her throat had suddenly closed on her. She nodded.

* * * *

"I'm leaving, Abby," Lina called out as she untied her apron. The customers had long since left and she was much too tired to stick around for another minute.

"Okay, no problem." Abby called from the backroom.

Lina groaned, her feet aching something fierce, her heart sick with fear for the sweet old mechanic, Willy, who had come and gone hours earlier. He'd been at the forefront of her mind all evening. Even her episode with the idiot Ty hadn't erased her desire to get to him. Lina knew time was of the essence. But when? She couldn't wait any longer than tomorrow afternoon, at the latest. She could only hope she'd reach him in time.

Someone knocked on the door, breaking her from her mulling thoughts, and she looked up to see Trent's devilishly handsome face smiling at her.

She went suddenly from being exhausted to elated, and as shy as a schoolgirl. Lina couldn't help the grin that took over as she walked outside. "Thought you'd forgotten about me."

He grabbed at his chest. "You wound me, Lina. I could never forget to walk home a girl as beautiful as you."

She tried to pretend that his pretty words didn't affect her, but her body hummed with pleasure. He was in good spirits, and for that she was grateful. Maybe they could even get back to where they'd been earlier in the day.

"So." Trent shoved his hands into his jean pockets and gazed at her. "You gonna tell me what happened with Ty tonight?"

Lina groaned and marched faster toward home. Why was it that the man always had an uncanny way of bringing up uncomfortable, unwanted topics of conversation?

Trent kept pace and cleared his throat.

Overhead the midnight blue sky glittered with millions of sparkling stars, a soft breeze rustled through her hair, and a pregnant, shimmering moon hung heavy and low. It was truly a beautiful night and she wanted to enjoy this walk. Especially this walk, with this man. She'd just have to figure out a way to steer the topic away from her misadventures with Ty.

"I don't know how that keeps happening to the man, luck of the Irish in him, probably." She shrugged.

Trent smirked and grabbed at her swinging hand.

"I can believe that. The man's a quarter Irish. Makes sense."

She froze, her heart hammering away in her chest. Lina licked dry lips, enjoying the sensation of his callused palm against hers. A flashback of Trent kissing the socks off her earlier flared through her mind, and her thighs trembled in response. Her breasts tingled and a delicious heat curled along her spine.

They strolled down the street toward her apartment in companionable silence. The only sounds stirring through the night was that of crickets and cicadas.

They walked up the dimly lit stairwell and stopped at her door. Lina licked her lips again. She wanted to invite him inside, but was that really wise with her grandmother hovering around them? The last thing she wanted was a repeat of Trent running from her apartment in terror.

But the temptation was too great. "You wanna come in?"

He stepped closer to her, enough so that she felt his body heat. He pushed a strand of hair out of her eye. "I'd like nothing more." His voice was gravelly, sultry. The heated promise in his dark eyes made her skin tingle.

Lina turned quickly, unlocked the door, and ushered him inside before he could change his mind.

Her grandmother's white eyebrows shot up, and a Cheshire grin curled her lips.

Trent ran his hands down her back and cupped her behind. "Mmm," he said, and pulled her toward the couch.

Merona lifted a fist to her mouth, her face drawing up into a look of mirth.

Don't you dare laugh, Granna. And I want you out of here this minute! And don't speak, you know that frightens him.

Don't you sass me, Lina. Merona waved her finger through the air. He's got the manners of an ape. But you like him, so I'll not toss any ketchup on him. Yet.

Trent leaned over and kissed her exposed neck, sending chills skittering down her arms. Lina leaned into him and moaned. She didn't want to, not in front of her grandmother, but when he touched her, she was helpless.

Period, Granna. You'll not toss any ketchup on him period. And what do you mean he has the manners of an ape?

Hmm. She lifted her nose in the air and sailed into the bedroom.

Lina breathed a sigh of relief. "You want any tea, Trent?"

He grimaced for a split second, enough time for her to realize just what he thought of her tea. "Um, no. I'm not really thirsty," he said in a low, sexy whisper.

She wrapped her arms around his neck, curls of heat spreading through her belly. God this was one sexy man. His sleeves were rolled up on his blue shirt, exposing tanned, corded forearms. She ran her fingers over them, stopping herself from purring aloud.

His blue eyes turned sultry and his full lips begged for a kiss. Lina leaned in, her lashes fluttering shut. His fingers kneaded her behind in a sensuous rhythm that stole her breath.

Trent groaned and pulled her in closer, letting her feel the evidence of his arousal. Lina wrapped one leg around his thigh and ran her hands down his pectorals. "Now," she whispered, "where were we earlier?"

Trent grinned and lowered his head. "Right here," he said.

Merona stuck her face over his shoulder. Lina, how unbecoming of you. You've only known this man for two days. I taught you better than that. A gentleman wouldn't be doing this yet. Not yet. You need more time to get to know him.

Lina yelped and stiffened in Trent's arms.

Trent pulled back a worried look on his face. "What's wrong?"

Shit, Granna! Look what you made me do. I said go.

Merona studied her nails, a bored look pasted on her face. I didn't make you do anything.

"Lina?" Trent waved a hand in front of her face, his blue eyes pensive.

"Oh." She threw her grandmother one last challenging glare and shifted toward Trent. "Leg cramp. I think I'll go get me some tea. You sure you don't want any?"

He sighed and shoved a hand through his hair, plopping down on the couch. "No."

Her heart ached for him. He looked like a sad little puppy. She narrowed her eyes at her grandmother and stomped into the kitchen.

That was evil. You made me look like the world's biggest jackass. Leg cramp. Like he'd really believe that.

Lina, I'm only thinking of you.

I thought you liked Trent. She fumed and threw open her cupboard with a powerful thwack. Lina grabbed a glass, squeezing it so tight, she was sure it would crack under the pressure.

I do. That does not, however, excuse your poor judgment.

Poor ... poor judgment? Her body trembled with rage and she slammed her glass down on the counter. How dare you? I'm a grown woman and I think I deserve a little fun every now and then.

I'm not saying you don't, Lina, sweetling. And if you don't stop slamming stuff around you're gonna run Trent out all on your own.

Lina bit her lip and gazed at Trent. His eyes were wide, his mouth open. "You okay, Lina?" he asked. "I mean, I could go if you want me to." Trent started to stand.

Lina blew out a quick breath and gave a tight smile. "I'm fine. Sorry. I just hate these damn leg cramps, don't you?"

"Yeah, sure." His gaze shifted and he rubbed his hands down his thighs.

She rolled her eyes and stifled the groan threatening to escape. What a colossal fool she was! And she really did need to calm down before she ruined this. Granna, please. I love you. But this is not the place for you. You can't just spy on me whenever you want.

Merona's lips quirked and she faded into a fine, white mist.

Satisfied that her grandmother wouldn't be bothering her and Trent any longer, Lina plunked two ice cubes into her glass, poured her tea, and walked over to Trent. Her heartbeat, along with her footsteps, much lighter.

"Sorry 'bout that," she said, taking a sip of the bitter brew.

"You sure you're okay?"

She nodded and smiled over the rim of her cup. "Much better now." Lina lifted her leg, loving the way his gaze homed in on it immediately, and rubbed her foot up and down his calf.

A transformation overcame him. Where once there was confusion, now she saw desire flaring and burning. Trent reached over, took the glass from her hand, and set it down on the coffee table.

Lina laughed, the stress of the last few hours rolling away. He pulled her down on his lap and nuzzled her neck.

"You sure your leg is fine?" he asked, planting soft kisses on her neck.

Lina inhaled his hot, spicy scent, her body screaming for his touch, for his nude skin on hers. All she could do was nod; her vocal chords had been paralyzed by desire.

His work-roughened hands slid up her bare arms. Goose bumps skittered like spider's feet up her flesh. She shivered and leaned into him.

Trent cupped the back of her head and laid her down on the couch, settling his weight over her. Then his lips crashed with punishing force against her own. She mewled and wrapped her arms around his neck.

Her world fragmented until all that remained was her and Trent. The here and now. No outside worries, no fears of running from the pitchforks and sickles, nothing but contentment and ardor.

Sage, wood and leather. He was all rugged. All man. Perfect. Her hands traveled under his shirt and she kneaded his tightly bunched muscles.

Trent groaned into her and deepened the kiss, his tongue mating with hers. Twisting and turning, nibbling and sucking. She lost herself in him.

His warm fingers slid under her shirt and he cupped her painfully sensitized breast. Lina whimpered, never wanting it to end. "Touch me, Trent. Everywhere," she whispered.

A loud crash sounded through the room, adrenaline zapped through her body, and Trent shouted so loud into her ear it rang. He shot up faster than she could take her next breath, his face set in a scowl. "What the hell?" he roared.

"What?" She gazed frantically, searching for Merona, knowing she was at the root of this. The old lady was hiding. Then she noticed her glass of tea had fallen over. Not just over, but off the coffee table onto the couch. Onto Trent. Her heart plummeted to her feet.

Lina turned toward him just as he plucked an ice cube from the back of his pants and threw it angrily to the floor. Her grandmother's beaming face came into view.

She ground her molars until they ached. How dare you! I told you to stay away.

I don't remember agreeing to such. I told you--Merona waggled her finger under Lina's nose--that type of behavior is unsuitable.

"I think I'm going home for tonight." Trent rubbed his wet rear.

"Oh no," she grabbed his hand, "are you sure?" All pleasure left her to be replaced by bitter disappointment.

His brows dipped and he nodded. "Yeah. Besides, I've got to check on Jess before I head out to Thornton's place." He leaned down, kissed her forehead, and then walked right out the door.

"Damn it all to hell!" Lina yelled, pinning her grandmother with her angry gaze. "You just couldn't resist. A kiss on my forehead, of all things." She poked her forehead with her finger. "He gave me a kiss on my forehead." She rubbed her stomach as the needles of pain coursed through her. Her body hummed with unrequited lust and aching regret.

"Next time you'll listen to me." Merona arched a brow.

Lina grabbed a throw pillow and chucked it toward Merona's head. Merona giggled and faded from sight a tenth of a second before the projectile landed.

"Arrgh!" Lina screamed. She stomped toward her bedroom and slammed the door shut behind her. Her body trembled with a mixture of fatigue, passion and anger. Her center was hot and aching. In the corner of the room, her grandmother snored with the sleep of mortals.

Lina punched her pillow and scowled.

Chapter Eight

From the Journal of Lina Brennen:
To save a person's life is the greatest gift ever granted me, and the greatest curse. Holding someone's future in my hands is a sacred thing. A scary thing.

* * * *

Lina hurried through the post lunch-rush cleanup and glanced at the clock on the wall over the door. One forty-five. Her heart raced, a cold chill settled in her bones. She had to get over to Willy's place and check on him.

"Abby," she called, heading into the kitchen.

"In here, Lina," Abby said from the storeroom. "I'm trying to figure out how soon we need to order napkins."

"The front's all clean," Lina said as she untied her apron. "Would you mind if I cut out a few minutes early? I need to run an errand."

Abby frowned. "I suppose so."

"I'm sorry, but this is very important." Her second day of work and she was asking to leave early. Not a good thing. But Willy's life was way more important than this job.

"Go ahead, then." Abby went back to counting packages of napkins.

Lina didn't waste any time dashing for the front door.

"Hey, Lina," Jess called from a half block down the street. "Where ya goin'?"

Lina fumbled in her jeans pocket for her keys. "Why aren't you in school?"

"Early out today. Teacher parent meetings, end of the year and all. Dad's there now."

Good, Trent wasn't around. Lina unlocked her door and slid behind the wheel.

"Can I come?"

"No." Lina slammed the door.

Merona unlocked the passenger door and swung it open. "Aw, let her come."

"Damn it, Granna. This is not the time!" Lina started the car as Jess plopped into the passenger seat.

"Why not? The child wants to learn, let her learn."

"Learn what?" Jess asked, and she buckled her seatbelt.

Lina peeled out of the parking spot and headed out of town toward Willy's garage. Jess grabbed the dashboard with one hand, the door handle with the other.

"Lina gets feelings sometimes. She's got one now."

"Enough, Granna."

"What kinda feelings?" Jess asked.

"Someone's in trouble."

"I'm warning you, Granna."

Merona chuckled. "Or what? You're always warning me, but you never do anything about it."

Jess laughed. "Kinda hard to control a ghost, huh?"

Lina shot Jess a glance. "You have no idea." She swerved onto the dusty one lane road, which lead to Willy's.

"Wow. You drive better than Dad."

Merona laughed. "Don't tell him that. He'd write her a ticket."

"Write me a ticket for you scaring the bejeezus out of him last night," Lina mumbled. "And that's another thing we are going to discuss, Granna. You need to mind your own damn business once in a while. Its my life."

But Merona wasn't in the back seat when she glanced into the rearview mirror. "Shit." She slammed on the breaks in front of Willy's Garage And All Around Fix-It Shop.

* * * *

"Willy!" Lina called and shot from her car--faster than Jess could blink--and ran toward the weathered and dilapidated auto repair shop.

Jess unhooked her seatbelt and ran after her. Her heart pounded furiously in her chest, her brain dizzy with fear for the sweet mechanic.

Jess skidded to a halt inside the dimly lit shop and stared at Merona's glittering gold and green form flitting in front of Lina's bowed head. And this time Merona was much more human looking than the ball of glow she'd seemed like yesterday. Jess could even make out the graying hair and her calico dress.

Merona shifted and Jess gasped when she saw Willy's sweat-soaked body sprawled against the wall. His hand lay over his heart, his shallow breathing interrupted only by the loud sounds of his retching. His lips were turning an alarming shade of blue.

Hot tears gathered at the corner of Jess's eyes and she stifled the sob that threatened to spill over. Not Willy. Not dear, sweet Willy. He can't die, he just can't.

"Lina." Jess's voice trembled. Her skin prickled and every strand of hair on her arm stood on end.

Her eyes widened as Merona's shifting colors exploded into a white ray of brilliance. Lina's hand whipped out and lay on top of Willy's, encompassing him in the great white light. Then a blast of heated air sizzled around Jess's head and Lina was enshrouded within a kaleidoscope of colors. Blue, red, purple, green, every imaginable color in existence seeped from Lina's pores. She looked like an angel.

In that moment, an overwhelming sense of peace nestled in Jess's heart, and she knew Willy would be okay.

Then the colors began to slowly subside, like high tide pulling away from the shoreline.

Willy's warm brown eyes opened. "Dear girl," he whispered to Lina.

Lina turned her face to look at him, her eyes glittering with unshed tears.

"You saved me," he said brokenly. A lone tear spilled down his cheek.

Frigid fingers gripped Jess's shoulders, her heart clenched in her chest and she jumped. She turned to see Merona smiling down at her. "I ... I see you," she said in reverent awe.

"Of course you do, child. Because you now believe."

The woman was gorgeous in an eerie, creepy kinda way. She reminded Jess of a Gibson girl, with her gray hair piled in a loose bun atop her head. Merona's blue eyes sparkled with keen wit and intelligence.

"How about we leave those two alone for a moment?" Merona whispered.

Jess looked back toward Lina and Willy, then nodded.

* * * *

Lina fought the waves of panic battering at her. It was one thing for Jess to know of her secret; children were more accepting of what they didn't understand. Willy, however, was a different matter entirely. She waited for his angry outburst. Each quiet second that ticked past seemed like a deathblow to her heart.

Willy's dark eyes studied hers, and then a smile tipped the corners of his lips. "I could never repay you for what you've done today, Lina." He lifted a trembling hand and trailed it along her jaw in an affectionate manner.

Lina bit her lip as a shiver coursed through her body. "You're ... you're not mad?"

He shook his head. "Lina, you've given me a second chance."

She sighed, the tight knot slowly loosening in her belly. "You have no idea what that means to me. You know who I am now, Willy. I've been running for the past fifteen years."

Willy stood ever so slowly and tested his left arm, rotating it from side to side. "You have a gift, Lina. Don't let anybody tell you otherwise."

"That's not what our town sheriff would say." She winced and shrugged. "He seems very afraid of me at times."

Willy laid a hand on her shoulder. "That boy's been through some rough times. Don't take the things he does or says to heart. He's a good man, and that's all that matters."

Lina stood and twisted a curl of hair around her finger. "That's what Granna keeps telling me, too."

His bushy brows gathered in a V. "Who?"

She waved a hand through the air and smiled. "Nobody."

"Well," he shook his head, "you have my word that I won't go tellin' anybody what happened here today, most especially not Trent Godfrey."

Lina exhaled, the cloying fear lifting from her shoulders. "Thank you."

Willy rolled his shoulders back and forth. "Damn, girl, I feel wonderful. Not a single pain racing through my old bones. I feel like I could run, even."

"Whoa, old boy." She wagged a finger under his nose. "Take it easy for a day or so. I can't stress this enough, Willy, you have to start eating better. I've healed your heart for now, but you could clog it up all over again with that high-fat diet you seem so fond of."

He shoved his fingers through his salt and pepper hair and grimaced. "I gotta start eating rabbit food?"

Lina cocked her head. "Yes, sir. Starting today when you come in for your evening meal, it's a salad for you."

"Ugh, you're worse than my mother used to be."

"Mmmhmm." She nodded. "I've got a personal interest in you now, Willy. And, by the way...." she narrowed her eyes.

He gave her a wide-eyed look. "Yeah?"

"Since you mentioned a second chance, how about you ask Abby out?"

"Wh...." he sputtered and scratched the back of his head, "What are you talkin' 'bout, girl?" A crimson streak trailed up his tanned neck.

The poor man wore his heart on his sleeve. "Don't even try to deny it, Willy. You've got the hots for a certain Ms. Abby Godfrey."

It wasn't possible for a man's skin color to turn a darker shade of red, but his did. Lina winked at him. "You'll hate yourself if you never try."

Willy yanked a soiled red kerchief from the back pocket of his oil-stained coveralls and wiped it down his face. "Mebbe you're right, girl. Mebbe you're right."

Lina patted his arm and walked away. Her job was done.

* * * *

Lina drove back in silence, every once in a while darting a glance at Jess. The child was chewing on her bottom lip and staring out the window.

Lina sighed and braked at the red light, the only streetlight in town. Figures she'd hit it. "Well, now you know all of it, Jess."

Jess turned her moss green eyes toward Lina. "Can I do that too?"

Lina's eyebrows rose. That was the last thing she'd expected to hear. Fear. Denial. Not this.

"No." She eased her car forward once more, the diner now clearly visible. "The healing touch is something directly related to certain bloodlines." Lina twisted her lip in thought. "You've definitely got something magical in your bloodline, but healing is probably not part of it, sweets."

"How do you know?" Jess persisted.

"Well...." Lina parked next to the diner and pulled the keys from the ignition. "Do you ever get a hot rush of awareness when someone has something physically wrong with them?"

"What do you mean?"

"Okay, say for instance,"--Lina shifted in her seat and gazed directly at Jess's thoughtful face--"when your dad catches a cold. Do you know beforehand that it's gonna happen?"

Her sparkling green eyes lost their luster and she gave her head a tiny shake. "No."

Lina grabbed Jess and hugged her. "Don't worry, sweetie. Like I said, you've got the magic strong in you. You've just have to figure out what exactly it is that you have."

Jess wrinkled her nose and nodded. "Yeah," she said finally.

Then a thought zapped through Lina and her eyes widened. "Hey. I have an idea."

That green sparkle was back in Jess's eyes.

"Have you ever attempted to contact your spirit guide?"

"What?"

"Everybody in the world has a spirit guide, but we have to be open to receive them. If you can see Granna, then you ought to be able to contact yours as well."

"Oh, Lina, sweetling, that's brilliant," Merona chimed in from the backseat. "Don't know why I didn't think of that myself."

"Really?" Jess asked.

Lina nodded and glanced at her wristwatch. Damn. It was time to clock back in. She shrugged. "Sure. Try it, Jess, and see. But be careful that your dad doesn't find out. The last thing we need is him banging down my door for exposing you to ghosts, ghoulies and witches. Which"--Lina held up a hand--"I'm not. I'm not a witch, I simply allow the spirits to speak with me." She winked at Jess. "Now, go on. I got to get back to work."

Jess smiled and exited the car.

She'd done a good thing, right? So why did she feel so nervous about it?

* * * *

The next week flew by with surprising speed. On Monday and Tuesday, her two days off, she and Granna went out to Jake and Junior Barnes's rundown little ranch. She packed a huge picnic to share with the sweet old men. The three of them went swimming in the little pond behind their house, a watering hole they fondly referred to as the "hot tub." They ate together at the water's edge, and she relaxed in the long, untrimmed grass as they told her amazing tales of their life in Unegi over the past three quarters of a century.

The brothers had been born among the hustle and bustle of a different kind of Unegi than today. Silver mining was in full swing, and the untamed Wild West was a living thing. Gunfights and dance hall girls, running moonshine during Prohibition, and watching the town fade into the near nothingness it was now.

Both days, when she got home, Jess was waiting for her on her doorstep. She was anxious to learn how to contact the spirit world. It wasn't as easy as Lina thought it would be. The girl still had doubts. Lina and Merona spent a couple of hours each afternoon teaching her relaxation and meditation techniques, but her cynical side hampered her progression. For such a young girl, she had very adult emotions.

And Trent.

Lina sighed as she slipped a pretty summer dress over her head and began buttoning the tiny seed buttons on the front. He'd been swamped with work. Mr. Thornton kept him busy out at his place searching for rustlers. He'd avoided her for a couple days after the iced tea incident, but he'd finally come around. Last night he'd asked her out on a date. A real date. He was taking her to the local saloon for drinks and dancing.

After that, well, she had plans for him. A slow smile curled her lips as she dabbed her favorite perfume on all the special spots.

Chapter Nine

From the Journal of Lina Brennen:
The one thing I miss the most in life is companionship. Someone to talk to, to spend time with. Someone with a flesh and blood body.

* * * *

Trent felt like a green kid on his first date. In a way, he supposed he was. This was the first time in more years than he could count that he'd gone out with someone who sparked him the way Lina did. He stood on the landing of Lina's apartment in the early evening's golden glow of the sunset, staring at the door. Switching the crystal bud vase with a single sterling rose from his right hand to his left, he let out a deep breath. This is it. He raised his hand and just as he was about to knock, the door opened.

Lina ducked, avoiding the hand coming at her, then laughed. "Right on time. I was going to wait out here."

Trent thrust out his left hand. "I got this for you."

Lina's eyes went wide, and then he saw the quick sheen of tears that formed in them. "Oh, Trent. It's beautiful." Almost reverently, she took the vase from him and brought the aromatic flower to her nose. Her eyes drifted shut as she inhaled.

Trent's body went rigid in an instant as blood rushed to his groin, pounded in his ears. "Sweet Heaven," he murmured. How could one little woman be so damn sensual? How was he going to get through this date without ripping that sexy little dress from her even sexier little body?

She sent him one of those knee-weakening, make-your-heart-pound-out-of-your-chest, crooked-toothed smiles before turning away. Her summer dress, an assortment of odd shades of pink and purple and ... plum, he supposed, swirled around her shapely thighs and ended almost illegally short of her knees. The bodice hugged her gentle curves, the tank-top style top left her arms bare. About a million tiny, pearly-blue buttons ran down the front.

He stepped into the apartment and shut the door. When she bent to place the rose on the coffee table, the skirt rode up in back, exposing about a mile of bare leg. Forget going out. He stepped toward her, arms held out as if to capture her before she got away.

"Hey Dad."

Trent turned his head, thwacked his shin on the edge of the coffee table, and nearly took a nosedive into the couch. "What are you doing here?" he asked, as he flopped down on the couch and rubbed his smarting leg.

Lina sat down next to him, her hand joining his as he rubbed his shin. His body and mind warred over the fact that she was touching him while his daughter was in the same room. And his body was winning, damn it all to hell.

Jess came out from the bathroom, Lucky the cat in her arms. "I came over to wash the cat."

"Wash...." Trent frowned, glanced at Lina who smiled sweetly at him, her hand gently massaging his leg now. He cleared his throat. "Okay." He shook his head. Why Lina wanted Jess to wash her cat was beyond him, but who was he to say anything? Jess had blossomed under Lina's attention. Her snippy teen attitude had lessened in the last few days. He should be grateful to Lina, not suspicious.

Then he glanced around the room at the candles, the crystals, the books on communing with the dead on the bookshelf, and the dead plants hanging upside down in the kitchen window. Suspicions. Yeah, he had them in spades where she was concerned. But, damn it all to hell, he was beginning to not give a good goddamn. He wanted her.

"Dad?"

He swung his gaze from the drying plants to his daughter who stood there, holding that mangy feline, and smiling at him with such a sweet, innocent expression, his heart did a little dip. He smiled at her. A smile he hoped conveyed all the love he felt for her. His baby, his Jessica.

He patted Lina on the knee and stood, then held his hand for her. "Ready to go?" he asked.

Lina smiled, nodded demurely, her gray eyes the color of polished silver, glimmering with humor. He wondered why. No, he didn't really care. He just knew that tonight was the night. He was going to bring her home and he was going to make love to her. The waiting was over. No one, and nothing--he narrowed his eyes and glanced around the room, waiting to hear a voice, feel that eerie sensation on the back of his neck--was going to stop him.

* * * *

"The Four Aces Saloon," Lina murmured as they pulled up in front of a clapboard building on the far outskirts of Unegi. "Cool name."

Trent turned the key, killing the engine of the police cruiser. She'd never been in a cop car before. High tech electronics in the dashboard, a tiny computer he said was for looking up criminals, a shotgun mounted between the seats.

A thrill of excitement rushed through her as he got out of the car and came around to give her a hand out. He looked so incredibly good in the tight, faded blue jeans that hugged his muscular butt, scuffed black western boots and western cut white shirt that stretched over the muscles of his pecs and shoulders.

She'd come real close to telling Jess it was time to go home so she could drag her father into the bedroom for a night of frolicking, preferable completely naked, in that huge bed.

Lina giggled to herself and took Trent's big, rough hand as he helped her out of the car. Sigh. Such a gentleman.

"There's something I forgot to do," he said seriously.

Her smile faded. "You have to go back to work?" Well, crap.

His smile was a little lop-sided, incredibly sexy. He shook his head. Then he reached up, ever so gently cupped her cheeks in his warm hands, and leaned down until his lips were just a breath away from hers. "I didn't kiss you."

Her soft little "ohh" died inside his mouth as he captured her mouth with his and dipped his tongue inside. Her knees went weak and she leaned into him, her hands fisting into the material of his shirt. Her skin tingled where he touched her. Her nipples tightened into hard little pebbles and ached for his touch.

Trent slowly ended the kiss with tiny nibbles and teasing strokes of his tongue. "Much better," he whispered, his voice gruff.

Lina could only nod. Not really better, she thought. Now she wanted to rip his clothes off and have her way with him. And they had this stupid date to get through. She took in a shaky breath and opened her eyes. He smiled down at her with such a tender look that she nearly melted, and the heated breezes of the late evening had nothing to do with it.

"Ready to go in?"

Again, she nodded. His hands trailed down from her face, along her neck, over her shoulders and down her bare arms. Goose bumps popped up at his touch and she shivered in anticipation of the night to come. No way was she going to let him get away again.

Granna had been dealt with. She'd work with Jess for an hour or so on her meditation, and then she'd head to Abby's house with Jess, and not come home until morning. She'd have him alone, totally alone, for the first time. And she was going to take every advantage of the situation. She looked up into his eyes and smiled. She'd take advantage of everything.

He laced his fingers through hers and turned toward the front of the Four Aces. Oh, yeah. She looked forward to taking advantage of him.

The saloon was everything she'd expect from this neck of the woods. The tables and chairs were solid wood, scratched and scarred from years of use. A bowl of peanuts, still in the shell, sat on each table. The floor was covered in sawdust. The long bar, brass rail and all, was worn from age, and looked like something out of an old west movie. Behind the bar was a shelf of booze bottles, and behind that was a long mirror, hazy from years of exposure to cigarette smoke.

Some of the tables were occupied by cowboys, a few she recognized from the diner. There were only three women in sight, all sitting at one table, talking loudly, obviously already well on their way to being drunk.

In one corner was a tiny dance floor and a jukebox that spouted out soft country tunes. From the back, she could hear the clack of billiard balls and the soft fwap of darts hitting a board.

"This place is really neat, Trent."

"Glad you like it." He eyed her as he led her to a table and held out a chair for her. "I wasn't sure if you'd feel comfortable here."

She frowned at him after he took his seat. "Why would I not be comfortable?"

He gave her a little shrug and didn't meet her gaze. "Big-city girl like you, you're probably used to fancier joints."

Big city girl, she thought and dropped her gaze to the scarred table. That wasn't the first time she'd heard that out of him. He seemed to have a problem with city people. As she traced ancient initials in the table with her fingertip, she asked, "Does it bother you that I'm from a big city?"

"Can't see why anyone from Chicago, with its nightlife, theaters, shopping and restaurants would want to hang around a dried up old cattle town like Unegi for long."

Because you're here. Because Jess and Abby are here. Because of Willy and all the other wonderful people I've met who made me feel like I fit in for the first time in my life.

"Maybe I need a change. Maybe I don't like big cities." She raised her eyes and didn't understand the look on his face. Concern, concentration, suspicion.

"What are you running away from?"

Her breath caught and she nearly choked.

"Are you in trouble? Is someone looking for you? Do you have an ex who's trying to find you?"

She shook her head. How she wished she could be honest with him. Tears prickled her eyes and she looked away so he wouldn't see them. She was not the weepy kind, what was up with all the tears? Her emotions were running away, and she needed to get them under control. Immediately.

He reached across the table and took her hand in his. "Sweetheart, you can tell me. I can help."

Lina pulled her hand away and reached for a peanut and slowly shelled it while she thought of an answer. Something that wasn't a lie, but that wouldn't reveal the pain of her past.

"Hey there, Sheriff."

Lina glanced up to see a woman standing at the side of the table. She was tall and thin, with huge blonde hair piled high on her head. Her tight black skirt just barely covered the essentials. The same could be said of her bright pink tube top.

"Hi, Carrie," Trent said, the exasperation in his voice unmistakable. "This is Lina Brennen, Mom's new waitress at the diner."

Carrie snapped her gum and gave Lina a little nod. "Nice ta meet'cha. What can I get ya?"

"Lina?" Trent asked, eyebrows raised.

"Um. Do you happen to have Guinness?" she asked.

The woman, with too much purple eye shadow and way too much dark rouge, frowned. "Don't think so." Her gum snapped again.

Trent chuckled. "They've got all-American beer. On tap or in the bottle. I'll take a Bud light, on tap."

Lina nodded. "Same, then, I guess." As Carrie walked off, she sent Trent a wink over her shoulder that Lina wasn't sure if she was meant to see or not. Had Trent dated that woman? Slept with her? Did she have any claim to him?

"You can stop shooting daggers at her back now, Lina," Trent said with a chuckle in his voice.

She snapped her gaze back to his. "I have no idea what you're talking about," she said in the haughtiest tone she could manage.

His deep rumbling laugh sent tension of another kind roaming around inside her. Tension she wanted to feel more of. "It's a small town, Lina. Everyone here has history. Carrie and I dated a few times. That's all. And it was a very long time ago."

"I didn't ask, did I?" She popped the peanuts she'd been fiddling with into her mouth.

"If looks could kill...." His blue eyes sparkled with humor.

Lina leaned her elbows on the table. "Kinda rude, don't you think, that she flirts with you while you're out with someone else?"

"Carrie's harmless," he said, propping his own arms on the table and leaned in closer to her. "Unlike you."

Her eyes widened. "What is that supposed to mean?"

He closed the space between them and planted a sweet, quick kiss on the tip of her nose. "It means, darling dear, that you are extremely dangerous."

Darling dear. She grinned. Couldn't help it. His playful mood was contagious. "Oh, how little you know," she whispered.

Trent's loppy-sided smile grew. "I hope you plan on showing me just what I don't know."

Her heart soared. She could see it in his eyes. He wanted her as much as she wanted him. She sat back in the chair, crossed her arms over her middle, and raised one eyebrow. "I don't know....." she teased. "What do I get in return?"

"Your wildest fantasies brought to life," he whispered, his voice all low and gravelly again.

A shiver of anticipation coursed through her, making her blood pound in her ears, the fine hairs on her arms prickle. Would it be rude to suggest they forget their drinks and head back to her place?

She glanced at his watch. Damn, Jess would still be there. And Granna. She'd have to just bide her time and enjoy being with him.

"In a hurry to get somewhere?" Trent asked, obviously seeing her gaze wander toward his wristwatch.

"Just wondering how long it takes to wash a cat," she muttered.

Trent leaned back in his chair and let out a laugh. "You make me smile, sweetheart. It's been a long time since I felt like that."

Her heart tightened, the air squeezed out of her lungs, those damn tears tried flooding her vision again. "You make me happy, too," she whispered, through a throat that'd tried to close down on her.

Carrie returned with their drinks. Trent handed her a bill and told her to keep the change. For service that slow, and the lustful way she stared at him, Lina wouldn't have given her a tip at all. Unless it was to tell her to keep her eyes off her man.

A loud group of cowboys sauntered from the back part of the bar, laughing and slapping each other on the back. Lina turned to look at them. One of them snagged her attention. Oh, wonderful. Why'd he have to be here? Mr. Rodeo Star Ty Brock was with the group, and his gaze immediately zeroed in on her. She turned back to see Trent's dark frown. She picked up her beer and took a hearty swig.

Poor Trent. If what she'd heard was true, that Ty had had relations with Trent's ex-wife, no wonder he hated the man.

"You play pool?" she asked, trying to get Trent's attention back on her, and to get him to stop glaring at Ty. Jeez, in a town the size of Unegi, you'd think that after so many years there'd at least be a truce between them. Or a duel at dawn. She almost giggled again, thinking of the town sheriff facing off against the local rodeo celebrity.

"Get outta my town and don't ya be comin' back, ya hear?"

Ty narrows his eyes as they stand toe-to-toe in the middle of the street outside the mercantile. "Yeah, and what if I don't?"

Trent draws his side iron, cocks it, the metallic click loud in the early morning stillness. "Then I take you out in a body bag."

"Yeah, I play. You?"

"Hmm?" Lina said as she tried to focus in on Trent.

He snapped his fingers in front of her nose and chuckled. "Where'd you go? You asked if I play pool. I do. Do you?"

"Oh. Yeah." Lina shook her head and smiled to herself. "How old is this place?" she asked, scanning the saloon, once again taking in the bar and mirror, and the sawdust floor, which she now realized had dirt underneath, not wood.

"The building has been around since the turn of the century. Unegi was a small mining town then. This was the local watering hole." He stood up, picked up their beers, and tilted his head, motioning her to follow.

Wow, she thought, as she followed Trent into the back room with the pool table. It'd been a long time since a place opened up to her like this. She could feel it. The spirits of long-dead cowboys and miners. She glanced at a staircase that went up to a short hallway. And a whorehouse madam named Sue. She was still around, watching over her men as surely as she had a hundred years ago.

Trent set their drinks on a small table by the wall and pulled a pool cue from the rack.

"Were there any duels at dawn on main street?" she asked innocently, as she pulled her own cue down.

Trent chuckled. "You could say that." He chalked his cue. "Legend has it that the sheriff ran more than one man out of town. And those that didn't run fast enough"--he waggled his eyebrows at her--"didn't get very far."

Lina laughed at his teasing. "Jake and Junior Barnes said this sheriff was a relation of yours."

Trent put a quarter into the slot and the balls tumbled down. "Great-great grandpappy Godfrey." he said, employing a cute little southern twang. He started racking the balls. He grinned at her and winked.

And Lina would bet that, if her little vision back there was any indication, Grandpappy Godfrey had wife troubles, too. But Lina wouldn't ask. She liked Trent's teasing, his smiles. She didn't want to have any serious conversations tonight. She just wanted--

"You break," he said as he leaned against the wall and picked up his beer.

"You sure you want to do that?" she asked.

"That good, are ya?"

"Better."

"What kinda wager you wanna make?" His royal blue eyes sparkled with laughter and lust. Heat coiled in her belly.

"Winner's choice."

His tongue moistened his lips, one raven's wing eyebrow cocked up. "I like that."

Lina suppressed her grin. She'd been on a billiard team for the two years she lived in Nashville. Granna had wanted her to make friends, to try out for a team sport of some kind. Billiards was the only thing she was good at. And she was damn good. "Get ready to lose your shirt, honey," she said as she leaned over the table to take her first shot.

Trent's chuckle went through her like a live wire against her skin. "Is that all you want? My shirt?"

She tilted her head, sent him a lusty wink. "For starters."

* * * *

Five and half games later, Trent knew he was about to lose his shirt. He chuckled. Not that he minded, not one bit. Lina was a damn good player. He'd managed to keep up, but she was clearing the table, and he hadn't gotten one shot this game. The cowboys, friends of his for the most part, had gathered around the table, placing friendly bets-- against him. Hell, he was ready to bet against himself.

Standing behind Lina as she bent over the table taking an extremely difficult shot, thoughts of the game flew from his mind as he watched her curvy little behind wiggle into position. Damn, she was one fine woman. And tonight, she'd be all his. He didn't care how good a pool player she was, or how much she enjoyed beating the pants off him. After this game, he was taking her home.

Jess was spending the night with his mother. He had the whole night to spend with Lina, and he planned to use every minute of that time exploring her body. His fingers itched to run over her skin, his mouth watered at the thought of tasting her. All of her.

"Eight ball, right corner pocket," Lina announced.

He pulled his gaze away from her backside as she sauntered around the table. She'd done it again. Third game she'd cleared the table, not letting him get a single shot in.

She missed. The cowboys groaned. Lina let out a surprised gasp. Trent chuckled as he took his position. "Eight ball, left center pocket." And he sunk the sucker.

Lina huffed and crossed her arms over her chest, pressing those delectable breasts against the front of her dress. She wasn't wearing a bra. He grabbed the edge of the table to stay standing as lust shot through him hot and fast.

"One more," she said with a frown. "I can't believe I missed that shot."

Trent shook his head. "Next time. Aren't you ready to go?"

"But we're tied up, three-three. We can't end on a tie."

The cowboys loudly voiced their agreement.

Trent leaned down and whispered in her ear. "If there's no winner, we both get our choice."

"Oh," she said on a quick little sigh that tickled his ear. "Okay."

When he pulled away and gazed down at her, her cheeks had flushed to a pretty pink glow and her eyes had darkened to pewter. "Be back in a minute," he said softly.

She nodded and sent him a tiny, shy smile. "Don't be long."

Trent made his way to the men's room. He quickly took care of business, washed his face and hands, then pulled out his wallet and checked to make sure he'd dropped in a couple condoms. "All set," he said to himself, as he pushed his hair back off his forehead.

He laughed at himself in the mirror. Damned if he didn't feel like a virgin on his first date. They were both adults, knew where this night was leading from the start. And now that it was within his grasp, Lord help him, he was so nervous he wondered if everything would work right.

"Jeez, don't think that way, Godfrey." He ran his fingers through his hair one more time, took a deep breath, and headed for the door.

When he turned the corner at the end of the short hallway, his feet stopped so quick he had to grab hold of the brass rail on the bar to keep from tripping. His throat constricted, his hands fisted, his gut clenched.

Lina was in Ty Brock's arms, snuggled up close and cozy with him on the dance floor.

Sonofabitch!

Chapter Ten

From the Journal of Lina Brennen:
Granna says my temper will get me into trouble one of these days. Maybe she's right. But then again, a woman has to do what a woman has to do.

* * * *

Stupid, stupid, stupid! Lina scolded herself, and for the first time that night, wished Granna was around to take care of the situation she'd gotten herself in.

She pressed her palms against Ty's shoulders to keep some space between them. What in the hell had possessed her to agree to dance with the man? He smelled of beer and sickeningly strong cologne. His eyes were glassy from too much alcohol. And his hands kept drifting lower and lower on her back. So far, they'd made it down the upper curve of her butt. If he went any lower, she just might have to hurt him.

Where the hell is Trent?

"Answer me a question," Ty said, trying to pull her closer to his body. "Why does Trent get all the really pretty girls?"

"Because he's a really good guy." She pushed a little harder on his shoulders. His hands inched down a little further.

"You know, we were best friends when we were young. He even rode the circuit with me the first two years."

Lina stopped pushing him away. This, she wanted to hear.

"He was good. Coulda been as good as me. But he decided to go off to Phoenix and become a cop." His hands slid a little lower.

Lina grabbed his wrists and lifted them up to the middle of her back. But removing her hands from his shoulders, she lost her advantage, and he pulled her closer. Her hips brushed his and she bit back the urge to gag. "So, why aren't you friends anymore?" She asked as she put her hands back on his shoulders and pressed him away slightly.

"His bitch wife."

Lina sucked in a breath and nearly choked on Ty's cologne. "Why do you call her that?"

"She came onto me. Showed up at my place in the middle of the night. Gave me all these sob stories about how bad life was with Trent." He shook his head, pulled her closer. "What's a man to do?"

"But you were his friend!" She pushed at his shoulders and drew her head back so far she thought she'd fall over if he let her go.

With a negligent shrug, he said, "She was one hot babe. She wanted it."

Lina's lip curled in disgust.

"Then she ran home and told him." His hands made the final foray down her back and cupped her butt. "You wouldn't do that, now would you, buttercup?"

That did it. Sick bastard. Lina slipped her hands up into his hair. His Stetson went tumbling to the floor. She gripped his hair in her fist and tugged his head back. At the same time, she leaned in to whisper in his ear. "I'm not, nor will I ever be your buttercup. If you don't get your hands off my ass this second, you won't have any fingers left. And if that isn't reason enough not to touch my butt ever again, just remember one thing. No more spilled coffee or ketchup. If you can't keep your hands off me, you will never, as long as you live, father any children."

Ty's hands came away from her. She released his hair and shoved him away. "Never again, Ty Brock. Last warning."

He gave a slight nod, bent to retrieve his hat, and stumbled into a table. Lina shook her head in disgust.

Poor Trent. The things that man had been through.

She turned to scan the saloon. There he stood, leaning on the bar, chugging a beer. His gaze locked with hers as he slammed the mug onto the worn wood. He looked ready to kill. And well he should. That little asshole deserved to be taken down a notch or three.

* * * *

Trent tried to control the rage burning a hole in his gut, but he wasn't too successful at it. Watching her lean in and whisper in Ty's ear, her fingers laced through his hair so intimately, he wanted to kill. And at the moment he didn't know who he was more furious at. Ty Brock, Unegi's local rodeo star, or the woman who'd started to wiggle her way into his heart.

Damn stupid fool.

He slammed his empty beer mug on to the bar and met her stormy gray eyes. She looked so goddamned innocent. How dare she.

Lina came toward him. She looked ... concerned. Yeah, she should be. Practically making out with Ty, right there on the dance floor, while he stood watching. She was just like Nancy. A loose woman with no sense of morals.

"I'm ready to go home," she said in that soft, gentle voice.

He stifled down the tender feelings that tried to push their way through his fury. "Really." He flipped a couple dollars onto the bar to pay for his beer. "Which one of us you goin' home with?"

Her porcelain face registered several emotions he was too worked up to try to interpret at the moment. But the one that settled in cold and hard, darkening those gray eyes back to the color of a winter storm, was anger. Her eyes narrowed on him, her lips flattened into a thin line. "You're a jerk," she hissed a second before she turned on her heel, her skirt flaring out to reveal more leg than should be legal, and headed for the door.

He went after her. Aching for a fight, there was no way in hell he was going to let her get away with that. The door nearly slammed him in the nose before he threw it open. He caught hold of her arm when she was halfway across the gravel parking lot. "Just where the hell do you think you're going?"

"Home." She jerked her arm free and spun away.

"It's three miles back to your place. You can't walk."

She turned on him, her finger coming up to point at his nose. She opened her mouth to lambaste him, but snapped it shut so hard her teeth clicked. She headed back across the parking lot and stopped next the cruiser, arms folded over her chest, foot tapping impatiently on the gravel.

What the hell has she got to be so angry about? She was the one making out in the middle of the saloon with Ty Brock. His damned archenemy. The man who'd ruined his marriage, stole his wife, made him the laughing stock of Unegi. And he was doing it again.

"Would you open the door so I can get in?" Lina snapped.

"Cool your jets, lady," Trent growled, as he unlocked the door and threw it open.

He didn't bother to shut the door after she got in, he rounded the hood, unlocked the driver's door and slid in behind the wheel. Lina let out a huff and slammed the door. Trent shoved the key into the ignition. "What the hell is your problem?" He backed away from the building then pulled onto the highway, gravel spraying out behind the car.

Lina didn't answer. She sat there, staring straight ahead, looking as warm and inviting as a marble statue. She wanted Ty. She wanted Ty, and she was trying to piss him off so that she didn't feel guilty about it. Well, it was working. He was good and pissed.

He slammed the car into park in front of the sheriff's office. The car had barely stopped moving when she jumped out and slammed the door so hard he was surprised his eardrums didn't pop.

He climbed out of the car and took the stairs up to her apartment three at a time.

She threw the door open then turned to glare at him. "What do you want?" she snapped.

"We're going to settle this once and for all. What's going on with you and Ty? Are you sleeping with him?" He pushed his way past her into the darkened apartment and flipped on the overhead light.

Lina growled. "Get out!"

"No." He spun around. "I don't share."

"Oh for the love of-- You are so stupid!" She threw her keys into the little mortar bowl thing on the shelf so hard they bounced out and landed on the floor where she left them. "You're the one who stood there watching while that--that--creep put his hands all over me!"

"You're the one running your hands through his hair and whispering in his ear!" Trent took a deep breath. His blood pressure, he was sure, was through the roof.

Lina brushed past him and he ignored the flare of sexual heat that warmed his blood. What the hell was it with this woman? He was furious with her, and all he could think of was getting her naked.

Lina stomped to the bathroom door and put her hand on the doorknob. "What I whispered in his ear," she ground out between clenched teeth, "was to tell him that if he ever touched my butt again, I was going to permanently disable him." She threw open the door, went through it, and slammed it shut behind her. "You know where the door is!" she yelled. "Use it!"

Trent turned to leave when her words sunk through the burning rage. "Shit," he cursed succinctly. "Shit." He'd really messed this one up. He replayed what he'd seen at the saloon. Her removing Ty's hands from her behind. Her pushing at his shoulders. Her gripping his hair in her pretty little hands. The look of fear on Ty's face when he let go of her. "Shit."

He went to the bathroom door. "Lina?" he called.

"Go home, Trent!" He heard the shower come on.

"Sweetheart, I'm sorry."

"Too late! You're just a big jerk and I don't want to see you anymore. Just because your wife--" Her words ended abruptly.

Trent's stomach tightened again. "What do you know about my wife?" he demanded.

No answer.

"Damn it, Lina, you talk to me! What did that little bastard tell you?"

"Go away. Go home. We'll talk about this when you're not so worked up."

She still sounded angry. Holy hell. He grabbed the doorknob and shoved the door open.

"Get out of here!"

Steam billowed from behind the shower curtain. Lina's skin--all her skin--glowed pink from the heat. Her dress lay in a heap at her feet. Her panties on top of it.

"Did you hear me? Are the men in this town deaf or something? Get the hell out of my bathroom!"

Trent's eyes widened, his blood roared like lions in his ears. His fingers twitched. Desire flared through his body with the force of a steaming locomotive.

"Lina," Trent croaked, all moisture leaving his mouth. She was stunning. The curls of steam weaving around her ankles made her look ephemeral and ethereal.

Her mouth parted and her tiny, pink tongue darted out, licking the corner of her lip. Trent growled low in his chest, the sound vibrating through him. Oh God. He was totally lost.

* * * *

Lina gulped, eyeing Trent warily. He looked fierce, untamable, his fingers twitching, his Adam's apple bobbing.

Lust, hot and primal, ripped through her. Her knees turned weak, and she ached to lose herself in his huge, muscular arms. To unbutton his shirt and run her fingers over his corded, tan chest. To unzip his jeans and grasp his smooth penis. To see his gorgeous blue eyes widen with lust and desire. She bit her lip. Liquid heat crashed between her thighs. Lina's breath sawed in and out of her lungs. She stood enthralled by the animalistic gleam in his eyes.

But she was furious with him. Or should be at any rate. And she wasn't going to give in so easily. She lifted a brow and affected a nonchalant attitude, though her mind was anything but. And boy, oh boy, did she enjoy his obvious reaction to her naked body.

"I said you could see yourself to the door, Trent Godfrey," she said. Lina set her mouth in a straight line and narrowed her eyes. Her heart pounded violently in her chest. She wanted him. Oh God, how she wanted him.

Trent's spine stiffened, and he took a step toward her. "You'll not get rid of me that easily, Lina."

"Oh really?" She lifted her chin, turned around, and stepped into the shower, drawing the curtain closed with a zing. The hot jets touching her sensitized flesh nearly made her moan. She was so ready. She'd never been this ready before, and the need rocked her to the core.

The bathroom door closed with a quiet whoosh. Her heart screamed for him to stay. To come back and take her now. But the words lodged in her throat and wouldn't escape. She hated him. She hated what he did to her and how she let him do it.

Lina laid her head against the cool tiles and let out a tiny groan. Why did he have to go and act all brutish again? This night was supposed to be special. This night she would have given him her all, and then some.

The curtain was thrown back, cool air mixed with the warm steam, and she yelped. Her heart pounded painfully behind her ribs. She stared into royal blue eyes filled with anger, lust, and some other emotions she couldn't quite grasp.

"I said you'll not get rid of me so easily," he growled. He stepped into the tub, grabbed her wrists, and pinned her arms above her head, pushing her against the wall.

"Oh ... God ... Trent," she whimpered, and rubbed herself against his still clothed body. The friction created a delicious heat inside her. Lina groaned and closed her eyes.

* * * *

Trent sucked in his breath, watching the tiny vixen rubbing herself against the evidence of his desire. Rivulets of water ran off her breasts, soaking him, and he gave into temptation. He lowered his head, encircling her nipple with his mouth.

Lina shuddered into him. "Oh ... so good," she squeezed out around a tiny moan.

Trent tasted her, licking and nibbling her dusky rose nipple. Lina arched into him, purring like a kitten. The vibrations of her pleasure traveled through his chest, straight to his groin, making him harder, hungrier.

"Lina, I've wanted to do this for so long," he whispered, and nuzzled the other breast. His clothing clung uncomfortably to his body, but he didn't care. She was in his arms, the goddess of his dreams.

"Then don't stop," she whispered back. Trent released her wrists and wrapped her long, lean legs around his waist. She peppered his neck with kisses; gooseflesh rose on his forearms and trailed along his spine.

Trent pushed her against another wall. The tiny bathroom exploded with the sound of shampoo bottles and hair supplies crashing into the ceramic tub.

Pressing his arousal against her, he wished he were as naked as she was. Needing to feel her flesh against his. He swooped down and captured her mouth with his, forced his tongue between her lips to taste her. Hot, sweet. Perfect.

He kneaded her soft round bottom with his hands, found the source of her heat. When he pressed a finger deep inside her hot, silky center, she threw her head back, crying his name.

"Yes, baby," he ground out, and pressed in again. Watching her face, he grew harder and thicker just seeing her response to his touch.

"Please!" she moaned, as she pressed against his hand, clutched fistfuls of his shirt. "More."

Too restricted by soaking wet clothes, Trent stepped from the pelting shower onto the mat next to the tub and gently set her to her feet.

She let out a sweet little whimper and grabbed for the buttons on his shirt. Her hands shook, her fingers fumbled.

"Just rip them off, woman, I don't care." He cupped her breasts in his palms, stroked her nipples to beautifully hardened peaks.

She fumbled some more. "I can't get it, Trent." Her voice broke.

He pushed her hands out of the way and ripped his shirt open. Buttons popped off in opposite directions like tiny missiles. And then she was in his arms, her soft, warm breasts pressed tight against his chest, as her mouth attacked his with urgency and need. She whimpered, speared her hands through his hair, and yanked him closer.

Male satisfaction coursed through his veins knowing she was as hot and sexually charged as he was. He held her hard against him, his tongue warring with hers. Her teeth scraped his lips, nibbled, bit too hard.

He landed against her, her back banging against the wall. She cried out but clung to him. She nibbled painful little bites down his neck, across his collarbone, over his pecs. When her teeth closed over his nipple, he shuddered and dragged his hand through her hair, lifting her face to him. "Wild woman," he growled, his breathing as erratic as his pulse. "My sweet wild woman."

She grabbed for his belt, her silver eyes never leaving his. "I've never wanted a man the way I want you," she whispered. "And I want you now."

His belt buckle clinked, his button popped open, his zipper ripped down, and then she shoved his pants and underwear out of the way. When her soft, tiny hands closed over his aching cock, he pressed against her. Closing his eyes, he leaned in, inhaling her sweet verbena scent as she ran her fingers up the length of him. "You're killing me," he rasped in her ear.

Her fingers squeezed with more force than necessary, making him jerk. At the same moment, her teeth closed on his shoulder. She growled. His blood pumped even harder.

Using her hair, he pulled her head back and ground his mouth against hers, punishing her, loving her. Ah, God. Loving her.

She squeezed his penis, rubbed her nipples against his chest, moaned when he nibbled the tendon on her throat. "Harder," she growled. He sucked her skin into his mouth and nearly came when she cried out with pleasure, squeezing him tight.

Her fingers on him were like molten lava, burning him, branding him forever with her mark. "Woman, if you don't stop now--" His breath hitched when she shoved him backward, his ass landing hard against the corner of the vanity. He gripped the countertop to keep from tumbling over. He had no idea what she was planning, but the feral, woman-in-charge gleam in her eye did things to him he didn't know were possible.

She threw open the drawer next to his hip and grabbed a box of condoms.

* * * *

Her hands shook as she fumbled with the box, pulled out a condom and ripped open the foil package. Blood thundered in her ears. Her body hummed with the delicious ache of arousal. She dropped to her knees in front of him and leaned in, taking his huge, throbbing penis between her lips.

A groan of pure male ecstasy ripped from his throat as his hands went unerringly to her hair. She loved the feel of his tugging fingers. The slight pain heightened her senses, pulling her own moan from deep inside.

Swirling her tongue over the tip, sliding her lips along the silky shaft, she reached up with her free hand and massaged his tightened testicles. He was so ... perfect. Never in her life had she been so aroused by a man. So needy to feel him inside her.

"Stop," he panted. "Stop, baby. I can't." He pulled her away from him, and she looked up into his midnight blue eyes. And the delight she saw there made her ache with something other than sexual need. He truly liked her. Wanted her more than just tonight. She could read it in his expression, feel it as if it were a tangible thing wrapping around her heart, making her part of him.

She extracted the condom from the torn package and slowly rolled it over him. As he watched her, his eyelids grew even heavier, his jaw flexed, his hands dropped away from her and fisted at his sides. His bare chest, dusted with soft black hair, rose and fell quickly with each labored breath.

She sat back on her heels, wrapped her fingers around his wrist, and tugged. He wasted no time in falling to his knees, wrapping his arms around her waist, and crushing his mouth against hers. Spiking her fingers into his thick, soft hair, she pulled him even closer, letting him take charge of the kiss. Of her body, as he pushed her onto her back and lowered himself over her.

His mouth was warm, wet, and wild as he ran burning kisses across her jaw, down her throat. The weight of him was magic. Pure, white-hot magic that singed her. His lips closed over one nipple. She whimpered. He brought one hand up and gently pinched her other nipple. She cried his name and arched against him.

"I need you." His voice rasped like a river bottom.

"Take me." She wrapped her legs around his waist and lifted to him, sacrificing herself to him, needing what he needed.

He slammed into her with a force that shoved her head against the wall. She screamed and clung to him. Her body vibrated with an intense tightness she wasn't sure she'd survive.

Chapter Eleven

From the Journal of Lina Brennen:
When Love knocks on my door. Will I answer? Will Granna shut up long enough so I can hear the knock?

* * * *

She was wild, rolling her head from side to side. Beads of sweat gathered above her brows. Trent pumped into her and she cried out, dragging her nails across his back. The pain only added to the sexual frenzy and he bucked, pushing himself to the hilt inside her warm, soft haven.

He captured her lips with his, stifling her moans. His tongue mated with hers. He suckled and nibbled on it. Not able to get enough, he wanted all of her. Forever.

Then her whimpers became long moans. Her silver eyes opened, and he drowned in their molten depths.

"Oh God, Trent!" she cried out.

Trent gritted his teeth as he felt her tighten around him. His breath came out hard and heavy. His body thrummed with orgasmic waves of pleasure as he joined sweet Lina in diving off the cliff to oblivion.

* * * *

The bathroom was steamy and Lina felt languid and satiated. Trent breathed heavily in her ear, making the tingles of continued pleasure dance along her skin. His heartbeat thumped hard against her chest. His body was heavy on hers, but not too heavy. Just right. She wanted to stay locked with him for about the next eighty years.

"I'm squishing you," he whispered, but didn't move.

A gusty laugh slipped out of her and she wrapped her weighted arms around him, ran her fingers down his spine. "Yeah."

He shuddered, then slowly pushed himself up on his elbows to look into her eyes. "You're an amazing woman, Lina Brennen."

His gaze had lightened, gentled. He smiled at her with such tenderness, her heart tightened in response as her body did the same. "You're not so bad yourself, Sheriff."

He chuckled, ducked his head, and lightly brushed his lips over hers. "And I thought only cowboys did it with their boots on."

Lina realized his jeans were still on, too, pushed down over his hips. The wet fabric rubbed against her calves as she slowly unwound her legs from his waist and stretched them out. She giggled. "I guess you were in a hurry, huh?"

He nuzzled her throat. "I think it was you who was in a hurry."

She rolled her head to the side, giving him more access to her neck. "You're the one who came barging into my bathroom looking mad enough to kill."

"Ah, babe. I'm sorry." He dropped his forehead to her shoulder. "I overreacted. I just couldn't stand seeing you in another man's arms."

He sounded so dejected she smiled against his shoulder. Running her hands down the hard, muscular planes of his back, she said, "I didn't want to be in his arms. Only yours. He's a jerk of the first degree."

"Why'd you dance with him in the first place? You should have known better. I mean--"

Lina shoved his shoulder and scooted out from under him. She narrowed her eyes at him through the cloud of steam that suffused the air. "Do you really want to go there? Do you really want to start this argument all over again? Jeez, Trent. He asked me for a dance and wouldn't take no for an answer. So to shut him up, I agreed, figuring you'd come save me. But instead, you stood there and got all pissed off because of what you thought you saw."

He flinched. Looked away from her. Started to get up. "I'm sorry." When he started struggling to pull up his sopping wet jeans, she grabbed his hand.

"Okay."

He looked down at her and she got to her feet. "Okay what?"

"Okay. You're sorry. I am too. I had no idea the history you have with the guy. Trust me when I say you never have to worry about him touching me again."

A small, almost sad smile curled his lips. She leaned in, placing her hands against his rock-hard chest, stood on her tiptoes and kissed him softly.

When she pulled back, he said, "I guess I should get going."

Disappointment, hot and fast brought stinging tears to her eyes. Maybe she'd been wrong. Maybe he didn't want more than ... this. She blinked back the tears, pulled a towel from the rack and wrapped it around her. "If that's what you want." She reached in and shut of the shower. The room fell deathly silent.

She couldn't meet his eyes. She stepped around him and opened the door, the cold, air-conditioned air hit her like a blast of winter. She sucked in her breath.

Trent's hot hand closed over her shoulder. "What is it you want, Lina?" His voice was low, rough, holding a world of meaning she didn't think she could interpret right now with her emotions tumbling about.

When she didn't answer, his arms closed around her. He pulled her back against his chest, laid a sweet, soft kiss on her bare shoulder. "Tell me what you want from me."

She was putting it all out there. She didn't know what he wanted, but he asked, didn't he? "Will you spend the night with me?"

Trent nuzzled her long neck and glanced at the clock near the door. Two in the morning. He thought about Jess. But she was a big girl now, and she was at her grandmothers, and he needed this. It had been too long. "I don't want to be any other place right now, Lina," he whispered.

* * * *

Lina rolled over and stretched her arms over her head, flexed her thighs, and straightened her toes. Mmmm she felt good. Tender in places. So alive. A soft snore came from next to her and she smiled into the soft light of morning that filtered through her lacy lavender curtains.

She rolled over and took in Trent's long, muscular body. The night had been hot, so he'd kicked the covers off. From his tousled hair to the soles of his big, sexy feet, he lay there in all his naked glory. Oh man, what an ass he had, she thought as she lightly traced her finger down the center of his back, over one firm butt cheek, and down the back of his rock-hard thigh.

His soft, even breathing hitched for a second, and then he let out a soft groan, snuggled the pillow tighter and fell back into deep sleep. Lina smiled.

"Now that is one very fine specimen of man."

Lina yelped and grabbed up the sheet, covering Trent's bare backside. "What are you doing here?" she whispered fiercely at Merona, who hovered next to the bed.

"It's morning. And if you don't get a move-on, you're going to be late for work. I didn't know he was staying all night."

Trent rolled toward Lina, a sexy, sleepy smile on his lips. "You asked me to stay the night. You don't remember?"

Granna. Leave!

To Trent, she smiled. "Of course I remember. Just a little out of it first thing in the morning."

He raised his hand, slid it into her tangled hair, and pulled her toward him. "I'll give you a little reminder, then."

"What a sexy voice he has first thing in the morning."

Get out! Go away!

Trent's lips touched hers and all thoughts of Granna slipped away. Renewed excitement from the night before flooded her. Her heart raced; her limbs felt heavy. She moaned against his mouth as his tongue teased hers.

"Well, my goodness, doesn't that look like fun."

Lina shoved Trent back and jumped from the bed. "Time for me to get ready for work," she said, forcing a smile. *And if you weren't dead already, I'd kill you! Who the hell cares about work when I've got this in my bed?*

Trent chuckled. "I'll tell Mom you had some trouble with the law. She'll let it pass this time." Propped up on one arm he patted the pillow next to him as his sleepy, heavy-lidded gaze roamed over her naked body. "Come back here."

She went to the closet and pulled out a pair of khaki shorts and a pale blue tank top. "Can't. Only been working at the diner for a few days. I can't start calling in sick,"--she turned and flashed him a smile--"or be in trouble with the law." *She was going to find a way to lock Merona out of the apartment. There had to be something that would hold a ghost at bay. Salt rings? Garlic?*

"Not a thing, sweetling. So how was he? As good as he looks?"

"Grrr," she growled as she searched through a drawer for a pair of matching socks.

"Hmm. You sound so sexy when you do that." Trent rolled to a sitting position and reached for her. "Come back here."

"Gotta shower."

"Sounds good. I'll join you."

"No!" She grabbed the sheet and draped it over his lap.

Trent's chuckle mingled with Merona's.

"Going shy on me now, are you?" He captured her wrist in his hand. "You get to run around naked, but I can't?"

He was so cute, Lina thought. She wrapped her arms around his neck and kissed him hard. "Later, okay?" she asked. "Please. This job means a lot to me."

"Okay. But later. For sure."

She nodded and kissed him one more time before dashing off to the bathroom. *You get in here, old lady.*

Merona floated into the bathroom behind her.

Lina turned on the shower then turned on Granna. "You keep your eyes off Trent," Lina whispered, her tone harsh.

"Sweetling, you know I'm just playing. You never cared when I made comments about any of your other men."

"My other men?" she asked, incredulous. "There's been two. And you were the one--"

"Who you talkin' to, sweetheart?"

Lina gulped and stepped into the shower. "Just myself."

She heard Trent's laugh through the door. Another wave of need and want and remembered pleasures from the night before crashed through her.

* * * *

Tent leaned back in his office chair, laced his fingers behind his neck, and stared up at the ceiling. He sat just beneath Lina's bedroom. The bedroom that he'd shared with her last night. She turned his brain to grits. He hadn't been able to concentrate on one blasted thing all day. Good thing not much happened in Unegi to occupy his mind.

He chuckled to himself and let his mind drift off. Visions of Lina's pale skin, shining hair, and flashing, stormy-sea eyes wound around him. He felt himself growing hard. Snapping his eyes open, he sat forward, leaning his elbows on his desk. Holy crap, he thought. How was he going to make it through the rest of the day without seeing her, touching her?

She was home now for her afternoon break. He'd heard her walking around up there a few minutes ago. He could sneak up and see her, but she undoubtedly needed some rest. They hadn't slept much last night.

A grin curled his lips as he propped his chin on his fist. Feisty little she-devil, she was. And a little kinky, too. Not that he was complaining, but he bore more than just a few marks on his skin from her teeth and nails.

She amazed him. She intrigued him. She aroused him with the slightest touch, her low, silky voice in his ear, that precious crooked smile.

The phone rang. He let out a quiet curse and prayed it wasn't Mr. Thornton with more stories of rustlers. He was getting mighty sick of being called at all hours, day and night, to come stand guard over his small herd of prize-winning beeves.

"Unegi Sheriff's department, Godfrey here."

"Skipping breakfast now, are you?"

Trent leaned back again in his chair and sighed. "Hi, Mom. No, I didn't skip breakfast. I ate today. I just had some stuff to do this morning."

"Tried calling you last night. You weren't home."

"I went out with Lina. As well you know, since Jess stayed at your place."

"I have a feeling you stayed in with her, too."

"Fishing, Mom? That's so unlike you." Trent smiled. He might be over forty years old, but Mom still tried to run his life.

"She's a city girl, Trent. Don't you forget it."

His smile froze. His gut clenched. Pain ripped through him with a fierceness he hadn't experienced in years. "She likes it here." Even to himself his voice sounded flat, his tone forced.

Abby snorted. "For now, she does." She sighed heavily. "Trent, baby, you know I love you. I'm so worried about you. I don't want to see you go through what you went through with ... her."

He sat forward and slammed his palm onto the desk. "She's nothing like Nancy! She...." She what? He didn't even know. He didn't know where she was from, why she was here, where she might be going. She'd only been in Unegi a little over a week, and already he was losing his heart to her. God, he could be so stupid.

But then he remembered how she'd looked at him last night. How she'd taken him, all of him, heart and soul. He was sure of it. She had feelings for him. And she wasn't about to run off with Brock, or anyone else for that matter.

"Just be careful, son. Be very, very careful. If not for your sake, for Jessica's. She's falling for the woman, too. Don't let that precious little girl get hurt. Or you'll answer to me."

That brought a smile to his lips. "I love you too, Mom." He cradled the phone and stared out the window at the old, clapboard building across the street that housed Stephen's offices. Next door was Bentley's Feed and Seed. And then the diner.

He loved this sleepy little town, where nothing ever happened. A few bar fights now and then was about as exciting as it got, if you didn't count the supposed cattle rustling.

If Lina didn't want to stay ... He sighed. If Lina wanted to move back to the city ... He scrubbed his hands over his face. If she left Unegi ... Too soon. Much too soon to think about this. Way, way too soon.

* * * *

Jess helped Lina cover all the windows in the living room and kitchen with thick blankets to block out as much light as possible. Her heart skittered with trepidation and excitement. It was finally time. Time to learn if she had what it took to be like Lina.

Merona hovered behind them, adding her two cents here and there. She was the one who said that the room needed to be dark, because this would be her spirit guide's first visit into the realm of the living, and too much light would hurt the guide's eyes.

"Okay," Lina said as they positioned the last blanket into place. "You ready?"

Jess could only nod. She'd practiced nightly the relaxation techniques Merona had instructed her in. Last night she'd come so close. She'd felt something, heard a voice. But it'd startled her and her concentration had been broken. Today she'd be with Lina, and that made her feel safe.

Lina picked up a butane candle lighter and moved around the room, igniting more than twenty candles set on every available surface. When she was done, she laid down the lighter and turned to Jess. "You sure you want to do this now? You're ready?"

"I'm ready." She smiled. "I'm excited."

"Of course you are, sweetie," Merona said softly as a cold hand touched Jess's arm. "Lay down on the couch and get comfortable. Lina and I are right here with you."

Jess laid down on the couch, her hands folded together over her middle.

Lina sat down on the floor next to her and reached up to pull her hands apart. "Keep yourself open, sweetheart." She placed Jess's hands next to her on the couch, palms up. "Open to accept your guide."

"Do you contact yours?" Jess asked.

"I have. And she's always with me." Lina quirked a little smile. "With Granna chattering at me all the time, sometimes it's hard for me to hear my guide."

Jess chuckled.

Merona tsked and shook her head. "You give me no respect."

"Hush now," Lina instructed.

Jess took a shaky breath. Her nerve endings tingled.

"Remember the one you seek comes from The Maker," Merona said as she settled in the corner of the room, dimming her own glow to no more than candle strength. "Your guide comes from a place of love and peace."

"Love and peace," Jess whispered. She closed her eyes and tried to relax.

"Deep breaths," Lina whispered. "Slow, deep breaths. Feel your toes relaxing. Your feet. Your calves. Your thighs. Light as air you begin to float on a warm sea of clouds."

Jess's mind settled. She began to ease into the soft cotton clouds that surrounded her. From far away she heard Lina's voice. "Your fingers. Your hands. Your arms." Jess's body floated on pink clouds, the special place she'd already told Lina about. "Your pelvis. Your stomach. Your chest. That's a girl."

"Clear your mind," Merona whispered. "No thoughts, just softness and light. Warm breezes and fresh spring air."

Jess could see it perfectly. Her imaginary place. Her warm hiding place. A place she'd gone to for as long as she could remember. Pink clouds, tall, lush trees swaying in the cool breezes, the scent of damp, freshly mowed grass.

"Do you see your bench?" Lina asked softly.

Jess nodded.

"Sit on your bench."

Jess pictured herself sitting on the pretty, white wrought iron bench. She smiled as she dug her bare toes into the prickly, dewy grass under her feet.

"Now send your request to your spirit guide, honey," Lina said. "Ask your guide to join you on your bench."

Please come to me. I need you. I want to meet you, to learn from you. Help me understand why I am the way I am.

Jess saw a shadow form behind one of her pink clouds. As she watched, the cloud parted, and a blinding white light flowed from within. She squinted against the harsh glare, but couldn't take her gaze from the person slowly walking her way.

"Hello, Jessica. I've been waiting to hear from you."

* * * *

Lina stifled a small gasp when she heard the deep, resonant, and accented voice from right next to her. She turned her head, her eyes wide as she watched the amazing appearance of Jess's spirit guide.

The candles burned brighter, filling the room with a blinding white glare. On the chair just across the coffee table from her, a shadow shifted, and a form began taking shape. First to solidify was long legs clad in tan buckskin pants. Moccasins on the feet. Then hands. Rough, tan, arthritic hands, folded on the lap. Then a body and a buckskin shirt with sparkling beads sewn in beautiful, intricate designs. And then long, gray braids hanging over each shoulder. And finally, his face. Deeply tanned, etched by age. Intelligent, deep brown eyes. He gave Lina a small nod and his face crinkled in a smile of welcome.

"Jess," Lina whispered. "Sweetheart, open your eyes. He's here."

Jess's eyelids fluttered open. "Who are you?" she whispered, more than just a touch of awe in her voice. Lina knew what she was feeling. He was a powerful spirit.

"My name is Dyami, Spirit of the Eagle," he answered in that deep, accented voice. "In your world I was a spiritual leader of the great Apache Nation. I was also your father's grandfather. I am here to help you."

Chapter Twelve

From the Journal of Lina Brennen:
I read a book on psychological disorders. That was a really dumb thing for me to do. I see ghosts, hear voices in my head, and can heal warm-blooded creatures by touch. I'm either a split personality, a schizophrenic, or seriously delusional. Add to that my temper and tears when things don't go my way, and you've got clinical depression. I've learned to stay out of the medical section of the bookstores.

* * * *

Trent shuffled around some paperwork on his desk and stretched out his long legs, enjoying the temporary calm and peace. In the background, the soft hum of the window unit lulled him into a quiet, trance-like state. Work had been hectic. What with the phone ringing every few minutes, people stopping by to ask him to settle ridiculous disputes, and hearing Lina's soft footsteps overhead, he was exhausted.

Last night with Lina had been amazing, but he was paying for it now. He could hardly keep his eyes open.

Trent's head lolled to the side. The shrill cry of the phone caused him to flail his arms in surprise, nearly throwing him to the ground. Jumping out of the chair, he glanced around the tiny room. His heart beat ten times faster than normal. The phone rang again. Never a quiet moment. He snatched the phone off its cradle.

"Yeah, hello. Uh, Sheriff's Office. Godfrey here."

"Trent!" A woman's high-pitched screech sounded on the other end.

He pulled the phone away from his ear and grimaced.

"You come out here this instant, ya hear me?"

Trent prayed for patience as he took deep breaths through his nostrils. Ms. Annabelle Butler, town gossip and meddling old bat, extraordinaire. "What's wrong this time, Ms. Butler?"

"I'll tell you what's wrong. Oh, I'll tell you...."

"Calm down, Ms. Butler. I can't help if you don't calm down," Trent said in a reprimanding tone. Some days he really hated being sheriff.

"Them witches, that's what's wrong," she huffed. "They done kilt six more of my prized laying hens."

Trent closed his eyes and rubbed the bridge of his nose in a furious motion. "Ms. Butler...." he began.

"Naw, sir. Don't you try to shush me up. I ain't takin' this, I tell you! If'n you don't do something 'bout this, then I will. Now, I had enough I tell you. Enough!"

"Ms. Butler," he said again, "Are you so sure it's witches?"

"Well now, Trent, you done lived around these parts for a good long time. The whole county knows about that there coven that meets not ten miles down the road from where I live." Her words came out breathless and full of anger. "It don't take an idiot to make the connection."

"All right, Ms. Butler, I'll be out there shortly." It took every ounce of fortitude Trent possessed to not groan aloud.

"Hmph," she said, then slammed down the phone.

Trent plopped down on the chair and shook his head. He was sure his blood pressure had just shot up to dangerous levels. That woman tried him to his very bones. "Well, hell," he said, and walked to his filing cabinet, frustration bubbling through his veins.

Glancing at his wristwatch, he realized Jess should be home from soccer practice now. He'd really wanted to spend a few minutes with her. Now it seemed he'd have to wait. Blowing out a disgusted breath, he rummaged through his files. This was the third time in six weeks Annabelle had called him claiming the witches had killed her hens.

Not that he'd put it past them blackhearts to kill innocent animals, but there was very little he could do about it. He didn't know much about witches or covens and all that crap, but surely anybody who danced naked around a bonfire and called down demons couldn't be anything but evil. And he'd had enough of that shit to last him a lifetime.

He stilled, his brows pulling together when he heard the voices. He straightened and stared at the vent above his head.

Lina's soft voice drifted down to him. "Deep breaths...." she said.

What? Trent walked closer to the vent and listened.

"Good, that's it. Slow deep breaths...." His eyes widened. That hadn't been Lina's voice. That voice was older, staid.

His heart began beating faster, the sound of his blood roared in his ears like a Tsunami. What the hell was going on? And who was up there with her?

"Clear your mind...." that same voice spoke. A chill passed up his spine, making the hairs on his arms stand on end. Trent didn't know why, but a nagging thought consumed him. Jess. Jessica was up there.

Goddamn it all to hell!

His fingers twitched, his pulse pounded, and a haze of red covered his mind. Trent slammed the cabinet shut and ran upstairs.

* * * *

"Lina," Merona's voice cracked. "Stop. He's coming. He's coming."

"Wh ... What?" Jessica croaked and sat up. The image of her grandfather slowly faded into a bright white mist.

Lina bit her lip, her heart caught in her throat. Oh God. What would he do? What would he think? Adrenaline rolled through her. Lina ran toward the candles and tried to blow them out. Her door vibrated with the sound of heavy pounding.

"Goddamn it, Lina, open up this door. Now! I know you're in there and I know my daughter is, too."

"Oh shit," she whispered, looking toward Jess's panic-stricken face.

Merona flicked her wrist toward the door. Open it now baby. Otherwise he's gonna kick down the door.

Lina licked her lips and tried to swallow the greasy ball of fear trapped in her throat.

"I said open it now or God help me, I'll kick this door down," Trent yelled.

Jessica sat up, her green eyes wide in her face, and grabbed at her head, wincing.

Lina sympathized. She knew from experience that breaking sudden contact with a spirit was painful and tantamount to having someone drag their nails across your skull.

She took a steadying breath and shot a glance toward her grandmother. Merona nodded.

Lina walked forward and opened the door. Her heart stuttered in her chest at the murderous gleam in Trent's royal blue eyes. His black hair was sticking up from his forehead, his gaze shifting back and forth. "Candles, incense...." he ground out. "What the hell was going on here?"

He pushed past Lina and grabbed Jessica off the couch.

"No, Dad!" Jess took a swing at his chest.

Lina's mouth dropped open. He was frightening, reminding her of a charging bear, ready to rip her limb from limb. She shivered and crossed her arms over her chest.

Trent stomped across the room and headed toward the door, then stopped and shot Lina a withering glare. "Just so you know," he said in a voice devoid of emotion. "Jess is never allowed back here again. You stay the hell out of our lives!" Then he walked out and slammed the door behind him hard enough to rattle the widows.

Lina blinked once, and blinked again. All she could do was stare from the couch to the door and back. A deep sense of loss swept through her. That's when the burning tears fell down her face. He hated her. He hated her.

Merona came up and laid a frigid hand upon her back. "Sweetling, it's okay...."

"No, it's not." Lina shrugged her off and ran toward the bedroom, her heart a tortured mess and she landed with a plop on the bed. On the same bed she'd shared with him last night. A great, choking sob wrenched from her throat. She hugged the pillow he'd used, his spicy scent still clung to it. It was over. Lina had been able to face many things in her life, but Trent's hatred was not one of those.

Merona sat on the bed and rubbed her back. "Sweet child," her grandmother crooned, "I swear to you it will be okay."

Lina sat up and hugged her knees to her chest, staring out the window. "We're leaving, Granna." Her heart ached at the thought of leaving Jessica and Trent. Especially Trent.

"Shh." Merona shoved a tendril of hair out of Lina's face. "Don't talk such nonsense. Give it a week. You'll make up."

Lina laid her head on her knees and gave a jerky sigh.

"Promise me, Lina."

Her mind was empty, her heart shriveled. She couldn't believe she'd dared to trust, to open herself again. What was one week? The way she felt now, nothing could be worse. "Fine, Granna," she whispered.

* * * *

"Daddy," Jess said on a disparaging sigh, with a good amount of eye rolling--to stay in character, she told herself. She had to convince him it was nothing. "I told you. We weren't doing anything wrong. Lina was just showing me how to meditate."

Trent leaned back in his chair, grabbed his coffee cup, and glanced around the brightly lit kitchen of their small home. For three days, she'd been trying to convince him that Lina hadn't forced her to do whatever he thought they were doing, that Lina was only trying to teach her how to meditate--which was mostly true.

"Why the hell do you need to meditate?" He stood up, collected their dinner dishes, and hauled them to the sink. "You're twelve years old." He dumped the plates and utensils in the sink.

Jess mumbled a single word.

He turned around, leaned his butt on the kitchen counter, and folded his arms over his chest. That Dad look that drove her nuts because he always tried to intimidate her. Well, she'd outgrown being afraid of him years ago. She knew he was just a big softy. A big softy who always thought he knew everything. "Come again?"

"Headaches."

Trent frowned. "What do you mean, headaches? You don't get headaches."

She'd had debilitating headaches for the past year and a half. But she'd never told him. Didn't want to worry him. She also heard voices and felt strange things in the air. Again, she'd never told him. He'd probably think she was having an aneurysm or something.

She knew she was different. She'd known it for a while now. Not until Lina and Merona came along had she realized it was okay. She wasn't the only one who heard voices. But now she was beginning to be able to see who--or what--those voices were coming from. For the first time in years, she was happy. And Dad was going to go and ruin it all. She'd been forbidden to see Lina. Not that she planned to listen to him.

"Yes, Dad. I get headaches. Bad ones. But you're never around to notice, anyway."

The stricken expression that crossed his face, along with the fact his hands dropped to his side and his shoulders seemed to sag, made her feel like a horrible little bitch. "Daddy...."

"I'm sorry, baby." He turned his back on her and started running water in the sink. "I'm sorry."

The slight hitch in his voice just about brought her to tears. She jumped from her chair and wrapped her arms around him, burying her face against his back. "I didn't mean it. I didn't. You're a good Dad."

His wet hands closed over her arms. "I know, Jess. I love you, sweetheart. I just worry about you. A lot." He turned around and wrapped his arms around her.

She hated to admit it, it wasn't a grown-up thing to do, but she missed cuddling with her daddy. He used to hold her on his lap, tell her silly stories, scary stories, sad stories. He used to tuck her in at night. Sometimes he'd even lay down with her and answer all the questions she had about her mother. It had been a long, long time since they really talked about anything besides school and his job, Nana or the diner.

He brushed his hand over her hair, cradled her head against his chest. "Tell me about these headaches, baby. Why haven't you told me about them before?"

"I didn't want to worry you." She leaned against him, breathed in his spicy cologne--the cologne she'd bought for him last Christmas--and smiled. "They only happen at night."

"Maybe we should go see Doc Webb."

Jess shook her head. She only got the headaches when she heard the voices. She wanted to talk to Lina about it before she went to see a doctor. She was beginning to suspect that she was hearing spirits, whereas before, she thought she was losing her mind. "The meditating was helping." She pulled back enough to look up into his face. He looked worried. "It's not fair that you're mad at Lina. She didn't do anything wrong."

"Well, she should have told me that you were having headaches. I'm your father. You barely know the woman."

Jess swallowed. She hadn't told Lina, either. And he'd never understand. The few times over the past couple years she'd tried talking to him about God, spirits, and the afterlife, he'd made it real clear that that subject was not open for discussion. Even Nana was a little weird about it. He'd totally freaked over Lina's books. Lina was the first person to ever come into her life that understood her. "I didn't tell her why I wanted to learn to meditate, Dad." She sighed and rested her cheek against his chest again. "Please let me see her. I really like her. And you really hurt her. I know you like her, too, and now you won't even talk to her."

* * * *

Trent sighed. Had he overreacted? Maybe. But what was he to think, walking into her place lit by dozens of candles, the windows blacked out, and his daughter lying on the couch. And her books ... And those crystal things hanging all over the place ... The drying herbs ... He shivered. No thank you. He wasn't going to let his daughter get involved with anyone who dabbled in ... whatever it was Lina was into.

"I just think she's a bad influence on you. I don't want to see you hurt, baby."

Jess sighed and pulled away. "Dad. Be reasonable." She flopped down in the chair at the table and sighed again. "She's not exactly an axe murderer or anything."

Ah ha! Who was to say she wasn't? He almost smiled. Yeah, right. Lina might be a little strange, but he didn't think she was a murderer, axe or otherwise. But she had all those books on the spirit world. Another shudder ripped through him. He did not want Jess involved in that garbage.

"We don't know anything about her. She doesn't talk about her past. All we know is she's from Chicago. Not what she did there, or why she left."

"She said she wanted a new start." Jess folded her arms over her chest and scowled. "What's so wrong about that?"

"Because a new start usually means you're running from something," Trent answered reasonably.

"Ha! Maybe she's just looking for a place to belong."

Trent frowned. "What are you talking about?"

"Maybe she doesn't feel welcome anywhere because she's a little different. Maybe she just wants someplace that accepts her for who she is. And maybe she doesn't want to have to answer too many questions."

He really did not like his daughter's tone. It sounded like she was the one who wanted to fit in, to not have to answer questions. "She tell you this?"

That annoying one-shoulder shrug. Trent almost growled. "Jess. Until I can talk to her, you are not to see her. Understand me?"

Jess narrowed her eyes. "I speak English, don't I?"

Now he was pretty sure he did growl. "Don't you take that tone with me, young lady. I am your father and—"

"Heard it all before." Jess pushed herself out of the chair and headed for the stairs. "But this time, you're wrong!" She stomped up the steps, down the hall, and slammed her bedroom door so hard the walls shook.

And don't slam the damn doors anymore!

He didn't yell it. What good would it do? Turning back to the sink, he started scrubbing plates. He remembered thirteen. He remembered the mouth, the attitude. How he'd driven his mother crazy with it. Now it was payback time.

He chuckled. "Thanks, Mom." On more than one occasion, she'd cursed him with the hope he had children just like himself one day.

After placing the last of the silverware in the dish drainer, he wiped his hands on the towel hanging from the oven door and headed into the living room to tidy up a bit. Neither he nor Jess were very neat people. He picked up a few articles of discarded clothing and grabbed her backpack off the floor by the couch, intending to take it up to her. If she wanted to sulk, she could at least put her stuff away since school had just let out for the summer.

The books tumbled out onto the floor. "Damn," he muttered as he dropped the clothes and started shoving books and loose papers back into the bag. And then his blood ran cold.

"Sonofabitch."

He picked up two books he recognized from Lina's bookshelf. *Contacting Your Spirit Guide* and *Life on the Other Side: A Psychic's Tour of the Afterlife.* "Sonofabitch," he said again. He knew it. Lina was corrupting his daughter with all that nonsense about spirits and shit. Enough was enough. And Jess was lying to him.

"Jessica Lynn Godfrey! Get your butt down here!"

She came stomping down the stairs. "What?" she asked, a scowl firmly in place.

"Don't you 'what' me, young lady. What the hell are these?" He held out the books, one in each hand, to show her the covers.

"Books?" she said, her eyebrows raised in a look of innocence.

He ground his teeth. "I told you that you weren't supposed to read this crap. Why do you have them?"

One-shoulder shrug.

"So help me, Jess. Answer me! You got these from Lina, didn't you?"

Jess's eyes went wide. She shook her head. "She doesn't know I have them."

His baby girl was lying to him. He hadn't been a cop for the last twenty years for nothing. He knew damn well when someone was lying to him. That hurt. Bad. And she was lying to protect Lina.

"You're grounded." He headed for the door. He was going to have this out with Lina right damn now.

"For how long?"

"Until I say so." He jerked open the door.

"Where are you going?"

"To find out what kind of bullshit that woman has been planting in your head, that's where. You"--he jerked open the door with one hand, pointed at her with the other, still clutching the evil books--"are not to leave this house." He slammed the door behind him, got in the cruiser, and headed into town.

Chapter Thirteen

From the Journal of Lina Brennen:
My thirteenth diary entry. I know Granna calls my belief in signs hogwash, but I know what I know. And thirteen can't herald anything good.

* * * *

Trent shoved a hand through his hair and pounded the steering wheel of his cruiser. When he found Lina--he clenched his jaw--he'd give her a piece of his mind.

How could Jess lie to him? His nostrils flared and his heart ached. It had felt like she'd rammed him with a red-hot poker when those words had fallen from her lips. To protect a woman that she didn't even know. A luscious, temptingly beautiful viper.

Trent ground his jaw when the sheriff's office came into view. Lina had hoodwinked him, too, and that almost hurt worse. It was his own damn fault that he'd brought that snake to his town. He'd fallen under her spell, her breathtaking beauty, inviting hips. "Damn it all," he spat.

Trent whipped into the parking slot and threw the car door open. His heart attempting to punch a hole through his chest, he stomped up the stairs to her apartment.

He pounded on the door. No answer. "Open the damn door, Lina." Nothing. No footsteps, no talking, no nothing.

Where the hell was she?

"Lina," he called one last time. But all that met him was empty silence.

The fury still burning in his gut, his heart a raw wound, he turned around. Staring at the street, he realized her car was nowhere in sight. I'll find you, come hell or high water, Lina. Trent stomped down the stairs and jumped into his car.

He took off in a cloud of dust and barreled down the road. He scanned the area, searching for her rusty blue escort. Spying the Chevron, he veered sharply to the right and parked. Maybe Louise would know something.

Trent took a deep, calming breath, not willing to give anybody the satisfaction of seeing him this way. Then he stepped from the car and walked with a steady, sure gait that belied the waves of fury roiling through him.

"Louise," he called as he stepped through the door.

"Well, my oh my, if it ain't Trent Godfrey. And to what do I owe the honor?" Her turquoise eye shadow showed up in stark relief to the pastiness of her face.

Trent scratched the back of his head. How could he ask this question without raising the suspicion of the one of the town's biggest gossips? Hell, all the women around Unegi were gossips. He blew out a disgusted breath. "Wondering who you saw driving in or out of town tonight."

Louise lifted a dark brow, her coral pink lips curling into a crescent-shaped smile. "Wouldn't happen to be askin' about anybody in particular would you?"

His lips thinned with irritation. "Lina Brennen."

"Ahh. Saw her heading toward Devil's Peak 'bout an hour ago."

"Thank you," he replied curtly, turned on his heel, and fled.

Louise's belly laugh trailed after him.

Trent got into his car, threw it into drive, and took off. His fingers gripped the steering wheel so tight they reflected a bright shade of white in the dashboard lights. What was she doing out at the mountain this late at night?

Then a thought ripped through him with the force of an arrow. That coven, the one that Ms. Butler was screaming about the other day, gathered every Monday night by Devil's Peak.

"Sonofabitch," he yelled, his heart rate pumping faster and faster. He knew it! How could he have been so fucking blind?

* * * *

Lina picked up a chunk of red rock and threw it down the cliff face. The shimmering waves of fading sunlight bathed the mountains in a crimson glow. A warm wind picked up the tendrils of her hair, and she inhaled the spicy scent of the desert. But none of it helped to soothe her aching soul.

She'd stayed as Granna had asked, hoping Trent would give her time to explain. Lina hiccupped and swiped the tears that kept leaking from her eyes. Explain what? That she'd been doing exactly what he suspected. That she wasn't exactly a witch, just a spiritual healer. Like anybody would understand the difference.

She'd finally gone out for a hike. Merona's constant words of assurance did nothing to assuage her guilt or pain. Merona had begged to come along but this was one time Lina had been forceful. She wanted to hear nothing, to do nothing but stew in her misery. It wouldn't solve anything, it wouldn't even help her feel better in the end, but nothing was helping at the moment, so what did it matter?

The tears blurred her vision, casting her surroundings in blurry shades of mixed watercolors. The warmth of the campfire she'd started seeped into her limbs, warming her body, but never quite reaching her heart.

"What now? Where can I go? What's the point?"

Two emotions warred inside her: disappointment at herself for being stupidly immature--how could she even think to teach Jessica things her father so clearly despised?--and bitterness that Trent would make her feel like a felonious freak.

The warm breeze turned suddenly brisk. Lina shivered and scooted further inside the cave, warming her hands by the fire. She was tired of fighting, tired of crying, tired of caring.

Lina traced the lines of the cave drawings she'd found when she arrived. This place was special. She drew comfort from the natural springs of energy welling around her. She closed her eyes, inhaled the desert bloom-tinted air, and listened to the lonely ballad of a coyote off in the distance.

Then another sound cut in. A harsh, grating sound that intruded on the quiet stillness. She snapped her eyes open as headlights rounded the bend. Lina turned her head to the side and knew, without knowing, who it was.

The lights were turned off, the engine cut, and she waited.

Trent's heavy footfalls pounded toward her, his breathing hitched and uneven. "You fooled me, Lina Brennen." His blue eyes snapped cold fire. "But I'll be damned before you poison my daughter with your sorcery."

Her brows dipped and her lower lip trembled, she bit down hard. If he came here to make her feel worse than she already did, he was doing a damn fine job.

"Take your fuck--" He shoved an angry hand through his hair. "You know what, you're not even worth it." He threw her books down on the ground and turned.

Lina shot to her feet and wrapped her arms around herself, trying desperately to hold in the cry of agony that clawed at her throat. "How dare you, Trent?" She trembled. "How dare you. You don't even have the decency to ask me what I was doing before you jump to conclusions."

His spine stiffened and he stood as still as a board, then slowly turned. "You're gonna tell me you didn't give my daughter that garbage?" Trent pointed to the books.

"Damn you, Trent! You wouldn't believe me even if the truth punched you in the face."

"Then tell me, Lina. Tell me the truth. Because right now I don't know what to believe." He took a step toward her, the light from the flickering flame behind her danced across his features, making him look sinister, like a nightmarish monster.

Regardless, she couldn't quell the simmering desire curling through her veins, making her want to kiss him and smack him all at once.

* * * *

Trent's hands fisted into tight balls at his sides. Believe her? She hadn't told him anything worth listening to, let alone believing. "Did you give Jess those books?" he demanded.

"No. I didn't know she had them." Her voice was little more than a whisper.

Damn it, he couldn't see her face. He took the three steps to her, grabbed her chin with his fingers, and turned her face toward the fire, looking for signs of deception. Of lies.

What he saw nearly buckled his knees. Misery and pain. Tear tracks down her cheeks. Her eyes were closed, and more tears fell from beneath her lids. Glancing at her posture, her folded arms, her hunched shoulders, his heart nearly shattered.

No! No, hell no! He wasn't going to fall for this. "Tell me! Tell me again. Look me in the eye and tell me the truth."

Her eyelids slowly fluttered opened. Her eyes were colored with shadows of anguish. "I didn't know she had the books, Trent." Her voice had lost all inflection. She sounded so ... lost. "I heard you tell her she wasn't to read them. I wouldn't have gone against your rules. She's your daughter."

His fingers tightened on her jaw. A reflex, nothing more. "Are you one of the witches? Are you part of the group of them that live out in the desert? Do you sacrifice chickens? Dance naked under the moon around a fire?"

Tears flowed from her eyes, but her lip quirked, as if she thought his questions were funny. "No. I've never sacrificed a chicken in my life. And I'm not part of some group who dances naked under the moon."

If she was lying to him, she was the best damn actress he'd ever seen.

She raised her hand to his. "You're hurting me," she whispered.

He released her and she stumbled back against the wall of the cave. She turned away from him and plopped down on the rocky floor. Then she buried her face in her hands and, over the soft crackle of the fire, he heard a quiet sob.

He ground his teeth. Spiked his hand through his hair. Paced a circle around the tiny cave. Looked at her dejected, forlorn position. He'd hurt her. Hurt her deep inside where it really mattered.

"Lina--"

She shook her head. "Don't." She swiped the back of her hands across her face. "Just don't say any more. I'll be leaving in the morning."

The pain that shot through Trent's heart did bring him to his knees. He landed hard right behind her, reached for her, pulled her against his chest. "No." She struggled against him for a minute, but he held her tight, his face buried in her sweet, cool hair. "No. Don't go."

The thought of her leaving, of never seeing her again, of never holding her again, ripped his soul open. Until the words left her lips, he had no idea they'd hurt so much.

"You don't want me here!" she cried and went limp against him. "I can't take this anymore. I can't!"

"I'm sorry." He kissed her neck. "Lina, don't leave me." He nuzzled his nose against her silky skin. "I got scared."

Lina turned in his arms, her stormy gaze snagging him. His heart. "Scared of what?"

Things I don't understand. Terrifying images from my past. My daughter being emotionally screwed like I was. He glanced around the cave, spotted the drawings that'd given Devil's Peak its name. Only, he knew who'd put those drawings there, and he even knew what they represented. He shivered and snuggled Lina against his chest.

"Trent?"

"Shh. I was wrong." He cupped the back of her head and held her so tight, rocked her back and forth. "I'm sorry I doubted. I'm sorry I hurt you. I didn't know about Jess's headaches. I didn't know...." He sighed. "Why do you have those books?"

"Knowledge, Trent," she answered softly. "Knowledge of the things in this world that most people can't understand." Her voice whisper soft, she said, "Refuse to understand."

"Like what?"

"Those that have gone before us. They're here, you know. They're all around us. Watching over us. Taking care of us."

Trent fiercely shook his head, cupped his hand over her mouth. "No. No, I don't want to hear this. And I don't want Jessica to be hearing this either. Do you understand me?"

Lina leaned back against his arm, met his gaze, and gently pulled his hand away from her mouth. "Why? Why does this frighten you?"

* * * *

Trent's eyes were dark, troubled. And she could feel the fear pouring off him in waves. "Nothing good can come of knowing such things. Evil lurks. It waits for when you're weak and defenseless."

Lina let out a slow breath. "What happened?" she whispered.

He shook his head, looked toward the fire. "It doesn't matter. All that matters is that I protect Jessica." His voice faded to a heart-felt softness. "That's all that matters."

He wouldn't listen, no matter what she said, she realized. There was nothing that would change his mind. He had to change his mind, she couldn't do it for him. "If Jess asks me questions, I'm going to answer her. If...." Her breath caught at the fierceness in his beautiful blue eyes when he looked back at her. "Trent. She's got to be free to make her own choices," she whispered, "or she'll rebel. Wouldn't you rather–"

"I won't let her be hurt."

Deflation. Lina slid off his lap and moved out of his reach. "You say you want me to stay, but you don't trust me not to hurt Jess." She shook her head and stood up, brushing the dirt from her bottom. "I love that little girl, Trent. She's very special. And if you think for one moment that I'd do anything to cause her harm...." All she could do was shake her head again. She swallowed hard as tears blurred her vision. "I think it's best if I leave."

She was almost to the cave opening when Trent said, "I don't understand you."

She stopped, stared out into the night. The stars sparkled over her, the moon glowed full and bright, casting eerie shadows over the bushes and cacti. "What's there to understand? I need a home. A place to feel safe." She shrugged. "I haven't found it yet. Maybe someday I will." She stepped into the night, into the cool desert breeze.

"You don't trust me either. Tell me what you're afraid of. Trust in me."

Lina stopped, turned back toward him. He still sat on his knees by the fire. The sight of his beautiful, hard body illuminated by the dancing firelight made her ache. "I can't.

"Don't go," he pleaded softly.

"How can I stay? How can I be someone I'm not? I know what you think of me. I know what most people think of me. I'm not all here." She tapped the side of her head. "I wear odd clothes. Sometimes I space out. Sometimes I talk to myself. I make my own soap, dry my own herbs. Make tea no one else likes." She took a few steps back toward him. "Well, Trent, that's me. That's who I am. That and a whole lot more. And I can't change. I don't want to change. I like me." Most of the time. Right now, she wished she could be someone different. Someone Trent could love, because damn it all the way to hell, she loved him.

"I like you, too." Trent came to his feet and closed the space between them. "I do." He gently cupped her cheeks in his rough palms, stroked the hair at her temples. "And that scares the hell out of me. Maybe I'm looking for reasons to push you away. Maybe...." He shook his head. "No maybe about it. You scare me. I'm terrified of how you make me feel. I've been asleep for so long, and you've woken me up."

She really wished she could stop crying. His words were tearing her apart. It wasn't a declaration of undying love, but it was more than she'd ever gotten before. She just wished he'd trust her. But then, how could she expect that when she was still withholding the truth?

"Please don't cry, baby." He leaned forward and placed the softest, most tender kiss on her forehead. "It kills me to see you crying. I need your smile. Your humor. Even your spaciness. You make me laugh. And, honey, I haven't felt like laughing in a whole lot of years."

"Do you trust me not to hurt Jess?"

Trent leaned in, just enough so he could meet her eyes. He was silent for so long, she started to pull away. He held her firm. "Yes." It was a simple answer, yet whispered with so much feeling. Lina threw her arms around him and buried her face against his rock-solid chest.

Her tears soaked his shirt, and right now, she couldn't have said why she was crying. She'd been crying for what felt like hours, days even. Since he stormed out of her apartment with Jess in tow. But now her heart felt light. She knew it shouldn't, there were still too many problems between them, but all she knew at that very moment was that she didn't want to live without him. She didn't know how she'd live without him.

"No more cryin', babe. Please." Trent rubbed his big, strong hands up and down her back, brushed them through her hair, snuggled her close. "Shh."

She pulled away enough to wipe her sleeve over her face. "Okay. No more."

Trent smiled down at her. "I'm sorry."

She nodded. "Yeah, you've said that."

He chuckled. "I mean it."

Lina's smile trembled a little. She sniffled. "Okay. Apology accepted."

"Really?"

She nodded.

"Good. Because I can't wait one more second to do this--"

Tenderly, his mouth claimed hers. She sighed against him. His tongue stroked hers. When his hands gripped her hips and pulled her tight against his arousal, she moaned.

"I need you," he breathed against her lips, his hot breath fanning her cheeks. "I need you so bad."

Placing tiny kisses on his jaw, she pulled his T-shirt from his jeans and ran her hands up his chest, lightly tugging at the curly sprinkle of hair there. "I need you, too, Trent."

He let go of her just long enough to pull his shirt over his head. Then his mouth crashed down on hers with pent-up frustration, fear, anger, and so many other emotions Lina couldn't even begin to know or understand. All she could do was feel. His hard body against her. His warm, moist mouth on hers. His tongue mating and dancing with her tongue.

Fingers fumbled with buttons and zippers, clothing melted away like magic until she stood naked in the firelight. She reached into the opening of his jeans and ran her hand along his hot, hard length.

He pulled away a fraction of an inch and grasped her wrist. "Easy, baby. Easy. I'm so damn close."

She smiled a wicked smile. "How close?"

He growled and lowered them both to the ground. She sucked in her breath when the cold rock touched her back. He chuckled and rolled to his back, pulling her over him. "What's the matter? Not into the whole nature thing?"

Lina propped her arms on his chest, loving the feel of the cool air, the warm fire, and his hot skin along her body. She smiled into his eyes. "I dunno. Never done it in the great outdoors before."

Trent's grin was mischievous, a little evil. "Oh, a virgin." His hands cupped her bottom, massaging her, making her blood hum deliciously through her veins.

She laughed. "Never did it on a bathroom floor, either, 'til you."

He chuckled, leaned up, and kissed the tip of her nose. "Little problem here, honey."

She raised an eyebrow.

"My pants are still on."

"So are your boots."

"Gonna fix that?"

She reached down between them, pulled his solid erection from his underwear, rubbed her hot, wet center over the tip until his head dropped back and he sucked in his breath. His hands tightened on her butt, his fingers dug into her flesh as he held her still. Her laugh was wicked. "You really need your boots off?"

He shook his head, his eyes closed tight.

"Condom," she remembered.

"Wallet," he groaned as he released her with one hand and tipped his body a bit to the side so he could reach into his back pocket. She clung to his shoulders to keep from sliding off and laughed. It felt good to laugh. Really, really good.

Business cards, cash, old receipts and a myriad other things tumbled from his wallet when he dumped it on the ground, grabbing for the small packet. Lina laughed harder and picked one up. One of five. Feeling frisky, was he?

"I need you," he whispered as he cupped the back of her head and pulled her to his mouth. His tongue was demanding, his teeth made her tingle and ache. "I've never needed anyone the way I need you."

And her heart ached at that. How she wished it could be forever. She loved him so much.

Pushing her darkening thoughts aside, she ripped open the condom, quickly rolled it on him and then, as she met his dark, tender gaze, she slowly lowered herself onto him.

As she slid down, he let out a long, low groan. Knowing she did that to him made her feel powerful. When she held him deep inside her, she knew that when this ended with him, she would never, ever find this feeling again.

His hands came up to cup her breasts but his gaze remained locked on hers. "Nothing has ever felt so perfect," he said, his voice gravelly. "You are perfect."

Without thought, she shook her head in denial.

He sat up, surprising her, and pulled her legs around his waist. Then he wrapped his arms around her. "Perfect," he whispered.

He was perfect. She tightened her legs around him, her chest pressed to his, her arms around his neck. Her other half.

Slowly he started to rock his hips. Shattering waves crashed through her until all she could do was cling to him and let him take her to a place she'd never gone before. To Heaven.

Their mingled cries of release echoed off the walls of the tiny cave. Their heavy sighs of completion surrounded them.

Trent laid back, bringing her down on top of him. His chest heaved, his heart thudded. "You're not leaving." It wasn't a request, it was a demand.

Lina smiled against his neck. Licked his salty throat. "I think you could persuade me."

He chuckled and held her even tighter. "Good."

Chapter Fourteen

From the Journal of Lina Brennen:
Life has a way of surprising me. Some good surprises, some not so good. But maybe that's why life is just a little bit exciting at times.

* * * *

In her bedroom, Lina hummed, rubbing a towel over her damp hair. She was due back at the diner in thirty minutes, but right now, priorities and real life couldn't intrude on the memory of her escapade with Trent in the dessert two nights ago.

Her backside still tingled at the thought of his warm, callused hands running up and down her nude, slick body. She shivered. The things that man did to her sanity.

She'd barely seen him yesterday, as he'd had to pull watch out at the Thornton Ranch again. Damn cattle rustler, she'd love to get her hands on him herself.

Merona chuckled. "That must have been some shag, sweetling, to have you still humming two days later."

Lina rolled her eyes and dropped the towel in the corner hamper. "Leave it to you, Granna, to spoil my mood."

"Oh pfft." Merona flicked her wrist.

Lina walked over to the bed and pulled on her denim skirt and pink tank top. Then she went into the bathroom and began pulling a brush through her tangled hair.

Lina stared at the woman in the reflection and chewed on her lower lip, butterflies diving in her stomach. She didn't want to give Trent or Jessica up, it was just that simple. And the only way she knew to keep them was to tell the truth. All of it, not bits and pieces, not little white lies, everything. The good, the bad, the ugly.

"Granna," she said slowly.

Merona's shimmering gold pulse glittered in the mirror and she gave a tiny shake of her head. "Sweetling, it's not time."

Lina set the hairbrush down. "Why?" she whispered. "He's got to know, Granna. Otherwise our relationship is based on nothing but a bunch of lies. And he's too smart to be fooled for much longer." Lina laid her head against the bathroom door, squeezed her eyes shut, and sighed.

All the lies, falsifying what she really was, had become an enormous burden. This was not the way to start a new life. Trent had told her he was sorry, but she wasn't foolish enough to think he'd be content to drop the matter entirely. This secret of hers would get her into more trouble than she'd like to think about. For the first time she was allowing someone--two someone's for that matter--into her life, her heart.

How could she hope to move forward with Trent when her past kept her locked in limbo?

Merona laid a gentle hand on her cheek, her blue eyes sad. "Sweet baby. Not now. You just can't...."

Lina straightened and threw her hair over her shoulder. "I know, Granna. I know. It was only a dream, anyhow."

* * * *

Three hours later, the diner was in full swing. The smells of sizzling burgers and crispy fries filled Lina's nostrils, making her stomach rumble with aching hunger. But on the bright side, she was becoming a damn fine waitress.

"I'll have your order up in a jiffy, Ms. Butler."

"Hmpf." She sniffed and planted a liver spotted hand against her chest. "See that you do. I ain't got all day. Gotta get back to the coop. Them witches been thievin', they have."

Lina smiled and patted Ms. Butler's blouse sleeve. "Yes, ma'am."

"Order up!"

The bell above the door jingled and her heart beat a little faster. When she turned to see who'd stepped through she blew out a frustrated breath. She'd hoped Trent would drop by and make an appearance.

Instead, Willy waved a quick hello and shuffled over to a table with a child no more than eight or nine. Lina grabbed her notepad and made her way over.

"Hey there, Willy. How you feelin' today?"

The brown-eyed miniature version of Willy laced his fingers together and laid his head on his hands with a big sigh. Lina held back a smile, already enchanted with the little guy. Children were so predictable, no matter what age they were.

"Feeling fine, Miss Lina. Mighty fine. Good enough to eat me a T-bone steak, even." His lips quirked and his brown eyes sparkled with hope.

"I don't think so." She shook her head and grinned amidst Willy's great sigh, sounding a lot like the kid. Men were just boys who never really grew up. "It's a grilled chicken salad for you."

Willy rolled his eyes and Lina chuckled. "So, Willy, you ever gonna introduce me to this handsome fella?"

The child sat up straight, his little chest puffing out. "I'm Bobby," he said before Willy could take a breath.

"Oh?" Lina lifted a brow. "Well, you're mighty handsome, Bobby. Anybody ever tell you that you look like old Willy here?"

"Reckon he would," Willy answered. "He's my great-nephew, out of school for the summer. Promised I'd take him to the canyon this weekend."

"Yup, you sure did." Bobby's cheeks glowed with childish enthusiasm. Willy reached over and tousled the child's honey-wheat hair.

Lina smiled even as that familiar ache spread through her gut. Would she ever be so lucky? "Well, you boys have a wonderful time. And what can I get for you, Bobby?"

The bell above the door jangled. Lina turned, holding her breath, hoping, waiting. Jessica walked through the door, her olive skin glistening from the sun's warm rays. Then much to her delight, the face she'd wanted to see all night stepped through. Her heart flipped in her chest then dove down into her belly.

His blue eyes shifted, his gaze firmly pinning hers, and that slow, sexy smile touched the corners of his lips. He wore a cowboy hat tonight, partially shielding his face. Oh Lord, but the man was sexy as sin.

"...and chocolate milk," Bobby said.

Lina snapped out of it and turned toward Bobby, shaking her head. She really needed to stop doing that. "I'm sorry, honey, what was that again?"

Willy shifted in his seat, caught site of Trent and chuckled. "He said a cheeseburger, fries and chocolate milk."

Lina threw Willy a grateful smile. "Thanks, Willy. Lemme go get you some coffee, and I'll put that order in right quick."

"Take your time, darlin'. We're not in any rush. Are we, Bobby?"

The child shook his head and resumed gazing out the window.

Lina hurried off. Her feet couldn't get her quick enough to Trent and Jess's side. They were seated at the counter, which was convenient for her since she had to grab the coffee pot anyway.

A callused hand ran along her backside as she walked behind the counter. "Missed you today, angel," Trent whispered low.

"Oh, brother," Jessica rolled her eyes.

Lina giggled. Her body hummed with excitement, joy, delight. She grabbed the coffee pot. "Oh really?" She shrugged and tried to walk past him.

Trent growled. His arms snaked out, entrapping her waist, and brought her closer to his side. "You better have a better hello for me than that."

"Get a room." Jess turned up her nose and jumped off the stool, walking toward the bathroom.

Lina laid her hand against Trent's chest, aware of the furtive glances being thrown her way. But being back in Trent's arms more than made up for it. The hairs on her arms stood on end as she inhaled the scent of leather clinging to his shirt. "You think we're making a scene?"

"I don't give a damn. Tell me hello, woman, and I want you to mean it."

Lina tried, but couldn't prevent the slow smile that curled her lips. "I missed you, too."

Trent nodded and let her go. "See you tonight?"

Oh God, a pack of wild hyenas couldn't keep her away. A shot of electricity coursed through her veins, turning her blood to molten lava. "Sure," she said, and sauntered off.

An hour later, the rush was slowly breaking up. Lina rolled her shoulders and caught sight of Trent in deep discussion with Abby. His brows were drawn low. His mother waved a hand through the air in agitation.

"Lina." Jess tugged on her arm.

"Hmm, sweetie?" Lina turned.

Jessica took a deep breath. "Well, I wanted to apologize for taking those books from your apartment the other night. If I'd have known what Dad would do...."

Lina shook her head. "Honey, I'm not mad, but you can't do that. Your father doesn't accept this, none of it. And we can't make him."

"I know." Jessica hung her head.

"And another thing. Why did you lie to your father about having headaches? I hate lying, Jess, loathe it in fact."

"You do it."

Lina grimaced at the truth of the words, they were like bitter poison to her heart. "Yes, and that's precisely why I despise it. But you know what, Jessica, it doesn't make it right. It never does."

Jessica scuffed the toe of her sneaker on the floor. "I wasn't lying," she mumbled.

Lina's brows bunched. "What do you mean?"

"Well. I do. I get these terrible headaches, feels like something's ripping through my brain sometimes. But when I talked with Grandpa the other day, the pain went away. I mean completely. I've never felt that good. Is that weird?"

"You say it went away when you talked to Dyami?"

"Uh hu." Jess nodded

"I'm gonna have to talk to Granna about this, but I've got an idea."

Jessica's gaze roamed around the room, her nose wrinkling. "Where is Merona tonight?"

"She begged off. Said she had a pounding headache."

"What?" Jess frowned. "I thought ghosts couldn't...."

Lina held up her hand, stalling Jessica. "Don't ask. My grandmother is a crazy old bat who does her own thing."

Jessica giggled and Lina joined in.

The bell above the door chimed and she nearly groaned aloud when Ty swaggered in. His oddly colored cinnamon eyes shifted around the room until they settled on her, and he walked over.

Out of the corner of her eye, Lina noticed Trent clench his fists and his jaw. Oh Lord, what now?

"Look, Lina, can we talk?" Ty started.

Jessica planted her hands on her hips and glowered.

Ty shoved a hand through his wavy brown hair and grimaced.

"Say what you have to say, Ty," Lina said with a raised brow. She was not in the mood tonight. The last thing she needed was another battle with Trent over miscommunication.

Ty blew out a deep breath while he gripped the brim of his hat in a white-knuckled fist. "I ... well I...." He shook his head. "Shit, this shouldn't be so hard."

Taken aback, Lina frowned. What could the man possibly have to say to her? This new behavior was alien territory, which made her wary. His cocky swagger she could deal with. This fumbling man, though, caught her completely off guard.

Ty gave her a crooked grin. "I wanted to apologize for my improper behavior on Friday."

What in the blue blazes? Had he really just said that? What a night this had been. What a strange and wonderful night.

* * * *

Trent turned back to his mother, a scowl pulling his brows together. What the hell? Ty apologizing for acting like an asshole? That was definitely a turn of attitude he didn't understand. That man had made a living of acting like a jerk for the past ten years.

"I still think snooping into her past is a bad idea," Abby said as she poured Trent another cup of coffee.

Trent shook his head. He should have kept his mouth shut. "You're the one who told me to be careful. You're the one who said she was a city girl and wouldn't be happy here. What other option do I have?"

"Why don't you try asking her?" Abby set the coffee carafe back on the maker, then folded her arms over her chest. "Maybe I was wrong."

He studied his mother's eyes, her frown. "Why the change of heart so suddenly?"

Abby shrugged. Trent ground his teeth. Great, now Mom was using the same lame little shrug his daughter used when she didn't want to answer a question. What was it about females?

"Maybe I'm getting to like her. She does seem happy here. She even seems to like her job. She works her scrawny little butt off every day, no complaints. And she's getting to know the folks around here. She greets them all by name, always has a kind word or smile for them. Maybe I was wrong, okay? Besides," she shifted her feet, glanced away for a second, "Willy really likes her."

Trent raised his eyebrows in surprise and nearly choked on his scalding coffee. "Willy?"

Her frown was fierce, and her blue eyes, so much like his own, narrowed and glared at him. "I ain't dead, sonny."

Trent threw back his head and laughed.

"What's so funny?" Jess asked as she slid onto the stool next to him.

"Nana's got the hots for Willy," he said with a smirk.

"Well, duh."

Abby flicked his ear, something she'd done all his life when she was ticked, and he laughed all the harder.

"And you watch yourself, missy," Abby said to Jess. "You're not too old to turn over my knee."

Jess grinned at her. "Why don't you just jump him and get it over with?"

"Jess!" All joking aside, Trent didn't like his baby talking like that.

Jess shrugged. "Well, jeez, it's not like they're not consenting adults or anything. Jeez, they're old."

"Smarty-pants," Abby said, and flicked Jess's ear.

Trent chuckled. "You behave, little girl. I don't want to hear you talking about anyone jumping anyone."

Jess giggled. "Sure, Dad. Like you and Lina—"

"Enough." But he still grinned. Yeah, that was something he and Lina did very well, but he still didn't like the idea of his baby growing up and knowing ... things.

Lina came up beside him and put her arm around his shoulders. "What's all the laughing about?" God, he loved it when she touched him.

He wrapped his arm around her waist and pulled her firm against his side. "Mom and Willy...." He broke off with a chuckle when Abby held up her fingers to flick him again.

"Oh, that." Lina waved her hand as if she knew it all. "He's getting up his nerve," she said to Abby. "Be patient."

His mother's eyes sparkled and the smile on her lips was one of pure happiness. Trent shook his head. How could he have not known? The old man came in every single day, twice a day, like clockwork.

"You guys coming over tonight?" Lina asked, directing her question to both Jess and Trent.

Well, hell, that wasn't what he wanted. He wanted Lina all to himself tonight. Preferably all night.

"Oh, yeah," Jess said. "Dad brought that spare little T.V. we had for you, and a VCR. I also brought some of my movies for you. We could make some popcorn and watch movies all night."

Trent almost groaned. That definitely was not what he had in mind for a night of fun.

"Well, come on, Dad. School's out. No reason I can't stay up all night."

"Lina has to be here at six in the morning," he answered reasonably. "She can't stay up all night

Abby obviously found humor in the situation. "She can sleep in an extra hour. You all go have fun." She pointed at Lina. "After cleanup of course."

Lina grinned and gave Trent a kiss on the cheek. "See you in a bit."

He wanted more, much more, than a little peck on the cheek. But now he was resigned to watching movies ... with his kid there. No make-out sessions in the plans for tonight. He sighed. Oh well.

Jess leaned over and whispered. "You guys can snuggle on the couch. I'll stay way-y-y across the room." And then the little imp had the nerve to wink at him.

"Mom," he said. "Flick her."

Abby chuckled, shook her head, and walked off.

The phone rang and Abby called from across the diner for Jess to answer it.

Jess ran around the counter and grabbed it on the third ring. Then she held it out for him. "It's for you, Dad. Ms. Butler."

Trent groaned and reached for the phone. "Hello?"

"Three more o' my best hens! You get out here right now and do somethin' about this, young man. They keep a killin' them and guttin' 'em right here on my land."

"Ms. Butler, I told you there's really nothing I can do. And I still believe it's coyotes doing it, not ... who you think it is." His gaze went across the room to Lina and he watched her refill saltshakers. Witches. He shook his head. No. Lina wasn't a witch. That he'd asked.

"You get out here or I'll make sure you're not the town sheriff any longer."

Trent stifled a chuckle. Like anyone else wanted the job. "Yes, ma'am. I'll be out there shortly."

Lina turned around and met his eyes. The look of disappointment wasn't lost on him. He hung up the phone and crossed the room to her. "I'm sorry, honey. Ms. Butler has more dead chickens."

"Tell her to build a higher fence," she said, sounding like a petulant child. She even had a cute little pout that he couldn't keep himself from leaning over and tasting.

"I gotta go. It's my job to soothe the angry villagers."

All the color drained from Lina's face, she shivered.

"What? What's wrong?"

She shook her head and turned back to the saltshakers.

"Babe?" He took her by the shoulders and turned her to face him. "I have to go."

"I know." She wrapped her arms around his waist and leaned against him, her head tucked under his chin. "I just was hoping...."

"Yeah. Me too. Tomorrow night, okay?"

She turned her head and looked up at him. "Promise?"

"Swear it on my badge, baby. Nothing's going to keep me away from you." He kissed her again, briefly. Then smiled and gave her a little wink. "'Til tomorrow."

She smiled back at him, went up on tiptoe, and kissed him again. "I'll be waiting," she whispered.

He slowly released her. "Come on, Jess. Change of plans."

"Ohhh," Jess whined.

"Wait," Lina said. "Jess can still come over. If you want to take the T.V. and stuff up to my apartment first. Do you have the time?"

God, she was wonderful. "I'll make the time. Keys?" He held out his hand.

She dug into the pocket of her skirt and pulled out her apartment key. "Thanks."

"No, thank you." He kissed her forehead, afraid that if he tasted her lips again, he'd be totally lost and never make it out to Butler's place. "I'll see you guys here for breakfast then?"

Lina smiled and nodded. "I'll be waiting."

Chapter Fifteen

From the Journal of Lina Brennen:
I've found that sometimes you gotta do what you gotta do. No matter what.

* * * *

"Isn't Daddy sweet?" Jess asked as she flounced over to the television set. "He even plugged it all in and everything. Even set the clock on the VCR."

Lina laughed. "Good thing, too, because I wouldn't have a clue."

"You don't watch television?"

Lina shook her head. "Nope. Never owned one."

Now it was Jess's turn to shake her head. "You're kinda weird, you know that?"

Lina laughed. "Yeah, I've been told so. Hey, Granna! Where are you?" she called.

Merona appeared right in front of her in a bright, shimmering display. "Right here, sweetling."

Lina jumped. "Jeez, don't do that." She rubbed her fingers between her brows. "Trent's busy, so we've got Jess to ourselves. She told me something interesting tonight." Lina turned to Jess. "Tell Granna about the headaches while I go take a quick shower."

"Okay." Jess plopped down on the couch and pulled a throw pillow onto her lap. "About two years ago...."

Lina hurried into the bathroom and stripped off her clothes. She jumped into the shower and stood under the cool spray for a few minutes. And thought about Trent. What else? He seemed to be the center of every worthwhile thought she possessed. She lathered her hair and remembered his hand in her hair. Soaped her breasts and remembered him kissing, suckling. She shivered with excitement at just the memory of him.

Deciding she'd better get back to Jess before her thoughts led to even naughtier things, she turned off the water, quickly towel dried, and slipped on her lightweight bathrobe, which hung on the back of the bathroom door.

When she went back into the living room, Jess had turned out all the lights and lit all the candles. She lay on the couch, obviously already starting her relaxation.

Merona smiled sweetly. She's going to try to reach Dyami again. I think he'll be able to open her up to the rest of the spirits trying to talk to her. She shook her head sadly. Poor girl has been so confused for so long.

Lina nodded. I just wish we didn't have to go behind Trent's back to do this. If he ever found out....

No luck getting him to tell you why he's the way he is? Merona asked.

Lina just shook her head. She really needed to know, so she could figure out how much she could tell him about herself.

* * * *

Jess found her bench among the pink clouds. The air was crisp and smelled strongly of freshly mowed grass. "I need you, Grandfather," she whispered. "Please help me." This time the connection was much faster. She felt his presence, and when she opened her eyes, he was there with her, sitting on the chair just across the coffee table.

She sat up and smiled at him. "Hello, Grandfather," she said.

His wrinkled face split into a grin, his deep brown eyes sparkled with humor and intelligence. "Granddaughter." He bowed his head slightly. "I am here to help."

"Grandfather," Jess said, then glanced at Lina and Merona. "I am wondering why I hear voices, but can't see who's talking. And why headaches come along with the voices."

The old man nodded slowly. "You have the gift that has been handed down through generations of our family, Jessica. Those voices are your ancestors, not unlike myself, who are here to help guide you through life. You must not push them away. Open yourself to them as you have to me. They will teach you much."

Jess felt a weight lifted from her shoulders. She could do that. She really could. Now that she knew she wasn't absolutely crazy.

"Ask your questions, Jessica," he said in that low, gentle, accented voice.

"I want to know why Dad is the way he is. Why he doesn't believe in the spirits."

Dyami leaned back in his chair, folded his hands together, and was silently thoughtful for several moments. "Many years ago," he began, "your father heard the voices you hear now. He questioned his mother--my daughter--on the ways of our people. Abigail turned her back on us and our ways, convincing herself not to believe. She told Trent that our traditions, our way of life, was not for him. That he was more than half white man. He should embrace the white way of life, as she had."

Jess gasped. "But why? Why would Nana do something like that?"

Dyami sighed and shook his head. "Your grandmother grew up in a time when racism was much more than it is now. Because she had the white man's eyes, our people reviled her. I guess in some part, she felt she'd be better accepted in the white man's world, and her son was raised as a by-product of that belief."

Tears gathered in Jessica's eyes, blurring the image of her great-grandfather for a moment. "That's so sad."

"Hatred is hatred, child," Dyami said. "She did what she thought best at the time."

"So that's why he doesn't believe, then? Was he just never raised to believe?"

"No. On the contrary. Your father was very interested in learning more of his heritage." Dyami nodded. "Trent took it upon himself to discover the secrets of communing with his ancestors. Only he did not have such help as you do now." Dyami's gaze touched on Lina, and then Merona. "You are a lucky child, Granddaughter. Never take your friends for granted."

"Yes, Grandfather," she answered respectfully, in awe of his wisdom, his calm. "What happened to Daddy?"

"He found the writings of an old ritual in a book, and he followed it. Only he didn't understand that this ritual was only carried out by the most learned of men, men who had studied and dealt with the spirit world for many moons. Trent drank an herb that opened his mind to the spirit world, only it was the dark side."

Lina gasped. "Was he harmed?"

Dyami shook his head. "Trent has, as Jessica has, many powerful ancestors watching over them. We took care that he was safe. Only his mind was harmed. Now he refuses to accept us. To hear us. To learn from us."

Jess blinked back tears and she wasn't sure why she was crying. Lina had opened a whole new world to her, one she would embrace. Her father, sweet, wonderful man that he was, was terrified because he'd made a mistake.

"Why did Nana turn her back so completely? Surely she'd want to keep a part of her heritage and who she was ... is ... intact."

Dyami smiled. "Ah, my daughter. Headstrong and beautiful." He stared off to the side, as if remembering something. When he spoke, his voice was low. "My wife was a stunning woman. She came from Norway. Spoke with a beautiful accent. Long blond hair and sparkling blue eyes...." His voice drifted off with a soft smile on his lips.

"Grandfather?"

"I'm sorry, child. I will tell you all about your great-grandmother some other time. She died giving birth when Abigail was just three years old. She was trying to give me my first son. Sadly, he did not survive, either.

"We lived on the reservation not far from here. Abigail wanted to live in the white man's world. I could not let her go, because she was not white, because I knew what it would be like for her out there. She left as soon as she was old enough, turning her back on her family and every bit of life she knew. She moved to Unegi and found a man. He was killed just after Trent was conceived. Town sheriff, he was. But the town was a lot wilder back then."

"Trent told me his grandfather was the sheriff of Unegi," Lina said, now sitting on the couch next to Jess.

Dyami looked infinitely sad. "Yes, his grandfather on his father's side was the sheriff of Unegi, but Abigail has never told him of her mother. The wonderful woman who fell in love with a redskin. The woman who turned her back on her culture to be with the man she loved."

"That's so sad," Lina whispered.

Dyami nodded. "It is. I hope and pray that one day both Abigail and Trent will open their hearts once again."

Jess nodded. "I hope so too, Grandfather."

* * * *

Lina slumped down on one of the stools along the counter and sipped a cup of hot coffee. She hated the stuff, but she needed the caffeine. Jess had kept her up well past midnight talking about Dyami, the spirit world, and how she was to open herself to it.

She was exhausted and missed Trent terribly. He'd stopped in that morning just long enough to grab a cup of coffee and run. He had a meeting with the sheriff from the next town over. He hadn't returned to the diner all day, hadn't come to see her during her break in the afternoon, and now it was time for her to go home and he hadn't appeared.

"Can I come over tonight?" Jess asked as she sat down next to Lina.

Lina sighed. She hated to say no, but....

"You're tired, aren't you?" Abby asked, leaning her elbows on the counter in front of Lina.

Lina nodded. "Yeah, I am. Maybe tomorrow?" she asked Jess.

Jess looked disappointed, but nodded.

The bell over the door tinkled and they all looked toward it.

Lina's tiredness vanished like smoke, and she grinned like an idiot when she saw Trent come through, wearing his sheriff's uniform. His gaze met hers and held as he walked toward her. She let out a yelp when he lifted her right off the stool and into his arms.

"Mom, Jess." He gave them each a nod then, still holding her in his arms, leaned down and kissed Jess on the forehead. "I'm kidnapping Lina."

Jess giggled.

Lina laughed.

Trent grinned. "Don't wait up." He winked at Jess then headed for the door.

Once outside, he carried her over to his cruiser, which was parked just down the street. Lina clung to his neck and laughed. "Where are you taking me?"

"Thornton's ranch. He lost another two head last night. He wants me to come watch his cattle tonight. And I swore that I'd spend time with you." He set her to her feet then pulled her close and kissed her long and hard. "Wanna join me for a stakeout?" he asked, a teasing grin playing on his lips.

"Hmm. Sounds a bit boring." She leaned against him, her cheek against his chest. She loved the way he felt, smelled, everything about him.

"It would be boring, if you weren't coming along." His hand slipped down to her hips, around to her behind and he pressed her close so she could feel the hard bulge behind his zipper.

She lifted her head and looked up at him. She wondered if he could see what she felt in her eyes. God, she hoped so. "You don't show up all day, and now I'm just supposed to get in that car with you, go out to some cattle ranch and--"

His lips brushed hers, lightly, tenderly. "You have no choice in the matter. I told you, I'm kidnapping you. You're going."

Lina snickered. "I think kidnapping is a felony, and you, Mr. Sheriff, are here to uphold the law, not break it."

He kissed her again, his tongue slid over her bottom lip, making her shiver. "Are you going to press charges?"

She slipped her hand into his hair and pulled his mouth down to hers. "Only if you keep me standing out here any longer." She kissed him hard, letting her tongue explore his mouth, reveling in the warm hardness of his body.

Trent chuckled when he pulled away. The sound went through her like a million little lightning bolts. "Get in the car." He reached around her and opened the passenger door for her. Then he went around and climbed in behind the wheel.

* * * *

He wanted to be in Lina's bed. A nice, soft bed, with a wonderfully soft woman climbing all over him and making him beg for mercy. But Mr. Thornton was adamant that he be out at the ranch, babysitting his damn beeves.

Reaching over, he took Lina's hand in his, brought it to his thigh, and laced his fingers with hers. She turned and smiled at him, then returned her attention to the spectacular sunset they headed toward.

Ms. Butler was just as adamant that the witches were killing her chickens. Sure looked like coyotes, wolves, or even wild dogs to him. They were killed and gutted, feathers everywhere.

"Lina," he said thoughtfully. "What do you know about witches?"

Her head whipped toward him so fast he was surprised she didn't get whiplash. "What do you mean?"

Was that a note of panic in her voice? He glanced at her and frowned, then concentrated on the narrow road ahead of him. "There's this pack of witches that live near Devil's Peak. Ms. Butler thinks they're killing her laying hens." He shrugged. "And Mr. Thornton's prize bulls keep going missing. I was just wondering what you knew about witches. Would they be doing this, by any chance?"

Lina's hand relaxed in his and she leaned back into the seat. He shook his head. Why had his question so startled her?

She took a deep breath. "Do you know what kind of witches? What do they call themselves?"

Trent thought for a long moment. "I think I heard the term Wicca mentioned somewhere."

Lina actually laughed. He turned to look at her. She was laughing so hard there were tears coming out of her eyes.

"What's so funny?" He didn't like being laughed at.

"They're not a pack, they're called a coven. And no, Trent,"--she wiped her watering eye with the back of her hand--"they don't kill chickens or steal cows."

"Well, what do they do then? I know they meet out at Devil's peak on Mondays, and certain other days, like the equinox and stuff like that. What do they do?"

"Well,"--she stared off at the pale pink and lavender sky--"I don't know a lot about them. I really don't know the origin of their religion, but some say it goes back to the ancient Celts." At his frown she said, "You know, the Druids that built things like Stonehenge."

He nodded. "They sacrificed things, didn't they?"

Lina shrugged. "I have no idea. It's ancient history. Not much is known about them. But I do know that Wiccans don't sacrifice things. The basis of their religion is grounded in the earth. They think that everything has a spirit; stars, planets, humans, animals, even rocks and trees. A lot of their rituals deal with bringing harmony and healing to nature." She leaned over and kissed his shoulder. "They're not going to kill some laying hens or steal cows. They respect life, in all its forms."

Trent squeezed her hand. "How do you know this? What if you're wrong?"

She laid her head on his shoulder. "If your witches are Wiccan, they are harmless."

"What other kind of witches are there?"

Lina took a slow, deep breath. "Well ... There are the Satanists."

Trent felt a cold finger run up his spine. "Tell me about those."

Lina shook her head. "I don't know much. I don't believe in dark magic. All I know is that Religious Satanists believe in Satan as a force of nature, not the red guy in hell with a pitchfork." She let out a little laugh.

He knew she was trying to lighten the mood, but he needed to know. Not sure why he needed to know, but he did. "What do they do?"

"I really don't know, Trent. All I know is that they have no problems in causing harm to their enemies. From what I've read"--he heard her swallow hard--"a lot of those kinds of people are not psychologically well."

"Charles Manson type thing?"

Lina nodded against his shoulder. He turned onto a long dirt roadway. At the end sat Thornton's ranch house.

"Thank you, Lina."

She sat up and looked at him in the fading light. "For what?"

"For sharing what you know."

Her smile was pure magic to him. He smiled in return.

* * * *

They parked beneath the only tree in the pasture, a huge elm. Trent leaned back in his seat with a heavy sigh.

Lina nibbled on her lip and stared at the vast amounts of land, stretching as far as the eye could see.

"How much of this does Mr. Thornton own?" Lina asked.

Trent raised an obsidian brow and turned to look at her. "Last I heard,'bout a thousand acres or so."

Lina whistled, her eyebrows shooting up her forehead. The large heads of cattle grazed by a nearby watering hole. "Well hell, he's a pretty rich man. What's he raising?"

He laced his fingers together and peered through the window. "Only the best. Angus beef."

"Jiminy Christmas," Lina said around a sigh. "I'm thinking Thornton owns a ton of cattle. Why's he getting in such a tizzy over a few missing ones?"

"If you look at it that way, then sure,"--he shrugged--"it doesn't make much sense. But think about it in terms of price. Good quality cow flesh can go for a hefty sum in those steer auctions. Now add to the mix that Angus is about the best of the best, and you're looking easily at a loss of a load of money per head."

"Wow."

"Exactly." He laid his threaded fingers on the steering wheel. "That's why Blake's been goin' nuts at the thought of any more of his cattle being stolen."

Lina sighed and rubbed her nose. "Yeah, I'd imagine."

She gazed at the silhouettes of the cattle, the night sky now a deep indigo, and fought the incessant call of sleep. Her lashes felt heavy and nearly impossible to keep open. Lina rubbed at the grit in her eyes and leaned her head back against the seat.

If she didn't do something soon, she was going to fall asleep. And that's the last thing she wanted to do. She had precious few hours with Trent as it was, she really wanted to enjoy this time together.

"I should have thought to fill a thermos with coffee before we came out here." Trent's deep voice rumbled.

Lina snapped her eyes open, unaware that they'd even closed in the first place. Frantically she gazed around for something, anything to keep her awake.

Then suddenly she had an idea, and her lip curled into a semi-smile. "Trent," she said in a deep voice, thickened by sleepiness.

He turned, his blue eyes looking at her questioningly.

Lina licked her upper lip in a slow, seductive move and shifted closer toward him.

His eyes flared with passion and lust, and suddenly sleep was the furthest thing from her mind. "You really think the rustler's gonna show up tonight?" She bit her lip and draped her arm over the back of the seat behind him, jutting her breasts out against her thin tank top.

His responding chuckle was all the encouragement she needed. Lina ran her hand through her hair, her body tingling with sexual need. The air in the car practically sizzled with it.

"You know," she said around a breathy sigh, "I've always been curious what those hard...."

He inhaled. The bulge in his pants become harder.

"...steel handcuffs would feel like." Lina narrowed her eyes, her finger toying with the neck of her tank top.

Trent groaned and shook his head. "Lina," he said in roughened voice.

She laid her finger against his lips, shushing him. "No. Don't say it." She shook her head. "Just say 'yes'."

He closed his eyes and took her finger into his mouth. His warm tongue sliding against her flesh made sparks ignite through her veins, and she melted beneath the onslaught.

"Oh, Trent," she moaned as the sensations overtook her body, wreaking havoc with her system. Lina gave herself up to the tempestuous waves of desire roiling through, making her ache and want and need.

"All right, baby. All right."

Lina opened her eyes to stare into his eyes, bottomless blue depths that sparkled with desire and need to match her own.

She fiddled with the buttons of his shirt, and he shook his head, pushing away from her slightly. For a brief moment panic surged through her with the force of a lightning bolt. Had she done something wrong?

"Let's hop in the backseat," he said. "We'll be a little more comfortable back there."

The earlier excitement slammed into her, making her breathless and antsy. Her stomach twisted in exciting knots. This was so exceptionally naughty. She jumped out of the car and flung the back door open with more force than was necessary. The car rocked for a second with the movement.

Over the top of the car, Trent lifted an amused brow and smirked.

Lina shed her clothing, dropping it on the ground, wanting to be naked, needing to feel the smooth planes of his body sliding against hers. Trent opened the other back door, then dropped his clothes too. The solid length of his cock jutted straight into the air. She sucked in a quick breath and slid onto the seat. The rough fabric running against her sensitized skin made her purr with satisfaction.

"Don't forget those cuffs," Lina said.

Trent chuckled, and her body hummed with shooting spikes of adrenaline. "What's going on in that devious mind of yours, Lina?" he drawled.

She quivered and pulled him into the car. "Give me the cuffs and the keys, and you'll see." A wicked smile tore from her lips.

Chapter Sixteen

From the Journal of Lina Brennen:
Precious moments in life. Small moments, large moments. Memories made and held close to my heart when it all comes crashing to an end.

* * * *

Trent's hot gaze devoured Lina, from the rosy flush covering her body, to the fathomless depths of her shining gray eyes.

"Well, come on, lover boy." A graceful smile tilted her lips and she hooked her finger in a come-hither motion.

His stomach clenched and his groin tightened at the sight of her tousled blonde hair. She was an erotic vision. And in that instant, Trent could deny her nothing. He didn't want to. He slipped the handcuffs and key toward her.

Lina slid her finger through the steel circle and lifted the cuffs in the air, one eyebrow arcing up. A robust laugh spilled from her lips and enflamed him even more.

Trent couldn't suppress the heat of desire that curled down his spine, and he raised a hand, trailing it along her smooth, tanned arm, delighting in the way goose bumps rose under his touch.

She shivered, a long, sexy sigh expelled from her lungs.

The sound vibrated through him. Never in all his life had Trent felt this way about someone. And he now knew he never wanted it to end. Lina was it. The perfect one for him.

He flexed his fingers as fire sizzled through his veins, a slave to his body's desires and to the sultry woman sitting before him.

"Lina." His voice was low, gravelly with sexual need. All his blood rushed toward his penis, making it jump in anticipation of her. God, how he wanted her.

Lina grabbed his hand. With a wicked gleam in her stormy eyes, she snapped open the cuffs and slapped one on his wrist. "Now I promise," she drawled, her voice a breathy burr, "that this won't hurt a bit." She snapped the handcuff to the wire screen in his back seat. "Unless you want it to."

He chuckled even as his body clenched in anticipation of whatever she had in store for him.

She bit her lip and lowered her head, encircling his nipple with her warm mouth. He hissed as her tongue drew tiny circles from one to the other and back again.

Trent let himself drown in wave after wave of euphoric ecstasy. "Oh, God Lina," he moaned and leaned his head back, squeezing his eyes shut, losing himself in the sensation of her. Her verbena scent surrounded him and he inhaled deeply. He'd never forget that scent. Ever.

Lina's hands slid up his chest. The touch of her fingertips on his sensitized skin was like being shocked with volts of high-powered electricity. She made him tingle and burn.

Her throaty laughter filled his head. "Having fun yet?"

"Uh-huh," he croaked, his brain incapable of forming words.

"Well, you haven't seen the best part yet. Just relax, Trent," she whispered, and wiggled her legs out the open door.

Trent spread his legs out on the seat, his head tilted back at an odd angle, his anchored arm already going numb from the awkward position, but he didn't give a damn. He couldn't move right now, even if his life depended on it.

Lina nuzzled his aching arousal with her chin. Just that simple touch alone nearly sent him spiraling over the edge. His chest began to tighten up; his breathing grew heavy and ragged.

Her strong, gentle hand trailed up his leg, gripping, kneading, until she encountered his cock.

He moaned, his gut clenched, and when she encircled him with her fingers, he bucked against her. "Lina," he pleaded, his free hand running through her hair.

She nuzzled him once more and then the warm heat of her mouth engulfed him. He nearly came on the spot at the intense pleasure.

Trent cracked open an eye, his heart flopping into his stomach at the sight of Lina's pert rear up in the air, her head bowed over him. The cascades of her blonde curls trailing along his abdomen and thighs.

She began to move up and down and his body trembled. Beads of perspiration slid down his chest. His insides quivered like a volcano ready to explode.

Then she started humming. The tiny vibrations traveled up his shaft, and fireworks of pleasure shot through his veins.

He gasped and pulled her up. "If you don't stop now, I'm not going to be able to hold back, Lina. Get on me now," he ordered through clenched teeth.

She glanced toward him, a wicked glint in her eyes. Lina slithered up his body. His breath caught until her moist heat was centered directly over him. She wrapped her arms around his neck and began nibbling on his collarbone, his throat.

Trent's legs started to shake, then a thought zapped him like a lightening bolt and it was enough to make him nearly cry out in pain. "Lina, I forgot the fucking condom."

Her tongue lapped at the hollow of his throat, and she shook her head. "Don't worry. I have some. I never leave the protection just to the man." His stomach clenched at her words. Not that he hadn't known she'd been with other men; it stung nonetheless. She hopped out of the car, grabbed a packet out of her skirt pocket, ripped it open and returned to him, quickly rolling it over him. Then she resumed nibbling on his neck, peppering a trail up to his ear.

But she was his now. And he was going to prove it.

He growled and shoved into her, parting the folds of her body with one hard plunge. Her heat was like a warm, velvet glove.

Lina sighed, her body moving in time with his, matching him thrust for thrust. Her nails raked down the front of his chest, her cries mingling with his grunts of sheer bliss.

He hissed at the pleasure her claws inflected and spiraled ever closer to the edge of ecstasy.

Lina was wild, throwing her head back, her hair flying around her shoulders, her shouts getting louder and louder. She gripped his shoulder. "Trent," she screamed.

Stars exploded behind his eyes, sweat trickled down his neck, and he shuddered inside her.

Lina threw herself onto his chest, burying her face against his neck and panting for air, her sweat-slicked skin rubbing erotically against his.

Trent grinned, and then all the hairs on the back of his neck stood on end. Someone was watching them. The gaze bored a hole into the back of his head. The rustler, Mr. Thornton, maybe. Shit, how was he going to explain this away? Maybe he really would lose his badge.

Suddenly nauseous, the enormity of their predicament became clear to him. His heart clenched frantically in his chest.

Lina stiffened and dug her fingers into his chest. "Oh God, Trent," she whispered.

The choking tension was tangible, he braced himself for whatever he might find. Ever so slowly, he turned his head and stared into huge, black, beady, bottomless eyes.

Mooo.

Lina's voice broke into a tight, hysterical giggle.

Trent groaned, his accelerated heart rate plummeting painfully back to normal. "Take these cuffs off me baby, it's time to head home. I think we did enough damage for the night."

She rolled her eyes and clutched at her heart as if she was as relieved as he was. "Well, we certainly made a memory tonight."

He snorted. "Yeah, I guess you could call it that."

Uproarious laughter erupted from both of them as they clung together. He wanted a lifetime of memories with her.

* * * *

"For a second there, I really thought we were goners." Lina shook her head and adjusted her top.

Trent parked the car in front of the now-deserted sheriff's office and leaned back. The dilapidated wood building looked frightening, like the entranceway of a horror house in the ephemeral blue glow of moonlight.

"Well, I can tell you one thing, baby,"--he rubbed his shoulder--"I ain't no spring chicken anymore."

She winced and nibbled on her lip. "Still numb?"

He rolled his eyes and smirked. "You could say that."

Lina bit the inside of her cheek, trying to contain the laughter, but it didn't work. "It seemed like the right thing to do at the time. You don't think we traumatized that cow, do you?"

His white teeth flashed into the darkness surrounding them. "Anything's possible." Trent reached out a hand and trailed it gently down her neck.

She sighed into him, and her lashes fluttered shut for an instant. She didn't want this night to end; it had been so perfect. After the laughter and excitement faded, being held in his arms was peaceful. Soothing. Wonderful.

But reality intruded. Tomorrow would be another hectic day. Her lips thinned, and she grabbed the door handle. "Thank you, Trent," she whispered. "For everything." As she leaned away from him to open the door, he grabbed her wrist.

"Lina, I was wondering,"--he cleared his throat--"if maybe you wouldn't mind some company tonight?"

Her lips curled into a semi-grin. Was he reading her mind or was she just that obvious?

Trent toyed nervously with the steering wheel, his gaze intense, and her heart melted all over again. His brows knitted. "I swear, no funny business, Lina. I um ... well, I sorta want to cuddle."

A giggle escaped her at the serious expression on his face. Never in all her life did she think she'd hear big, bad Trent saying he just wanted to cuddle. Wasn't that just a pick-up line?

He twisted his lips and turned away, his hands dropping to his lap.

Tenderness spread through her body, reaching out its warm fingers and touching the life back into her heart and soul. She grabbed his hand and lifted it to her mouth, pressing a tiny kiss against his knuckle.

"Oh, Trent, I swear, any woman in the world would die to hear those words fall from her man's lips. But...."

He shook his head. "But what, then? What is there to think about?"

"I was going to ask you about Jess. I'm sure she's bound to wonder why her father isn't around when she wakes up in the morning."

He chuckled, dots of shimmering moonlight dancing in his eyes. "Honestly, Lina. Do you think for one minute that our meetings have been that clandestine? I had a very enlightening talk with my daughter the other day, and she's given us the go ahead, if you know what I mean?"

"She didn't." Lina didn't know why anything Jess did surprised her. That child was the spitting image of Merona's temperament, and how that was possible was beyond her. She knew one thing, though--Jessica was spending way too much time with her grandmother.

He cocked his head and shrugged.

She snorted. "Well who am I to argue with that, then?"

* * * *

Trent stepped through the doorway just as Lina clicked on the light. His stomach twisted and knotted up. It wasn't as if he hadn't spent the night with her before. But this time felt much more ... intimate. Before, they'd fallen asleep after hot, exhausting sex. Now--he licked his lips--it just felt different.

She dropped her keys into the little mortar on the tiny shelf by the door and turned toward him, a radiant and slightly self-conscious smile touching her lips. He was glad to see he wasn't the only one suffering from a case of nerves.

Lina pushed her blond bangs out of her face and shrugged. "So."

He lifted a brow. "Honey, if this makes you uncomfortable, I could go."

"No." She shook her head quickly, walked toward him, wrapped her arms around his back, and laid her cheek against his chest.

He sighed and nuzzled her hair. This felt so right. Better than anything ever had with Nancy. Suddenly that wasn't such a startling revelation. It all made perfect sense. Lina was the woman of his heart, and always would be.

Trent scooped her up, clutching her tight to his chest.

"Oh, how lovely," a soft, melodic voice sounded in his ear.

Trent cast his gaze around the living room. Lina stiffened in his arms. "Did you say something?" he questioned slowly.

"Um. I said that this was lovely...." her words trailed off.

He was sure the voice hadn't been hers. He heard the same one sometimes when he was around Lina. Trent shrugged it off. Obviously, he was just tired and his mind was playing tricks on him. Again.

He planted a tender kiss on her forehead and walked toward the bedroom. She sighed into him.

"I have to take a shower," she whispered.

"Mind if you have company tonight? I'm feeling the need for a hot shower myself."

"You rub my back, I rub yours?" She lifted a blonde brow, her gray eyes twinkling.

"Wouldn't have it any other way."

* * * *

Lina inhaled the scent of the desert sage soap still clinging to Trent's body and ran her fingers down the arm encircling her waist. She wiggled her bottom further into him and listened to the steady rhythm of his deep breathing. If only she could sleep as peacefully as the man behind her.

She glanced at her bedside clock and sighed. Already way past two, and she'd yet to catch even a minute of shuteye. Her mind wouldn't let her; she really needed to tell Trent everything and at least give him the chance to accept who she was before automatically reconciling him to the angry villagers category.

"So he really said cuddle?" Merona's golden form shimmered with the tinkling of her laughter.

Lina nodded, barely listening to her grandmother's chatter.

"Well, hell's bells, sweetling." She snorted and rocked faster in her rocking chair.

"Granna," she began slowly, her heart pounding painfully in her chest.

Merona stopped rocking and bore her steely blue gaze into Lina, her aura now a glittering pink. "Oh sweetling, you still haven't given up on that, have you? You can't, Lina, simple as that."

"But you know what, Granna? I'm doing myself a greater disservice by not telling him. Trent is not one of those that will ever accept lies, no matter how justified I think it might be."

"Lina, I love you. More than you'll ever know. That's why you have to trust me. Now is not that time. Have you heard nothing Dyami told us? Trent is not spiritually ready for a conversation of this magnitude."

Lina shook her head, anxiety burning a hole in her stomach. Surely this was not the way, either. Trent had already proven to her time and again that he did not take kindly to lies. And yet--she admitted grudgingly--Merona was right. Trent would likely take even less to the fact that she dabbled in sorcery, at least in his eyes, anyway.

Her heart ached and hot tears gathered at the corners of her eyes. Lina's lips trembled as she said, "Take this curse from me, Granna. Make me normal."

Merona patted Lina's forehead, leaving a frigid trail of goose flesh behind. "Someday, sweetling, you'll see...."

"Yeah, right," Lina choked and buried her face in her pillow.

The shrill cry of the phone ripped through the still silence of the room and Lina nearly jumped out of her skin. Her heart squeezed in her chest. She cast a gaze at Merona.

Merona shrugged a slender, pale shoulder.

"Hello," Lina said.

"Help me, please." Willy's broken voice echoed over the staticy line.

"Willy, what's wrong?" She sat up in bed and clutched at her nightshirt.

"It's Bobby. He's dying," he said around a choking sob.

Lina threw the covers off and glanced at Trent. He gave a gentle snoring sigh, rolled over, and snuggled her pillow against his chest. Oh god. There was no way Trent wouldn't find her secret out now.

"Hold on, Willy. I'm coming."

* * * *

"What happened, Willy?" Lina asked as she ran through the garage into Willy's living room.

The faint hum of the television rang in the background. A trail of blood led the way along the beige carpeting lining the long hallway and into a bedroom. Lina's heart caught in her throat, all sorts of terrible thoughts flashing through her mind.

Tears streamed freely down Willy's wrinkled face and he swiped his hand across his eyes. "He ... he had to go to the outhouse."

Lina pushed through the door and went to the tiny figure lying on the bed. Bobby's body was sweat-slicked, his honey-wheat hair clung to his forehead, his face contorted in a mask of agony. His pitiful whimpers brought tears to her eyes.

His swollen, bleeding foot was propped on a pillow.

Oh, heavens. Merona's words were clipped. Snake bite, sweetling. He hasn't much time.

Lina peeled off her jacket and laid her hand over Bobby's heart. Knee-staggering waves of pain cut through her instantly. Her breath came in short, hard gasps, and her stomach rolled with waves of nausea. A strangled cry escaped her throat and she jerked away from the child.

She closed her eyes and waited until the rocking pain subsided.

"Please, Lina," Willy's voice cracked, "tell me you can do something for my nephew."

She swallowed hard, knowing this healing would drain her completely. *Granna, I'll need your assistance on this one.*

Merona nodded and flitted forward. Already her aura began to glow a brilliant green color.

"I'll help him, Willy."

Bobby's teeth clattered and his tiny body began to convulse, his fingers clenching in an automatic response.

Lina gazed at the puncture wounds in Bobby's ankle, noting the deep slash marks gouging into the flesh. She snapped her attention toward Willy. "You cut him?" she snapped, not so much furious at Willy as at the situation.

His brows knit. "I tried to draw the poison out."

"Damn it all, Willy. You never, ever, cut someone with a snakebite. And you most certainly don't raise the leg above the heart. All that's gonna do is draw the poison faster to his heart."

Angrily she snatched the pillow out from under Bobby's leg. Mercifully, he'd sunk into the deep abyss of unconsciousness. Already, red lines were creeping up his calf. His ankle was a furious purple-blue color.

"I panicked. I ... I ... ," he stuttered.

Her heart twisted in her chest. "God, Willy, I'm sorry. I'm didn't mean to snap at you. I know you didn't understand."

All right, Granna. I'm ready.

Merona laid her hands over Lina's. She gasped at the frigid pain of icicles forming in her blood. Lina closed her eyes against the disconcerting sensation, and set her hand over the puncture wound.

In her mind, she saw the red, angry tissue beneath the skin, the sidewinder's poison tracking ever closer toward Bobby's tiny, barely beating heart. She hissed, her brows dipping low as beads of sweat trickled between her breasts.

Merona's soft, fluttering powers infused Lina, giving her the extra strength to hold on, to work the toxins out and rid Bobby of near death.

The poison's forward progress stopped and reversed course. Black waves of exhaustion crashed against her, and she clenched her teeth. "Granna, I need more. Give me more." She breathed against the overwhelming pain wracking her body.

Merona's light flared and heat traveled with the force of a freight train down Lina's hands, through her fingertips, and into Bobby's ankle.

Willy gasped and Lina opened her eyes.

Clear sprays of venomous poison flew through the air like shimmering drops of rain. Bobby grunted. His glazed eyes opened to stare at Lina's face.

With one final push of power, she closed the wound, seeing in her mind's eye the red flesh sealing together, becoming whole and free of imperfection. The swollen ankle began to deflate, and the two tiny pinpricks closed over as if they'd never been.

Lina cried out, her body trembling with fatigue, and laid her head against the side of the bed. She gulped oxygen into her burning lungs, and her heart beat an unsteady tattoo in her chest.

Merona patted her back. "You did good, sweetling. You did good."

Willy dropped to his knees, a strangled cry escaping his lips, and he gathered Bobby to his chest. The child sobbed, his tiny fingers clutching at Willy's shirt.

Lina blew out deep breaths as she silently thanked the Maker for helping her make it in time. Little Bobby had been close, very close to death. Another few minutes and his heart would have stopped.

She sighed and wobbled to her feet. The walls shifted in and out of focus. Every fiber, nerve ending, hell, even her skin, hurt to the touch.

"Lina, I can never repay you," Willy said.

Bobby sat up, his body still shimmering with sweat. Confusion and awe reigned in the depths of his mahogany eyes. His tiny lips quirked into a semblance of a smile, and her whole being melted. Lina gripped the windowsill for support and returned the grin with as much force as her tired body would allow.

The child jumped off the bed and ran toward her, his arms outstretched, and threw himself against her body.

Warmth spread through her heart and she closed her eyes, imagining for a moment that Bobby was hers.

"Thank you, Ms. Lina," his little voice whispered.

She tousled the tendrils of his silky locks and knuckled a tear from her eye. A huge lump formed in her throat and all she could do was nod in response.

Willy walked forward and grabbed hold of Bobby's shoulder. He gave her one last, fierce hug and walked toward his bed, a huge yawn sounding from his lips.

Every part of her body tingled. Emotions never buried far below the surface flared to life, and she ached all over again for the one thing she'd never have. Children. A son or daughter to hug her with as much love and devotion as Bobby just had.

"Come on, Lina," Willy whispered. "Let me make you a cup of coffee."

She shook her head, pinching the bridge of her nose. Her head felt thick with sleep. "I can't, Willy. I really need to get back." Lina bit her lip and glanced at the clock hanging above Bobby's bed. Three thirty in the morning. She groaned.

"No. Absolutely not." Willy held up a restraining hand. "You're about to melt into my carpet. Your eyes are much too black, and you need a jolt at least so that you can drive home."

"He's right, sweetling. Last thing we want is for you to wreck and die in a car crash," Merona said.

Thanks for that comforting thought, Granna. She turned toward Willy and nodded. "All right. I'll take you up on that offer. One cup, then I really need to head home."

Lina knew, deep down, that Trent was more than likely awake, pacing a hole in her floor, and ready to wring her neck when she got back. Suddenly the need to get back wasn't so pressing. She didn't relish the thought of walking into that hornet's nest.

* * * *

Lina leaned back in the cushioned seat, blowing the curling tendrils of steam aside so that she could take a sip of the black coffee.

"Lina." Willy blinked twice, gazing at her over the rim of his cup. His Adam's apple bobbed up and down. "Thank you."

She smiled and nodded.

He cleared his throat and looked away.

She knew what he was going to ask her. Lina sighed and took a deep swig of the burning brew. It scalded her tongue and throat, but she didn't care.

"I heard you talking to someone in that room," he finally said.

Lina met his gaze, looking for any signs of fear, contempt. All she saw was open curiosity. "That was my grandmother. She's my anchor to the spirit world and helps me with especially tough cases."

"What a wonderful gift," he breathed, and ran a hand down his face. "I knew when Bobby had been bitten that you were the only one able to save him. You've done me a mighty service tonight, Lina. Twice you've helped me, and I want you to know I'll never forget that."

She ground her teeth. The kindness of his words cut deep to the heart of her. "I wish I felt the same way about my gift as you do, Willy. It would make my life a hell of a lot easier."

She set the coffee aside and turned to study his home. She needed something to distract her from the keen intelligence glittering in the depths of his brown eyes, those eyes that seemed to penetrate deep into her soul and make her want things again. Like friendship and trust, things that could never be.

Because deep down she knew once Trent figured out who she really was, it was over. This mask of normalcy would shatter to reveal that she'd never really been a part of them, of this life, of these people.

She bit down on her lip, her chin quivering at the thought. She wouldn't cry. She'd done enough of that to last her a lifetime. Lina crossed and uncrossed her legs. Merona glided toward the window, her golden form shimmering.

Willy's home was sparsely furnished. A couple of ragtag recliners faced a television. Potted plants hung from the ceiling. Shag carpeting. This place definitely needed a woman's touch.

She plastered on a tight smile and switched subjects. Because if she didn't, she would surely crack. "So, how are things between you and Abby?"

At this, Willy's neck began to gather with hot, red streaks of color. She giggled at the sight, her mood lifting immediately.

Willy grimaced and scratched the back of his head. "Been thinkin' 'bout it a lot and well, I reckon I'm gonna ask Ms. Abby out to the Canyon with me and Bobby."

Lina pushed away from the table, the chairs legs squealing loudly against the linoleum, and stood. "I think that's a lovely idea. And I'm sure she'll say yes."

Willy's eyes widened and he gulped. "You really think so? I mean, Lina, I'm well over sixty, these old bones just aren't what they used to be. She's so beautiful and wonderful. What can I possibly offer her?" He spread his hands wide, his mouth turning down into a frown. "I'm only a mechanic. She deserves so much better."

"Oh, Willy." She walked toward him, leaned down, and kissed his whiskered cheek. "You just be yourself and you won't go wrong. You're so much better than you think. You're a good man. A really good man." Again her heart twisted in her chest. Willy was everything she'd ever dreamt a father could be, a father she'd wanted so badly her whole life.

He grabbed her hand and laid a tender kiss against her knuckles. "Thank you, Lina. For everything."

She nodded and stalked toward the door, seconds away from sobbing her eyes out.

Chapter Seventeen

From the Journal of Lina Brennen:
Have you ever had one of those moments when you just know something terrible is about to happen? Maybe not today, maybe not even tomorrow. But all the hairs on your arms rise up and the breath is literally knocked from your lungs. Let me tell you, it ain't fun.

* * * *

Trent clenched his fists as he paced between the bathroom and the bedroom. His stomach ached as he imagined what Lina was up to at the moment. Truth be told, his mind couldn't come up with one damn good reason for her being out of the house at four a.m. Unless....

The squeal of metal on metal heralded her arrival, and he stalked to the window, pushed back the white curtain, and gazed into the pitch-black of night. Her shoulders were slumped forward, her hair hanging down her back in disarray. For a second he felt a twinge of sympathy, but he pushed the unwanted emotion aside and steeled himself for the confrontation sure to come. He was ready for a fight. He'd had enough of this. Of the sneaking around, the strange voices he always heard around her. Her eccentricities, which, at the moment, he hated to admit that he loved. But she had a lot of explaining to do. Lina was an enigma for him, a complete and utter enigma. And that just didn't sit right with him. Not if he wanted to take the next step in their relationship.

He shook his head and muttered under his breath. "Shit. I can sure pick 'em."

Trent threw himself down on the couch and ran a hand through his hair.

The rattle of keys sounded loud through the stillness seconds before the door opened. He turned his head, fury burning a hole through his gut. Lina sighed and pushed the straggly strands of hair out of her face.

"Where have you been?" he asked in a low, even, growl.

Immediately her spine stiffened. "Trent," she squeaked.

"Who else? Answer me, Lina, where you been? I've been awake over an hour. You left no note, no nothing. Now you've got a lot of explaining to do, and I don't aim to leave until I get it from you." He stood, towering over her by a good six inches and using every one of them to his advantage.

She turned steely gray eyes toward him, her face an unreadable mask, though her features were pallid and exhaustion oozed off her in waves. He felt it; he saw it in her movements, in her posture. His heart turned over at the sight. But he wouldn't back down. He needed to know. Not that he wanted her to prove his suspicions correct; he wanted her to prove him wrong. That she hadn't been high in the mountains dancing nude and sacrificing Ms. Butler's chickens to some heathen god of nature. Or whatever the hell.

All he wanted from her was for her to tell him, to bring him into her life, a life he felt such a tiny part of. An afterthought, really. And that stung, more than he cared to admit.

For once, he wanted to know that his heart hadn't screwed him over again. He wanted fervently to believe that Lina felt for him the way he did for her. That she wasn't hiding some deep, dark secret.

"For God's sakes, Lina," his voice broke and he grasped her chin roughly, hauling her closer to him. "You can tell me. Whatever it is, I don't care. But tell me."

Her eyes sparkled with intense misery and sadness, so much so, that he felt it to his very bones. That was nearly his undoing. He pulled her to his chest, burying his hands in her hair, inhaling the spicy-sweetness of her.

"Oh, Trent," she finally said. Her body shuddered into his, and she clutched at his naked back, dragging her nails down his flesh.

He moaned, overwhelmed by the depth of her emotions. They engulfed him, turning him to flame.

"I ... I ... ," she stuttered and pulled back from him, gazing deep into his eyes, as if she was trying to read his mind, see what he was thinking. He broke eye contact, unnerved by the intensity of her gaze, and she let out a tiny sigh.

"I was at Willy's," she finally said.

"What?" He shook his head, his brows knitting. That was the last thing he'd expected. Willy's? But why? What could she possibly have to do there at four in the morning?

Lina grabbed at her head and winced.

He couldn't take anymore of this, seeing her in pain, so tired. It was as if his heart had been forcefully ripped from his chest; Lina was his life, and seeing her in pain made him feel it as well. Trent scooped her off her feet and walked toward the bedroom. Her body trembled in his arms, and he laid a tiny kiss on her forehead. "Baby, it's all right. I'm sorry. I just got worried."

Not that he wasn't still curious, he was, but suddenly none of it mattered. All that did matter was that she was safe, in his arms, and back home with him where she belonged. He lay her down on the bed, her blonde hair cascading around her shoulders like a pale halo. The sight made him weak in the knees. She was so beautiful. He'd wait for her to come to him. If she loved him, she would. She would be honest with him and he'd wait. He'd wait for her to make that move.

He prayed she'd make that move, because the thought of not having Lina in his life was too painful to bear.

Lina let out a tiny sigh and snuggled her head into the crook of his neck. Already her shivers were subsiding.

"Baby, you can't go into work like this tomorrow. I'll call Mom later and tell her that you're sick."

"No," she muttered. "No. I can't do that. I have...."--she yawned--"responsibilities. Just let ... me sleep ... for a little bit." She closed her eyes, and within moments, she slept the sleep of the dead.

Trent closed his eyes, rubbing her head and listening to the soothing sound of her breathing. His mind burned with a million questions that he couldn't think of decent answers for.

He stared out the window, getting lost in the pale glow of predawn. What was this secret? This gaping, yawning secret? He loved her, but they had trust issues. Big ones. And that hurt more than being stung by a dozen scorpions.

* * * *

The pounding in her head was a ravenous beast. Lina rolled over and groaned loudly, clapping her hands over her head, as if that would do any good. "Oh," she moaned pitifully. Lina cracked open an eye and knew immediately that Trent was gone. Emptiness washed through her. She'd screwed up big time. But it wasn't as if she'd had a choice in the matter.

Merona glided toward her, concern etched into every fine groove lining her face. "Sweetling, you really look awful."

"Thanks for stating the obvious, Granna," she grumped, and slowly headed toward the bathroom. Each footstep she took jarred her body, sending tendrils of pain to slither up her spine and stab into her brain.

"Lina, you are going to make things worse for yourself if you go to work."

"I don't have a choice," she hissed and grabbed at her head. "Oh God, it feels like my brain's on fire." Lina closed her eyes and attempted to push the pain away. But unlike the people she healed, she wasn't capable of doing so for herself.

This was going to be a long day. A very long day.

* * * *

The bell dinged over the door and Lina swung around to see who it was. Along the way, the glass coffee pot she held slammed into the edge of the counter, shattering and sending coffee flying all over the counter and Mr. Jacobs, who sat on the other side of it.

"Oh no." Lina grabbed a stack of napkins from the dispenser and tried to sop up as much as she could. Mr. Jacobs, a sweet old man, helped her clean up the spilled coffee, murmuring soothing words to her as he did so.

"Lina," Abby said from over her shoulder. "I'd like to have a word with you."

Lina's heart sank to her shoes. She knew what was coming. Since starting work this morning, that was the second coffee pot to break, and she'd also taken out three water glasses and a plate. She should have stayed home, called in sick, but she thought she could make it. She'd been wrong. Exhaustion made her hands shake and her stomach queasy.

After cleaning up Mr. Jacobs and the counter, Lina followed Abby into the kitchen. Abby turned toward her and planted her hands on her hips. "I didn't think I'd be having this discussion with someone of your age, Lina. I'm very disappointed in you. You're obviously exhausted, yet you came to work."

Lina could only nod in agreement as tears stung her eyes.

Abby shook her head, her lips pressed tight in disapproval. "I don't care if he is my son, Lina. You need to keep your priorities straight. You have a job, and if you can't do it, I'll have to let you go."

Lina swallowed back the tears and nodded. "I'm sorry, Abby."

Abby shook her head. "This isn't the first time you've come to work too tired. I don't like it."

Lina's bottom lip trembled and she bit down on it.

"My employees need to give everything to their job. I can't have my waitresses dropping food and scalding coffee all over–"

"Abby." Lina and Abby turned to see Willy standing in the doorway to the kitchen. "Can I have a word with you?"

Abby scowled. "Right now, I'm having a word with my waitress, Willy. You'll just have to wait."

Willy ambled up to Abby and put his arm around her shoulders. He sent Lina a gentle smile and winked. "Abby, darlin', I really must have a word with you."

Abby's mouth dropped open and her eyes went wide. Then her lips slowly curled into a shy smile and she dipped her head. Lina thought it was about the sweetest thing she'd ever seen, and if she weren't ready to fall asleep on her feet, she might have appreciated it.

"Okay," Abby said, and she let Willy lead her further into the kitchen.

Lina practically collapsed against the wall, slid down, and pulled her knees to her chest, dropping her forehead to them. Her hands shook, her insides shook. She'd had several cups of coffee since coming to work. The caffeine hadn't helped her sleepiness, it just made her whole body vibrate and her stomach turn.

"Babe?"

Lina snapped her head back so hard she conked it against the wall. Trent stood over her. She wondered if she'd actually fallen asleep for a minute.

"Hey, sweetheart." Trent hunkered down in front of her and touched her cheek. "Are you okay?"

The softness in his voice had her blinking back tears. She wasn't sad. It was just that every time she got really, really tired, she turned into a blubbering mess. She'd been fighting tears since Willy's.

"Hey, don't cry. What's the matter?"

"I'm just tired," she said, and swiped at her tears.

"You're going home to rest," he decided.

"But your mom...."

Trent shook his head at her and stood up, pulling her up with him. "You need to sleep, you've been up for a good twenty-four hours, haven't you?"

She leaned against him, needing the support, his strength, and nodded against his chest.

"It's settled then. Mom," he called.

From the other side of the kitchen, Abby called back.

"I'm taking Lina home."

"Good."

* * * *

Trent could just barely see his mother and Willy on the other side of the kitchen, partially hidden behind the open door of the storeroom. Willy had his hands on Abby's arms and he spoke in low tones.

"Come on, honey." Trent put his arm around Lina's shoulders and led her out through the diner. It was still early, just after nine, but the sun beat down with amazing heat. Lina leaned heavily against his side, her head on his shoulder as if she hadn't the strength to hold it up on her own.

Something was going on. He'd approached Willy this morning outside the diner and asked him why Lina was at his place in the middle of the night. Willy was evasive, only saying that he needed her help, and she'd come when he called. Then Willy went on to sing Lina's praises.

They crossed the street to the sheriff's office, and still supporting her, they went up the steps to her apartment. Lina fumbled in her pocket for her keys. He took them from her and opened the door.

"You go get some sleep, okay?" he said softly.

She nodded, but instead of going in, she turned into his chest and buried her face against him. His heart melted. Sometimes she seemed like the strongest woman he'd ever met, and then there were times like this. She was weak and gentle and so damn sweet it brought a lump to his throat.

He hugged her for a moment, then gently set her away. "Come on." He took her hand and led her through the door, then shut it behind them and pulled her along to the bedroom. She sat down on the edge of the bed and kicked off her tennis shoes. She had yet to say anything, and he doubted she would. Her eyes drooped and her skin was pale.

She went to lay back on the bed, but he caught her wrists and held her in place. "You'll be more comfortable if you take off your shorts and blouse."

She looked down at herself and gave a little shrug.

Trent couldn't help but smile. He knelt beside the bed and started unbuttoning her blouse. The poor thing was dead on her feet. He had to tamp down the excitement that undressing her caused him, but she was so damn beautiful she made him ache for her.

He pulled off her short-sleeved blouse, then lifted her up, and gently set her down on the bed, her head on a pillow. She sighed. He couldn't help himself as he unzipped her denim shorts; he laid a small kiss on her belly, right next to her sexy little navel.

She sighed again and lightly touched his hair.

He pulled her shorts off and then her socks, and dropped them on the floor.

"There you go, babe. You get some sleep now."

"Trent," she whispered, her eyes already closed.

"Hm?"

"Hold me?" Her voice was almost childlike and his heart twisted, his gut clenched. He could deny her nothing.

He moved around to the other side of the bed, stretched out next to her, and pulled her into his arms. She burrowed into him and sighed again. Within two heartbeats, she was asleep.

"My precious Lina," he whispered. "I wish you'd tell me your secrets. I want to know you." Her only answer was the tiniest of snores that made him grin. "I need to know you."

* * * *

Trent kicked his booted feet on the desk and idly toyed with a paperclip. Work was slow, so he had time to chew on his situation with Lina. And that was by no means a good thing. Already his mind was working overtime. He wanted desperately for Lina to trust him enough to tell him who she was, who she really was. The side of her nobody knew. But the more he thought on it, the more he suspected that wouldn't happen. And he couldn't live like that.

The sound of a squeaking bedpost filtered through the ceiling and he ground his teeth. His body automatically responded to the suggestive image of her lying in the bed, wearing nothing but those lacy pink panties and bra.

"Damn it all to hell." He stood and began pacing back and forth. Since when had he picked up this nasty habit? Last night in Lina's apartment, now in his office. Trent stopped and frowned. She was driving him crazy.

He glanced toward the silent phone.

For some time he'd debated whether to call and get Lina's personal records. He'd mentioned it to his mother days ago, and she'd talked him out of it. But with what had happened last night, he couldn't continue to remain idly in the dark.

Sure, it broke just about every ethical code in the book, but that's just how insane she made him.

Trent stalked toward his desk, snatched the receiver off the cradle, and dialed the Phoenix police station before he had a chance to change his mind.

"Charlie, how's it goin'?" Trent asked his former partner and long-time friend.

"Trent. What have you been up to lately? Been a long time since I've heard from you."

Trent clenched his jaw, uncomfortable with the lie he was about to tell. He toyed with a sheet of paper on his desk. "Oh, you know. Same crap, different day."

"Boy do I ever," Charlie chuckled. "Anyhow, I'm sure this isn't a social call. What do you need?"

Trent wiped the smile off his face. Charlie knew him too well. "Truth is, I do need something." He paused. "Got me a woman in this town, real suspicious. A drifter."

"Ah ha. Strange that you'd get a drifter in a small town like Unegi."

"Exactly." Trent lifted a brow and squirmed, his heart clenching painfully in his chest. "Anyhow, I need some background info on her."

"Like what kind of information?"

"Places she's lived, if she's ever been convicted, stuff like that." He rubbed his fingers over his chest, guilt eating at his gut.

"You got any grounds for suspicion? Other than the fact that you got an outsider in your midst?"

"She's got a shady past, Charlie. I'm sure of it. And I need to find out if this woman is a danger to this community before anything does happen." He swallowed the lie, a ball of tension settling in his stomach, making him nauseous. Had he really just said that about Lina? His sweet Lina?

"I don't know, Godfrey. This sounds to me...."

"Look, Charlie. I'm asking this not as a cop to a cop, but as a friend to a friend. You know what this town means to me. I'd do anything for it and its people."

"Ah shit, Trent."

Trent scrubbed a hand down his face. "Look, never mind. Last thing I want to do is make you uncomfortable--"

"I'll have the necessary information to you in a few days. Give me her social security number."

Trent ticked off the numbers, all the while a sinking feeling of self-loathing coiled down his spine. He was no better than a rat's ass for doing this.

* * * *

The air conditioning had gone out at the diner, and Lina couldn't wait to get home and take a nice cold shower. As she headed out the door of the Tumbleweed, Abby called to her. She turned around and Abby handed her a big bag of lemons.

"Hope you can use some of these. The delivery driver left an extra case."

Lina smiled. "Ice cold lemonade sounds wonderful right now."

Abby grinned. "Maybe we'll offer some free lemonade with supper tonight." She swiped her arm across her forehead. "Providing we get any customers. Darn this heat."

Lina winked. "Bet Willy still comes in."

Abby blushed like a schoolgirl. "Hush, you."

Laughing, Lina bid her a goodbye and headed down the street. As she walked past the big front window of the sheriff's office, she peeked in, as she did every day, and saw Trent on the phone. She smiled and waved. He grinned, sent her a wink and an air kiss.

She wondered if she looked as silly in love as Abby did. With a sigh, she rounded the corner and climbed the stairs to her apartment. She and Trent hadn't had any time alone in days. She let herself in, shut the door, dropped the lemons on the counter, then went straight to the air conditioner and cranked it up to high. Trent had been so busy chasing chicken killers and cattle rustlers that they'd only seen each other at the diner. And man, she missed him.

She shed her clothes as she walked to the bathroom. Yanking her ponytail holder out, she turned on the cold water. It was a short shower, but she was revived and squeaky clean by the time she stepped out and pulled on her lightweight robe. Now, for some icy lemonade.

"Didn't hear you come in."

Lina let out a little yelp and grabbed her chest. "Would you stop that," she growled at Merona who followed her into the kitchen.

"It's not like you didn't know I was here. My goodness, if I went out in that heat, I'd dissolve."

Lina rolled her eyes as she tore open the bag of lemons. "You're a ghost, Granna. You can't even feel the heat."

"Where's Jess?"

Lina sliced four lemons in half and began searching drawers for her little plastic juice extractor. "She was smart and stayed home today in the air conditioning. Ah ha! Here it is." She held up the juicer in triumph. "Besides, I'm wondering if you're a bad influence on her."

"You wound me, sweetling. I love that little girl just as much as you do."

"I know, but she's only twelve, and I get the feeling you discuss things with her you shouldn't discuss with a child." Lina pulled a glass pitcher from the top shelf of one of the cupboards and set to work squeezing lemons.

"I don't talk to her about anything I didn't talk to you about at that age."

Lina held up a lemon and pointed it at Merona. "See, and I'm so well adjusted."

Merona laughed as she floated to her rocking chair. "I think you've turned out just fine, sweetling."

"A lot you know," Lina mumbled.

"He's coming up the steps," Merona said.

"Who?" Lina asked.

"Who? Who do you think? Who else comes here in the middle of the day looking for some quick loving?"

Lina dropped the rind into the pitcher as Merona's words registered. "Don't talk about him like that," Lina whispered just as the knock came. "And go ... away."

With a sparkling laugh, Merona faded into nothingness.

"Come in!" Lina called.

The door opened and there he stood, all six feet plus of gorgeous male perfection. And, oh yum, in uniform. Gun belt and all. Her heart tripped a bit. "Hi."

"Hi there, beautiful," he said as he closed the door and moved toward her. "Jeez." He glanced toward the air conditioner. "It's like an icebox in here."

"Yeah." She sighed and smiled. "Isn't it great?"

He chuckled and pulled her into his arms. "Lemonade?"

Lina nodded as she raised her hands to his shoulders. "Uh-huh. Want some?"

He shook his head. "Maybe later."

"Why not now?" she asked, wondering at the gleam in his eye. Hoping that maybe Merona was right and he'd come over for an afternoon of–

"I have plans."

"Oh." Disappointed, she tried not to let it show.

"Yeah." He slowly backed her against the refrigerator. "I have something very important that needs taking care of."

"Okay." He was playing with her. The tilted grin, the laugh lines crinkling at his eyes gave him away. "What would that be?"

"Payback." He reached up, took hold of her wrists, and brought them down to her sides, then behind her back.

"Wh-what kind of payback?"

He clamped both her wrists in one of his big palms, then reached behind him. "The kind I've been fantasizing about for several days now. The kind that is going to make you squirm."

"You think you can make me squirm?" she challenged with a sly smile.

Click.

Handcuffs closed over her right wrist. Her eyes widened and as she tried to pull away, the other side closed over her left wrist. She tried to move, and realized he'd handcuffed her to the door handle of the fridge. "You didn't," she said in surprise.

Trent chuckled. "Oh, baby, but I did."

Lina laughed and expectation zinged through her. "Now what?" she asked.

He untied the belt at her waist and pushed the sides of her robe back, exposing all of her. "Now I have my way with you."

"Oh, my," she breathed.

He leaned in and kissed her hard, hot and demanding. "I've missed you," he whispered, trailing wet kisses down her neck.

Lina moaned and tried to lean into him, but he took the smallest step back and chuckled again. The vibrations sent tingles shooting down her arms to her fingers. "Don't tease," she begged, dropping her head back against the fridge.

"Ah," he said as he flicked a tight, sensitive nipple with his tongue, "teasing is ninety percent of the fun."

"Meanie."

He laughed, then sucked her nipple into his mouth. She felt the tug all the way to her womb.

"You always smell so damn good." He went down on his knees in front of her. "Like flowers and spice."

"Verbena and cinnamon," she answered absently as she trembled with need for him.

He trailed his tongue down her belly, dipped into her navel, then lower. His hands spread on her hips; his callused fingers sent another wave of pleasure through her as they rubbed against her sensitive skin.

She sucked in her breath and whimpered when his tongue slid over her aching center. "Trent!"

He glanced up, even as his tongue and lips tugged at her. "Hm?"

The vibrations of his voice had her gasping. "Please."

He tilted her hips toward him more, then slid one long finger into her, sending her over the edge. She cried out his name and gripped the refrigerator handle as her knees nearly buckled with the force of her climax.

Chapter Eighteen

From the Journal of Lina Brennen:
There are times when you can stand and face the music. And then there are those times when you just want to tuck tail and run. Lately I've been particularly fond of the second option.

* * * *

Trent quickly stood and wrapped his arms around her, holding her to him, holding her up. "Shh, babe," he whispered in her ear as she sucked in big gulps of breath. He hadn't meant to upset her, and the tears running down her cheeks had him beyond concerned.

"Undo my hands."

Trent quickly uncuffed her and she threw her arms around his neck and held him tight. Her body shook.

"Baby, baby, I'm so sorry. Shh."

She shook her head against his shoulder and held him even tighter.

"What is it? Did I scare you?"

She shook her head again, then turned her face into his neck and kissed his skin. "No one has ever...."

Trent let out a slow breath of relief. Then a smile of pure triumph curled his lips. So, once again he'd been the first at something for her.

"You okay?" He slid his hands up and down her back. She was so soft. So perfect.

She nodded. "That was...."

"Hm?" he prodded, his male ego getting just a little too big, he knew.

"Wow."

He chuckled. "Yeah."

"Let's go to bed."

He groaned. "No."

She rubbed her abdomen over his raging arousal. "Yes."

"No, babe. This was just for you. Besides, I'm on duty."

Lina laughed, and the sound went through him with the force of a tornado. And that's when he knew. He'd fallen in love. One hundred and ten percent in love, with Lina Brennen. And surprisingly, it didn't even scare him. He opened his mouth to say the words.

A sound from the bedroom had the hair rising on the back of his neck. Lina pulled away. "Lucky." She rushed off.

Trent sighed and followed. The thing sounded like it was dying.

"Oh," Lina said. She was down on all fours, peering under the dust ruffle of the bed. Her beautiful bare behind sticking up in the air didn't help his condition any. "She's having her babies. Come look."

He leaned down, grabbed her around the waist, and hauled her to her feet. "Do me a favor first," he said when she turned wide eyes on him. "Put some clothes on or I'm going to throw you on this bed and make love to you for the rest of the day."

She giggled, stood up on tiptoe, and kissed him quickly. "Gotta see to the babies. And you're on duty."

Trent gave her a slap on the rear when she turned away. "You are such an imp."

She flashed him a sexy grin. "And you love me that way, don't you?"

He just smiled. When he confessed his love, he wouldn't be teasing with her.

* * * *

He hadn't agreed with her, she thought as she tugged on a pair of cotton shorts and a tank top. She'd left it open to him to say, "yes, I love you that way," but he hadn't said anything. He just smiled at her. Tears prickled her eyes. Damn me and my stupid fantasies.

Dropping to her knees, she buried her head under the dust ruffle of the bed to hide her misery from Trent, who was just standing there watching her. Go away, she wanted to shout. Just get out and leave me alone.

Her own misery was forgotten when she looked at Lucky. The pitiful cat was whining like a lost child. Lina reached out and touched her, but she felt nothing. Her hands didn't begin to heat or cool. The pain of birth was something Lucky would have to go through on her own. Poor thing.

"Why don't you bring that cat out here, so you don't have to crawl under the bed?" Trent asked as he knelt next to her and peeked under the bed.

"She likes the dark," Lina stated as she tried to sooth Lucky.

"I forgot you had the thing. Never see it when I'm here."

"She's not a thing!"

Lucky yowled.

"Sorry, baby," Lina crooned to the cat. "Shh. Trent didn't mean anything by it."

"Sorry," Trent mumbled.

When Lina didn't respond, he reached over and touched Lucky's head. The cat leaned into his big hand and mewed at him. More tears stung Lina's eyes, this time at his gentleness.

"It's okay," she whispered. "I've just never had a pet before."

"Not even as a child?" he asked, sounding incredulous.

She shook her head. Most animals didn't take to Merona. Dogs barked, cats hissed. She even saw a Guinea pig throw a fit over Granna once. But Lucky was special. Merona had helped save her.

"Well, as much as you care for this cat, I think you'd do great in a house with a big yard and a dozen animals."

The first kitten was being born, so Lina didn't have to respond. Thank goodness.

"Ohh, kittens. I just love those little buggers." Merona's glowing aura appeared under the bed, opposite Trent and Lina.

"What?" Trent asked.

No talking around Trent! How many times do I have to say this?

"What, what?" Lina asked, playing dumb.

Trent shook his head, his brows pulled down in a frown.

Lina quickly examined the first baby born, and grinned even as tears fell. Perfectly healthy and just as black as his momma. She tucked the baby next to Lucky and waited for the next one who was just being born. Lina picked this one up, and her heart stuttered. "Oh, no." The baby was barely breathing. Her hands began to warm instantly against the kitten.

"What is it?" Trent asked.

"Uh." Her hands were going to start glowing any second. "I need hot water," she blurted out, the first thing she could think of.

"Honey, is that kitten ... He doesn't look too good. Kinda limp."

Merona reached across the cat bed and laid her hand on Trent's forehead. He jerked up, hit his head on the bed frame, and then scurried out from under the bed. "Right. Hot water."

"Thanks, Granna," Lina whispered as she let herself feel the kitten. There was a small tear in its tiny heart. She pictured the heart, the tear, the mending of it, the healthy pink tissue stitching back together, the blood pumping through the heart.

Mew.

Lina laughed with relief. "That's right, baby. All better now, aren't you?" She put that kitten next to Lucky, to let the momma cat take care of him now.

"Here's your water," Trent said as he came back into the room.

"Thanks, but he's okay now." She scooted out from under the bed.

Trent stood there with a dishpan of steaming water and the most confused look on his face. "I thought it was dead."

Guilt assailed her. She held up her hands and opened her mouth to explain, when Merona came out from under the bed and tipped the pan of water right out of Trent's hands.

Granna!

Water soaked the rug, splashed up on Lina's front and Trent's legs.

"Shit," Trent cursed. "I'm sorry." He turned and fled the room.

You need to keep your mouth shut, missy, Granna scolded. He's not ready to hear it yet.

I have to tell him. I have to.

Trent rushed back into the room with a couple bath towels and began mopping Lina's chest. For some reason, this broke the tension for Lina and she burst out laughing.

And then they were both laughing. She wrapped her arms around his neck and hugged him. "It's okay. It was just water."

Trent chuckled and held her tight. "Water that is now soaking my uniform."

"Maybe you'll have to take it off so it can dry."

"You're a bad girl, Ms. Brennen."

"Am I?" She chuckled and pulled away. "Well, anyway, I have some babies to look after." She kissed him on the cheek.

He pulled her into his arms and gave her a long, tender kiss that just about curled her toes. When he released her, he said, "Okay, take care of your babies. I'll see you tonight at the diner."

She nodded.

He sent her a wink, then ambled out the door.

"One catastrophe diverted," Merona said.

"He's not an idiot," Lina whispered. "These diversionary tactics will only work so long."

"Long enough," Merona said softly.

"What's that supposed mean?"

Merona shook her head and then dissolved into a sparkling shimmer.

"Answer me, Granna. What are you talking about?"

Nothing but the sounds of kittens mewing for their first meal came back to her.

* * * *

Trent rolled over and grabbed the phone. "Godfrey," he answered in a sleep-roughened voice.

"Trent, this is Blake Thornton. Them rustlers are in my pasture. If you don't get out here, I'm going to get my shotgun and go af'er 'em myself."

Lord above, here we go again. "Mr. Thornton, what makes you think they're in your pasture?" Trent glanced at the clock on the nightstand. Just after three a.m. And all he'd wanted was one good night's sleep.

"I seen the lights. They're takin' my cattle. You commin' or am I a shootin'?"

He rolled out of bed, cradled the phone between his ear and shoulder, and grabbed his jeans off the floor. "I'm coming. You stay in the house."

"Alrighty then. I'll be awaitin'."

Cradling the phone, Trent had no doubt the old coot would be awaitin'. Saw the lights, he thought, as he pulled on a uniform shirt and grabbed his gun belt from the back of the chair in the corner of the room.

He stopped off at Jess's room and woke her up to let her know he was heading to Thornton's. She mumbled a reply and pulled the covers over her head.

At the door he stomped into his boots, and grabbed his jacket and keys. "Saw the lights," he mumbled. "Probably a stray UFO from New Mexico."

Ten minutes later, he pulled onto the road leading to Thornton's ranch. And he saw the lights, too. On the western edge of the pasture there was a truck with its running lights on. Behind it was a horse trailer. "I'll be damned," Trent said, cutting his own lights. He drove slowly along the boundary fence, keeping an eye on the vehicle. When he reached a gate for the pasture, he got out, unlatched it, drove his car through, turned the cruiser off, and then fastened the gate. Fresh tracks had recently turned up the earth.

Trent jogged the rest of the way, not wanting to alert the thief he was coming. He drew his handgun from the belt, having no idea how many men he was approaching.

The truck was running, a shiny black Ford F-350 dually. A truck Trent would recognize anywhere. And there was the owner, silhouetted by moonlight, loading one of Thornton's prize-winning steer into the horse trailer.

Trent lifted the pistol, aiming it at the center of the man's back. How long had he wanted to get him in his sights? "Wife thievin' ain't enough for you, Brock? You take cattle, too?"

Ty stopped, his spine stiff, but he didn't turn around.

"Come on, Ty. You're caught red-handed. Though, only God knows why you'd be needing to take these beeves. You, Mr. Rodeo Star." When he realized his hand was shaking, he lowered the gun and waited. As much as he detested the man, he wouldn't be shooting him tonight. He'd once been his best friend.

Ty dropped the lead rope and turned around. "I guess I'm under arrest?"

"You don't sound real surprised."

Ty jumped down from the ramp into the shadow of the trailer. His voice was low when he answered. "It's a relief."

"Come out here where I can see you."

Ty stepped out of the shadow, his hands held up in surrender. "I'm not armed, Trent."

Trent slowly approached Ty, visually searching for any sign of a weapon; though, deep down, he believed him. Even so, Trent kept his own weapon in his hand. "You have the right to remain silent–"

"Shit, Trent, give me a break. I know the routine."

"Give you a break?" Trent grabbed him by the collar as fury shot through him. "You've taken a dozen of Thornton's highest dollar cattle. He's going to press charges. You've committed a major crime around these parts."

Ty met his gaze evenly as years worth of anger and hurt crashed through Trent.

"You're not pissed about the cattle. The courts will deal with that. You're still mad about Nancy, aren't you? And then Lina--"

In one motion, Trent dropped his handgun and punched Ty right in the face. Hard.

Ty staggered back and gingerly touched his cheekbone with his fingertips. "Nice one. Better than when we were kids, anyway. You never could fight worth a damn."

Something snapped inside Trent. Something that'd been brewing for the last ten years. He wasn't a cop right now, he was a man. A man who'd been wronged. He charged Ty, and when his shoulder connected with Ty's chest, they both went sprawling to the ground.

Fists flew, and a few connected. Trent took a blow to his jaw and one to his stomach. Ty took a couple more.

"I never slept with Nancy!" Ty croaked when Trent had him pinned to the ground, his hands around the man's throat. "I never had sex with her!"

It took a few seconds for his words to sink in. When they did, Trent slowly released Ty's throat. "What?"

Ty raised his hands to his neck. "I never had sex with your wife. Jesus, man, you were going to kill me."

"What do you mean, you never had ... sex with her?" Trent said through heaving breaths. He sat back on his heels, still straddling Ty's waist, hands fisted, ready for more. "She was out all night, came home with hickies all over her neck, told me you screwed her brains out. Her words, not mine."

"Let me up, I'm lying in cow shit."

"Answer me," Trent growled. "God damn you, Ty, tell me the truth."

Ty threw his hands out to the side. "She showed up at my place in the middle of the night. I was drunk. I'd been out celebrating my third gold buckle. She came on to me. Yes, the hickies were from me. She was a gorgeous woman and she was hot for me."

Trent almost went for Ty's throat again but he held himself back. He needed to hear this. He wasn't sure why, but there was something important in this.

"But then she started talking about you. You. The man I'd called best friend for most of my life. I couldn't do it. Wouldn't do that to you." Ty rubbed a hand over his eyes. "She didn't love you, man. She used you. She wanted out of the marriage. She told me these things. She said the only way you'd give her a divorce was if she cheated on you, and what better way to get to you than with your friend."

"I don't believe you."

"Yes, you do. Think about it. She'd asked you for a divorce, and you said no."

"She was going to take Jess from me," Trent said quietly, his anger draining away. "I couldn't let her take my baby."

Ty nodded. "She wanted out. She wanted away from you, and away from Unegi. And you wouldn't let her go."

Trent rolled off Ty and sat on the ground, staring at him. "Why you? Why didn't you ever tell me? How could you let ten years go by without a word?"

"I tried telling you once, right after she left. But you weren't ready to listen. You just walked away." Ty sat up and faced Trent. "I could never understand that. I'd expected a sound beating if nothing else." He chuckled and gingerly touched his cheekbone again. "I swear to God, Trent. I never had sex with her. But I let you believe it because I was so damn jealous of you. You had everything. The respect of the entire town, a beautiful little girl who adored you, a mother who practically fawned over you."

"Jealous? You're the rodeo star, the local celebrity. The local bad boy."

"Even then, I knew it couldn't last. But what you had--family, love--that's forever.

He should still be furious with the lies, but it felt as if a huge weight had been lifted from his shoulders. Betrayal is the worst thing a man has to ever deal with, and he'd thought the woman he loved had betrayed him along with a man he'd once called brother. He'd come to terms with Nancy's infidelities years ago. It was Ty he could never look past.

"Hey, man, you okay?"

Trent let out a sigh. "Yeah. I am." He even chuckled. "I sure can be an ass at times, can't I?"

Ty joined in his laughter. "First class, grade A."

He shook his head. "Shit. Ten years."

"Yeah."

"I tried to be a good husband."

"She didn't want a husband. She wanted the prestige of being the wife of one of Phoenix's finest. When you took the job of sheriff here, she couldn't handle it."

"Big city girl," Trent said, more to himself than to Ty.

"Yeah. Now Lina,"--Ty grinned at Trent's growl--"she fits in here. I have a feeling she'll be stayin' around for a while."

"And if you ever touch her--"

Ty threw back his head and laughed. "Save it, bud. She already threatened my life, er, manhood, if I ever laid a hand on her again. That lady is all yours."

A smile stole over Trent's face. "Yeah, I think she is."

"You deserve the happiness, man. You really do." Ty slapped Trent's shoulder in a way they'd done thousands of times, years ago.

Trent returned the gesture, his heart light for the first time in more years than he could remember. Then he remembered where they were, and why they were there.

"You wanna explain the cattle rustling?"

The smile left Ty's face. He stared off into the night for a long time before he answered. "I'm in trouble. I needed cash, and I needed it fast."

Trent's stomach tightened. "What kind of trouble? How much money?"

"Serious trouble. Several thousand. I borrowed some money I couldn't repay."

"Damn. What happened to all the money you won on the circuit? There were hundreds of thousands."

Ty turned his head and met Trent's gaze levelly. "I've got a gambling problem."

Trent shook his head. There was nothing he could do. He had to arrest Ty.

"I know you gotta take me in. I understand."

"I'm sorry, man. But, yeah, I gotta take you in."

Ty nodded and got to his feet, then held out his hand to Trent. When Trent took his hand, Ty pulled him up, and then gave him a back-thumping hug. "I've missed you."

Well, this was new, Trent thought. Getting all choked up over a guy. He chuckled to himself. Great, now he'd found his friend again, he was going to lose him to jail. "Yeah." He stepped away and picked up his gun, holstered it.

"I'll follow you back to your place so you can park your rig. The bed at the jail isn't too bad. I've spent a few nights on it. And mom'll cook you a good breakfast before we head into the county seat to file the papers."

Ty nodded and headed for his pickup. "One other thing, Trent."

Trent stopped walking and turned back. "Yeah?"

"You smell like shit."

Trent shook his head and chuckled as he headed across the pasture to the cruiser. Sonofabitch. He never would have guessed that Ty had a gambling problem. He hoped that Thornton and the courts weren't too hard on him.

* * * *

With only three hours of sleep, Trent shouldn't feel this good. But as he drove back to the sheriff's office, he felt on top of the world. He hated the fact that Ty was going to jail, but that wasn't really his problem. It was his job to see that the citizens of Unegi were cared for. That he and Ty had settled such a long-standing argument ... Well, he was happy, truly happy for the first time in a very long time. He hadn't realized how much he missed his friendship with Ty, or how much he'd been hurt when he thought Ty had betrayed him.

Trent pulled up in front of the sheriff's office and got out of his cruiser. He'd really hated making Ty spend the night in a jail cell, but the law was the law. He trusted Ty, to a point. But he couldn't guarantee he'd still be in Unegi in the morning if he'd let him go home to sleep.

Unlocking the door to his office, he saw a thick manila envelope on the floor that'd been shoved through the mail slot. He picked it up and turned it over. It was from Charlie in Phoenix. This was the information on Lina he'd requested. His heart did a little double thud before it settled into its normal rhythm. He laid the envelope on his desk before he went into the back, where the single jail cell was located.

Ty was asleep on the cot, covered by a thin blanket. "Hey," Trent called.

Ty's eyes slowly opened and he rolled to his side, facing Trent. "Hey," he responded, sounding tired and depressed.

"You sleep okay?" Trent unlocked the cell door and opened it.

"As well as can be expected, I suppose." Ty sat up and scrubbed his hands over his face.

"Why don't you go get cleaned up? We'll go over to the diner and get some breakfast before we head into Florence."

"I can't face your mother. She already thinks I'm pond scum. Now she'll know I am."

Trent chuckled. There was no love lost between his mother and Ty. She hadn't cared for him when he was kid, and liked him even less as the local rodeo celeb, but after Nancy, she had no time for the man. "I haven't said a word to anyone. And I'll straighten things out with her later. Come on."

Ty threw back the blanket, stood up, and stretched. "What about Thornton? You tell him yet?"

Trent shook his head as Ty passed by him, heading for the bathroom down the short hallway. "No. I'll call him after breakfast. I know he's going to press charges."

"Yeah," Ty said as he went into the restroom. "The old geezer's never liked me much, anyhow."

"Don't suppose you know anything about Ms. Butler's dead chickens?"

Ty chuckled from behind the door. "If you mean have I been running naked through the fields, biting the heads off her prize hens, the answer is no."

Trent laughed as he headed back to his desk. He supposed that was too much to hope for, anyway. The hens were being killed by a damn coyote. Why Ms. Butler refused to believe that was beyond him.

As he sat at his desk, the thick manila envelope caught his eye. He picked it up, turned it over and over in his hands. He'd been so anxious to get it, to learn all her secrets, but now that he had it, he didn't want to know.

No, that wasn't true. He still wanted to know, but he wanted her to tell him, in her own time. He wanted her to trust him enough, love him enough, to open herself up to him.

Love, he thought. When had that happened? He wasn't foolish enough to try to convince himself what he felt for Lina was anything but love. It was deep within him, warming him in parts of his heart and soul that had been so frigidly cold for so long.

A slow smile spread across his lips. Lina was special, and she truly liked Unegi and the people who lived there. Would she consider making it her permanent home? Would she consider a home with him?

"What's got you grinnin' like a cat?" Ty asked as he came down the hall toward the front desk.

Trent grinned. "I think I'm going to ask her to marry me." He swiveled in his seat and flipped on the paper shredder.

Ty raised an eyebrow. "Good for you. I don't think you could go wrong with her."

With a low chuckle, Trent opened the manila envelope, extracted the hefty sheaf of papers, and sent it through the shredder. He crumpled the envelope and dumped it in the trash. "Even if every time she serves you food, it winds up in your lap?"

Ty followed him to the door. "Even so, brother." He stood on the sidewalk in the blazing sunshine and waited for Trent to lock the door. "Besides, I deserved it." He rubbed his whiskered chin as he walked down the sidewalk next to Trent. "Though it's been a long time since any woman turned me down. I wasn't expecting that."

"Maybe your approach needs a little work."

Ty laughed. They crossed the street to the Tumbleweed and went through the door. The breakfast crowd had cleared out to just a few regular patrons and Trent quickly spotted Lina poring coffee for Willy.

She turned her head and flashed him that endearing, crooked smile. Then she spotted Ty next to him and her smile slipped a notch.

"Have a seat," Trent said to Ty, then he moved across the diner toward Lina. She met him halfway, right in the middle of the diner. He didn't care who was watching, he had to kiss her. He pulled her into his arms and she held the coffee pot away from him. Her smile returned. "Mornin' baby," he said in a low voice as he gazed into her dove-gray eyes, eyes he wanted to spend the rest of his days getting lost in.

"Good morning," she returned.

"Sleep well?" he asked.

She nodded.

"I missed you," he whispered, and lowered his head toward her.

"I missed you, too."

When he touched her lips with his, the electrical current that'd always been between them sparked to life. When he slipped his tongue into the warm, sweet depths of her mouth, lightning bolts were dim in comparison to the heat that shot through him. Yes, he thought. She's the one. The only one.

Chapter Nineteen

From the Journal of Lina Brennen:
Fear of discovery always hangs over my head. Once discovered, life as I know it ends, and a new one begins. I hate that.

* * * *

"Oh, my goodness, someone get a hose."

Trent's head snapped up and he looked around the diner.

Shut up, Granna!

"Did you just hear something?" Trent whispered, his brow furrowed.

Lina shook her head.

His frown relaxed and he chuckled and nuzzled her cheek. "I'm hearing voices."

Lina let out a nervous little laugh. "You should really have that checked out by a doctor." I'm going to kill you, Granna!

Merona chuckled. I'm already dead, dear.

"I've got to drive into the county seat today." Trent slowly released Lina and stepped back, but his eyes remained riveted on hers. His intensity made her blush, made her tingle.

"Okay."

"And then I need to go into Phoenix."

She nodded, wondering why he was giving her so much information. He didn't normally do that. Usually, she saw him when she saw him. She couldn't deny how much she liked that he wanted her to know what he'd be doing all day.

"I should be back by suppertime. But ... I need some time with Jess tonight. I hope you understand."

"Of course," Lina said, feeling a little pang of disappointment, but she did understand. The wonderful way he was with Jess was only a part of what made him the man she'd fallen so madly in love with.

"If I clear it with Mom, would you like to spend the day with us tomorrow? Just the three of us? Maybe a drive into the desert and a picnic up at Devil's Peak?"

Lina's heart thudded with excitement. "I'd love that."

"Great." Trent gave her one more hard, quick kiss.

"Where's Jess?" she asked as he slowly released her and smiled.

"She didn't want to get up this morning. She said she'd ride her bike in later."

She probably stayed up too late talking to Dyami, Merona said.

Lina nodded. It's good for her. She needs him.

"Lina," Abby called from behind the counter. "You've got customers waiting."

Trent chuckled. "Sorry to keep you from your work, babe."

Yeah, he looked sorry, she thought as she grinned at him. She turned to see a table of three tourist-looking people that'd come in while she was in Trent's arms. He had a way of turning her mind to mush and lighting a fire inside her that seemed unquenchable.

Figuring the coffee in the carafe she still held was cold by now, she went behind the counter and grabbed a fresh pot.

"That boy has something up his sleeve," Merona said, following Lina to the table of customers.

Hush. "Coffee anyone?" she asked.

The man and woman turned over their mugs on the table. The teenaged boy with them shook his head and said, "Coke, please." Lina smiled. It was nice to see manners in teens these days. It didn't come often.

"I think he's made a major decision, and he's planning something for tomorrow's little picnic. I can't wait." Merona clapped her hands and laughed. "I knew it. I just knew it."

"I'll take the Tumbleweed special," the man said.

"Same for me," the woman said as she shut her menu.

"Cheeseburger and fries," the boy said as he collected up the menus and politely handed them to Lina.

"Two tumbleweed specials, a cheeseburger and fries for breakfast." She grinned. "My personal favorite. Anything else?" she asked as she took the menus.

The boy chuckled and they all shook their heads.

Lina nodded and smiled at them before heading back to the order window. "What do you mean, big decision?" she whispered as she put the order ticket on the counter and filled a glass with ice and soda.

"Oh, like I'd tell you and ruin the surprise."

As she returned to give the boy his Coke, out of the corner of her eye, Lina saw Abby throw her arms around Trent in a big hug. "That's wonderful, son. Of course she can have the day off."

"Shh," he said as he hugged his mother back. "It's a surprise."

"Told you so," Merona said with a laugh.

Lina's heart skittered all around her chest as she walked back behind the counter. Could it be? Would he? No. She hadn't known him long enough. At least, she figured that he would feel that way.

"Is he going to ask me...."

"Hey, sweetheart," Trent said as he leaned over the counter and grabbed the coffee pot off the warmer. "You talkin' to yourself again?"

Lina forced a chuckle. "You know me."

He winked. "Stop daydreamin' and get back to work, Missy. Got a couple of really hungry guys that need feeding."

Lina's gaze traveled over to where Ty sat, his head in his hands, at a corner booth. Then back to Trent. For the first time, she noticed his jaw was a little swollen, a little dark. Ty had a black eye. "What happened with you two?"

"Well, let's just say we settled some old problems." Trent leaned over the counter and kissed her cheek. "I'll take the Tumbleweed special, and bring Ty his regular."

Lina nodded. How very odd, she thought as she watched Trent sit down across the table from Ty. From what she'd gotten out of Jess, they were practically mortal enemies. Now they were having breakfast together? And she'd bet her life savings--which granted, wasn't a whole lot--that the bruises each sported was from the other.

"Well, now," Merona said as she settled herself at the counter as if she were a patron. "Isn't it nice to see the boys have made up? Shame when two friends fight over stupid things."

I wouldn't call someone having sex with the other one's wife a stupid thing, Lina replied as she scribbled out Trent and Ty's order.

"A misunderstanding," Merona shrugged. "The woman was as bad as Jess said, but Ty isn't. He's just misunderstood."

"Order up!" Mac called.

Lina picked up the warm plates from the order window, frowned at Merona, then headed to the table holding the little family. How do you know it was a misunderstanding?

"Dyami told me."

Lina rolled her eyes. Great, now the spirits were talking behind their backs.

Merona chuckled. "Yes, we do talk behind your backs. You'd be surprised what can be learned that way."

Lina placed the order in front of the family. "Would you care for anything else to drink?"

"No, thank you," the man said. "Would you happen to know where we could find Lina Brennen?"

"Who?" she asked, stunned that strangers would be asking for her. She threw a quick glance over her shoulder at Trent. He was deep in conversation with Ty, thank goodness.

"Lina Brennen. We're from Tampa, and we've traveled all this way to find her. We think she might be able to help us."

"Help you how?"

"Be careful, sweetling," Merona whispered in her ear.

"Well, we'd rather talk to her personally," the woman hedged as she reached across the table to take the man's hand.

Lina's heart thumped against her ribs. She'd lived in Tampa four years ago, but only briefly. She'd only been there for a month, had just started a job working as a concessions worker at a baseball field. A child had fallen off the stands and she'd helped her. These people must know about her.

She glanced back at Trent, and he was watching her this time. Someone needed her help. But she couldn't let Trent learn about her this way.

"Can you stay here for a while?" she asked the man and woman. "I'm Lina Brennen," she said softly. "But I'm working, so--"

"Oh, thank the Lord." The woman covered her mouth with her hand and tears sprung to her eyes. "We'll wait. We'll wait as long as you need us to."

"Ma'am, I--"

"Back to work, Lina," Merona whispered fiercely. "Trent's getting suspicious."

"If you want to look around town for a while, I get off work at two."

The boy stared at his burger, not touching it. The man and woman smiled at her. "Of course," the man said. "By the way, I'm Jeddiah Thomas, and this is my wife, Carol, and son Paul."

Lina nodded. "Nice to meet you."

"Trent's coming," Merona hissed.

"If you'll excuse me," Lina said. "I have to get back to work."

She turned and came up against Trent's chest. She sucked in her breath and stepped back.

"Everything okay over here?" he asked.

Lina nodded, but she couldn't bring herself to meet his eyes. Damn, but she hated lying to him. "Everything's fine. I was just telling this nice family all about Unegi." She finally looked up at him and he raised an eyebrow at her.

"Not much to tell." He stepped around her and extended his hand to Jeddiah. "I'm Trent Godfrey, town sheriff. Is there something I can help you folks with?"

Jeddiah and Carol shook their heads. Jeddiah said, "Just on vacation, taking in the sights."

Relief flowed through Lina as she hurried back to the counter.

"That was a little too close for comfort," Merona said as she settled back on a stool.

Go home, Granna. Go ... play with the other spirits or something.

"It's the boy. He's sick. Something in his blood."

How do you know? Lina watched as Mac put Trent and Ty's orders in the pickup window.

"His ancestors hover around him. You didn't see or hear them? They know you can help him."

Lina shook her head. She hadn't picked up any psychic vibrations. That was so odd. She could usually feel ... something. She picked up the plates and headed toward Ty.

"Don't worry about it, sweetling. You've got a lot on your mind."

And if you would have just let me tell Trent the truth when I wanted to, I wouldn't have to sneak around like a criminal right now. Damn it anyway. I hate this! She clunked the plates onto the table and glared at Ty, only because he was in her line of sight.

He chuckled and raised his hand in surrender. "I swear, Lina, I won't lay a hand on you ever again."

Lina sighed and rubbed her forehead. "Sorry, Ty. It's just one of those days."

He reached over and picked up the bottle of ketchup. He very slowly opened it and positioned it over his hash browns, and carefully squeezed.

Lina chuckled. "No more exploding ketchup," she said. "I promise."

He grinned at her. "Truce?"

She nodded.

Trent slipped past her into the booth and caught her hand in his, pulling her down next to him.

"I've got to work, Trent," she said, but smiled.

"Yeah, me too." But he put his arm around her shoulder and pulled her closer. "Wish I didn't." His other hand ran up her bare thigh, under her skirt.

Ty cleared his throat. "Need a little privacy?"

"Lots of it," Trent responded with a wicked gleam in his eyes. He gave her a sweet little kiss on the lips before releasing her and picking up his fork. "Mom said you can take tomorrow off, and the day after that, too, if you need it."

Lina frowned at him. "Why would I need two days off?"

He gave her a negligent shrug, but his lips turned up in a teasing smile. "Recuperation?"

"I thought your daughter was going with us."

He chuckled then. "During the day...." He let his words trail off and a tingle of pleasure stole down her spine at his meaning.

"We'll see, big boy." She scooted out of the booth. "What time are you going to pick me up?"

"About ten?" he asked, then took a sip of his coffee.

Lina nodded and grinned. "Sounds good." She turned back to her work, and did her best to ignore Merona's ramblings for the rest of the morning.

* * * *

A little after noon, Trent was on his way to Phoenix after dropping Ty in Florence at the county sheriff's office. Thornton did indeed wish to press charges. Trent had filled out the necessary paperwork, and waited with Ty through booking. He would have hung around until a lawyer showed up, but Ty told him to go, knew he had things he wanted to do.

The sun blazed down on the highway ahead of him. Waves of heat danced and shimmered above the black surface. His heart felt light. For once in his life, he knew he was making the right decision.

When he thought back on all the mistakes he'd made over the years, he realized he'd never once listened to intuition when it came to matters of the heart. He'd married Nancy because she was beautiful, because she was the epitome of everything he'd always thought he wanted in a woman. Tall, dark-haired, with sultry gypsy eyes. She was cultured and proper. A true lady.

Trent snorted as he pulled off the freeway onto a smaller highway that would take him downtown. A true lady until she didn't get exactly what she wanted. She'd wanted the big city life. Fancy dinners and parties you had to wear a tux to. She wanted a husband she could show off and brag about. God, they'd been so young and stupid.

But he had Jessica. His precious little girl. He laughed as he turned onto another, smaller road nearing the center of town. She wasn't a child any longer. She was almost a teenager. An adolescent. Someone he wasn't sure he knew anymore.

As he pulled his cruiser to a stop along the street, he prayed that his baby wouldn't grow up too fast. He also prayed that she'd be open to what he was going to approach her with tonight. And if she wasn't? Well, all he could do was cross that bridge when he came to it.

Trent climbed out of the car and headed for the shop right across the street. Gold and Stone Jewelers. Now, to find the perfect engagement ring for his mysterious, beautiful, flaky, wonderful woman. He chuckled as he pulled open the door and entered the cool air-conditioned interior. Something that sparkled, something a little unusual. Something that screamed Lina to him.

* * * *

At two o'clock on the dot, Lina took off her apron and hung it on the hook in the back room. She came out front and bid Abby a "see you later," and then nodded to Jess.

"I'm gonna hang with Lina for a bit, Nana."

Abby nodded from the booth where she sat with Willy, holding his hand across the table. "No problem. I doubt there'll be much business until supper hour."

Lina smiled to herself. Willy and Abby were seeing a lot of each other. She'd heard from another one of the regulars that they were out at the Four Aces the night before, kicking up their heels.

Jess joined her at the door and they went out into the stifling mid-afternoon heat.

"So, what's up?"

"I'm not sure," Lina answered. "A family came in today looking for me. They said they think I can help them."

"You can," Merona said confidently as she floated along beside them. "The boy is about your age," she said to Jess. "He's got a problem with his blood. It's killing him."

As they passed the Mercantile, Lina spotted the family inside. She waved through the window, and Carol spotted her. The three came out the door and smiled at Lina as if she were their savior. Her nerves jangled. She couldn't do anything here, out in the open.

"Why don't you come up to my place? Its cooler there."

They fell into step behind her, and she wondered what the busybodies of Unegi were thinking about this. She wondered how fast this would get back to Trent, and how much explaining she'd have to do.

Damn it, she was going to tell him tomorrow, no matter what Merona said. He had a right to know the truth, and if tomorrow turned out to be about what she hoped it was about, he had to know the truth about her.

The family of three followed Lina and Jess up the steps to Lina's apartment, and she let them in. "All right, please have a seat." She shut the door behind her. "I'm Lina Brennen, and before we go any farther, I'd really like to know how you found me."

"That little girl you saved a few years ago in Tampa, that was my niece," Jeddiah answered. He lowered himself into the chair opposite the couch. "We've been searching for you ever since. You see, our son has a very rare blood disorder, and we were hoping...." His voice trailed off as if he'd become too emotional.

Lina sat down on the couch beside Paul. She laid her hand over his. Pain shot through her and she jerked away. "Oh, dear. You hurt badly, don't you?"

Paul nodded shyly and looked away. "This is dumb," he said to his mother. "Some lady can't do anything for me. I've seen all the doctors there are to see."

"Hush," Carol said softly. "We've got to try." She turned imploring green eyes on Lina. "Please, Ms. Brennen, if there's anything you can do...."

"We'll pay you anything you ask," Jeddiah added.

Lina turned a scowl on him. "No money. I don't take money for helping someone. All I can do is try, but sometimes...." She hated the sometimes. The times when the Maker wanted to take his souls back, when a life couldn't be saved. But she also knew that's the way it was.

"Not this time, sweetling," Merona whispered. "You can help this child."

Lina nodded. "It'd be best if he could lay down on my bed. Sometimes this takes a while, and it works easier if he's relaxed. Jess, would you show him where the bedroom is?"

Jess nodded and held her hand out to Paul, who was about her own age. With a shy smile and a slight flush to his cheeks, he took her hand and followed her from the room.

When the bedroom door shut behind them, Lina turned back to Jeddiah and Carol. "This is very important to me," she said carefully. "I only ask for one thing, and that's your complete secrecy. I can't have people knocking on my door in hopes that I can help them all. I've had to keep moving my whole life because most people don't accept what I do."

"Of course," Jeddiah said with a nod. "We understand."

"How did you track me down here? I need to know this."

Carol spoke up. "I have a cousin that works for the IRS. He was able to find out where you work. We traveled to Chicago, but you'd gone by the time we got there. Our finances were so poor, we took too long getting there."

Lina nodded and let out a deep breath.

"We promise, Ms. Brennen," Jeddiah said, his tone pleading. "We won't say a word to anyone. Just please, please help our boy."

"I can't always help."

Carol nodded. "We understand, but we had to try. He's our only child."

Lina nodded. "I'll try." She stood up and motioned them to lead the way to her bedroom.

Paul was lying in the middle of her big bed, his eyes closed, lines of pain etched near his mouth. Her heart went out to the boy. Please God, please let me help him.

* * * *

Lina was exhausted as she made her way back to the diner, Jess skipping along beside her. There'd only been two other terminal patients she'd tried to help, and this one had been the hardest. Part of it was the boy refused to believe. The other part was that so much of his body had deteriorated from the disease.

"That was so cool, Lina," Jess said as she skipped over a crack in the sidewalk. "I still can't believe you fixed him. He was so sick, and in so much pain, and then the pain was gone and he smiled."

Lina smiled then and draped her arm across Jess's shoulder. "Yeah, it is pretty cool when I can help someone. Did Dyami reveal all of your gifts?"

Jess wrinkled her nose and shook her head. "He said that I'd find out what they were when they're needed. He talks in this weird code, like only saying half of what I want to know, and then he smiles and shakes his head, refusing to say more."

Lina laughed. "Yeah, spirits are that way, sometimes."

"I'm not," Merona piped in.

Jess giggled.

"No, Granna, you certainly aren't. You say everything that's on your mind."

As they reached the door of the diner, Trent drove up in the sheriff's cruiser. "There's my girls," he said with a grin as he turned off the car.

Thank God Lina had finished with the Thomases before Trent returned.

"Are you ever going to tell Dad?" Jess whispered.

"Yeah, tomorrow," Lina answered softly as Trent came toward them. "Everything will be out in the open tomorrow."

Jess hugged Lina. "Good."

"Maybe," Lina said. Only if he believed, she added silently.

Trent wrapped his arms around her and hugged her tight and she reveled in the feel of his hard chest, his strong arms. "Miss me?" he whispered against her ear.

"Lots," she answered truthfully.

"Good." He kissed her softly, his tongue tracing her lips.

Jess groaned and turned away.

Trent chuckled and pulled back. "See you in the morning, okay?" he asked softly as he ran his thumb over her bottom lip. His hard, warm palm caressed her cheek.

For some reason, a lump formed in her throat and the beginnings of dread began to settle in the pit of her stomach. She could only nod.

He leaned down and kissed her again before he took a step away, his hand trailing down her arm. Holding her hand in his, he gazed at her, as if he couldn't bring himself to let her go. She smiled. She understood the feeling.

"Bye, babe," he whispered, and gave her fingers a tiny squeeze before he released her.

Her stomach coiled in a tight knot. Something wasn't right. "Trent," Lina said just as he turned to collect Jess. He turned back and raised a raven's wing eyebrow at her, a half-smile curving his lips. "Be careful."

His brow pulled down into a frown and Jess turned around, her eyes wide, frightened.

"Careful?" Jess asked. "What's--"

Lina shook her head. She wanted to tell him she loved him. She wanted to hold him close. Her heart thumped too hard. And then as fast as it came, the feeling passed and she sighed with relief.

Trent pulled her into his arms again and held her tight. "Sweet Lina," he whispered. "Being a sheriff in a place like Unegi isn't all that dangerous." He chuckled against her hair and she clung to him. "Peeping-Tom cows are about all I've had to deal with in the past few years."

Lina laughed against his shoulder.

Trent pulled back and kissed her forehead. "That's better. I love it when you laugh."

And I love you, Lina thought. But the words stuck in her throat. Something held her back. She glanced over his shoulder and saw Jess standing there, arms folded across her chest, a Cheshire cat grin on her lips. Maybe she just couldn't tell Trent her feelings for the first time in front of his daughter.

"See you in the morning." Trent gave her another quick kiss before he released her. "Come on, Jess, let's head home. We've got some talking to do."

Jess groaned but headed for the passenger door. "Talking to you is never a good thing."

Lina laughed at Trent's scowl. He shook a finger at Lina and narrowed his eyes. "I'll get you for that one."

She was still smiling as she watched his car disappear down the road.

Chapter Twenty

From the Journal of Lina Brennen:
That feeling is back. The one that tells me I'll be moving on again. I keep pushing it to the back of my mind, hoping I'm wrong. But I've never been wrong before. And that scares the hell out of me.

* * * *

"So what did you want to talk about, Dad?" Jess asked as they prepared a salad together for dinner. It felt a little strange to be hanging out with her father, especially when Lina would be off work soon. That her father was hanging out with her as opposed to Lina made Jess suspicious. Something was up, that was for sure.

He clenched his jaw and ran his hand through his already disheveled hair, his blue eyes glittering with nervous anticipation. Trent dropped a few grape tomatoes into the salad bowl, strode toward the grill sitting out on the patio, and flipped the burgers.

He licked his lips and Jessica wanted to scream. What in the world was going on? The whole drive back from the diner he'd been acting all fidgety and out of sorts.

"Dad. You ever gonna tell me what's up? Or you gonna just make me stand here and guess all night long?"

He blew out a deep breath and gave her a crooked smile. "Well, honey. See, it's like this." Trent leaned against the white kitchen counter, crossed his arms, and then uncrossed them.

"You know what? Maybe we ought to sit," he suggested.

A slow grin spread across Jessica's face. Suddenly it all made sense. If this was what she was thinking it was, then she'd let him tell her in his own way. But trying to contain the burgeoning excitement growing inside her would be another matter entirely.

Jessica's insides clenched with happiness, her stomach doing strange fluttering movements, and she plopped onto the kitchen nook. Trent walked over and sat next to her, looking at everything but her face.

"You see, Jess, I'm planning to ask Lina to ... um...." He cleared his throat and gazed at her. "Marry me." He said the words so low she could hardly hear them.

"Say that again, Dad?" She had to make absolutely sure.

He gave her a droll look. "Marry me. I want Lina to marry me."

"Oh, my god!" She threw her arms around him, her heart threatening to burst from her chest with excitement. "Are you serious?"

He reached inside his jeans pocket and extracted a tiny, black velvet box.

"Oh, my god." Jess knew she was sounding like a broken record, but she could hardly believe it. And at the moment could barely make out a coherent thought, let alone string together an intelligent sentence. She'd never even dared to hope that her father would marry again, or that she would find a woman she approved of one hundred and ten percent.

"I'm very serious, Jess." He lifted a brow and opened the box. Inside, a princess-cut diamond refracted the rays of sunshine, spilling a kaleidoscope of rainbow colors throughout the room.

Jessica bit her lip, her breath catching in her throat. "This is so beautiful, Dad."

He sighed. "Oh good. I was hoping you'd approve. But I wanted your approval for something else."

"You have it." She nodded.

"Jess, I haven't even asked you yet."

She smiled and patted his shoulder. "You don't need to. You've always known how I've felt about, Lina. I love her, well, like the mother I never had."

Trent wrapped his arms around her shoulders and dropped a kiss on the crown of her head.

She pulled back. "I can't believe it. When are you going to ask her?"

"Tomorrow," he sighed and pushed to his feet, heading toward the grill.

Tomorrow. Jessica blinked. Lina had said she was going to tell her father everything tomorrow. Oh god. Why did the word tomorrow conjure up nothing but terrible feelings? Jess rubbed at her chest as shooting spikes of pain left her breathless, the word tomorrow echoing in her head.

As the pain subsided, so too did her fears. She was just being silly. After all, she didn't deal with premonitions. All she could do was talk to Dyami. Still though, that nagging thought persisted.

Tomorrow.

Tomorrow.

Tomorrow.

Jess shuddered. She really needed to stop doing that. Getting up, she pushed the unsettling thought to the back of her mind. Nothing was going to happen. Everything was going to be perfect. She hoped.

* * * *

At ten o'clock on the dot, Trent knocked on Lina's door. Anticipation and a little too much caffeine had his hands shaking. Oh, who was he kidding? He was about to propose to a woman. He was a damn basket case.

Lina pulled the door open and smiled at him. "Good morning," she said in that sweet, sexy voice that made his knees weak and his groin tighten.

Trent pulled her into his arms and kissed her hard. His tongue delved into the warm, moist recesses of her mouth, tangling with hers. He pulled her closer, her body flush with his, wishing clothes didn't separate them. He didn't think he'd ever get enough of her. Yeah, he thought, he wanted to spend the rest of his life with this woman. He had Jess's blessing. Now all he needed was a yes from Lina.

When she slowly pulled back and smiled up at him, her eyes darkened to a soft pewter, he almost popped the question right then and there. But he wanted it to be special. He wanted to ask her in their little cave up on Devil's Peak.

"Dad!" Jess yelled from the bottom of the stairs. "Come on. You can do all that stuff later."

Lina giggled and the sound went straight to his heart.

"We're coming," he called to Jess. To Lina he said, "Mom packed us some fried chicken and salad and stuff. We just need to stop and pick up some sodas."

Lina nodded at him, then went up on tiptoe and laid a soft, sweet kiss on his lips. "Sounds good."

"Mmm, baby," he whispered just before he took her mouth in another deep kiss.

"Da-a-ad!"

Lina laughed against his mouth and Trent groaned. "Maybe I shoulda left her at home."

"Don't be mean," Lina said as she pulled the door shut behind her and followed him down the stairs.

Trent laughed. "Me? Mean? Never." He tweaked Jess's nose when he reached her. "Get in the car, brat."

They drove to Louise's gas station and went in, laughing and teasing. Trent sent Jess off to find something, then dragged Lina down another aisle. When he had her alone, he pulled her in for a kiss.

"Stop that." Lina giggled and playfully pushed him away. "Your kid is right over there."

"She can't see. And I can't keep my hands off you." He grabbed her around the waist when she turned away, and pulled her back against his front, running his hand up under her tank top.

Laughing, Lina slapped at his hands and pulled away. "Behave."

He grabbed for her again. "Can't."

She sidestepped him and ducked around the end of the aisle. "If you're good," she said as she backed away from him with a wicked gleam in her eyes, "I'll let you come over tonight."

"Oh?" he asked as he stalked her down the aisle between bottles of motor oil and candy bars.

She nodded, holding her hands out in front of her as if to ward him off. "If you bring the handcuffs again."

Trent chuckled. "Only if you're the one who gets handcuffed this time."

Lina laughed. "You'll only find out if you're good."

He grabbed for her again and dragged her into his arms. "Ah, but I also know how to be very persuasive." He nuzzled her neck, loving the feel of her silky smooth skin.

"Oh, my. You sure do."

"Lina!"

Trent's head snapped up at the woman's voice. He glanced around but saw no one.

"Trouble's coming."

Trent scowled and looked down at Lina. She frowned and started pulling away.

"Who said that?" he growled, tired of hearing these strange voices. And it only happened around Lina.

Lina visibly swallowed. Her face had lost all color. He gripped her shoulders. "Answer me."

The bell over the door dinged and a young man walked in, right up to the counter where Louise was.

"Give me your money."

Trent's heart nearly stopped. He shoved Lina behind him and moved silently up the aisle. He reached for his handgun before he realized he wasn't in uniform. He hadn't even worn his off duty piece. He'd wanted to leave that all behind for the day. Damn stupid thing to do!

The kid was in his late teens, with shaggy nondescript brown hair, baggy shorts and T-shirt. He waved a pistol in Louise's face as she stared in horror at the boy.

"Hey there, son," he said calmly as he rounded the end display and walked toward the kid.

The boy turned on him, holding the gun up, his hands shaking. Louise slipped from behind the corner and dashed out the door. Good girl, Trent thought.

"I don't want no trouble, dude, just the cash."

Trent nodded. "I understand, but this isn't the way to go about it."

* * * *

Lina watched in horror from behind a display of bottled water. The robber waved the handgun frantically at Trent.

"Come on, man. You don't want to do this," Trent said with a calm that Lina couldn't understand, couldn't grasp. There was a gun pointed at his chest, and he just stood there, a look of supreme confidence on his face.

"Like hell I don't," the robber shouted. "Just get down on the floor, and nobody gets hurt!"

"Can't you do something?" Lina whispered to Merona who hovered nearby, her aura glowing a distinct mustard color that Lina had never seen before.

Merona shook her head. "I can't. I tried. This is his destiny. I cannot intercede."

Lina's heart constricted with pain. "He's going to die?"

When Merona didn't answer, Lina knew the truth. Tears gathered in her eyes as she prayed like she'd never prayed before. She begged the Maker to let Trent live. She begged to keep him safe.

"Come on, son," Trent said in that cool, calm voice of his. "Give me the gun. Don't make this any harder on yourself."

"Lay down on the floor!" the robber screeched hysterically.

"Dad?"

"No!" Lina and Trent shouted at the same time. Jess stood at the end of the aisle. She dropped the box of crackers she'd been holding.

The gunman swung toward Jessica and Trent pounced on the boy. Lina ran for Jess, jerking her behind the next row of shelves as the grunts and groans of the fierce struggle went on just feet away.

"Shh, baby," Lina whispered to Jessica as the girl sobbed. Lina held Jess tight. Her own tears couldn't be stemmed.

The sound of the gun blast echoed through the store like thunder in a cave. Jess screamed. Lina held her breath and heard the sound of footsteps running. Lina peered around the shelving toward the door. Just as the robber reached it, the door swung open, catching him square in the face. He went down with a thud and lay motionless.

"Jess." Lina gripped the sobbing child by the shoulders. "Go out to your dad's cruiser and call this in on the radio." Jess nodded but didn't move. Lina gave her a shake. "Now!" she shouted to get through to her.

Jess stumbled to her feet and ran for the front door.

Lina rounded to the next aisle and saw Trent lying in a pool of his own blood. With a choked scream, she fell to her knees at his side. "No," she cried as she laid her hands on his chest over the seeping wound. "No, Trent. You can't leave me. Not now. Not ever."

Trent's beautiful blue eyes opened. "Lina," he whispered.

"I'm here."

"Lina." His voice was raspy. He was in so much pain. She could feel his pain, and the bleeding wouldn't stop, it flowed through her fingers hot and sticky.

"Granna!" she shouted.

Merona instantly appeared across Trent's body.

"Granna, help me! If you help, we can save him. I know we can."

"Child," Merona said to her. "You must be sure."

Lina pulled her eyes away from Trent to stare at Merona. "Of course I'm sure! Help me!"

"He is the one?" Merona asked, her voice so calm, so gentle, that it took Lina a moment to realize what she was asking. The prophecy. It had come true. She'd heard the stories all her life, of course, from Merona and from Jane.

When you save the one who can't be saved, your heart will be bound to him forever.

"Lina, sweetheart," Trent rasped. One hand over the wound on his chest, desperately trying to stop the flow of blood, she brought her other hand to his cheek. Tears blurred her vision of his handsome face. "Take care of Jess...." His voice trailed off into nothingness. She felt his life force leaving his body.

"Granna!" she cried. "Yes! He's the one! Now! Before it's too late!"

Merona's aura began to brighten, to glow brilliant silver as her hands joined Lina's over the wound on Trent's chest. Merona's lips moved in silent prayer. Lina joined in the prayer as she watched Trent's face. Merona became so bright Lina squinted against the intensity of her, never taking her eyes away from Trent. He had to live. He had to! She loved him with all her heart.

The bleeding stopped. The wound began to close. Merona's light was blinding.

* * * *

On a harsh, painful gasp, Trent forced himself to breathe. The next breath came easier. Then the third.

"He's alive, Granna," he heard Lina say on a sob.

"Yes, my darling child," another voice answered. "And now I must go."

"Go?" Lina asked. Trent felt Lina's hands on his cheeks, moving over his brow, over his chest.

"This is how it is done, sweetling. It is time for you to live on your own."

"No, Granna. You can't leave me now."

Trent forced his eyes open to see who was causing his Lina the distress he heard in her voice. What he saw made him shake with fear. A woman. A phantom. A glowing silver form hovered over him. That form reached out a translucent hand and stroked Lina's cheek. Trent tried to move away, but couldn't. His body had no strength.

"Read the last page of your book, my child. You will learn the truth. I will be watching from afar from now on." The glowing shape of the woman began to rise farther up toward the ceiling. "Make us proud,

Lina. You are a warrior." The apparition turned her eyes on Trent. "She is a special one, Trent. She needs extra care." And then, it was gone. Like a light switch being turned off, the glowing lady vanished.

"Lina!" Jess cried as she ran down the aisle toward them.

"He's all right," Lina said through her tears. Trent still couldn't move away, though he wanted to. Needed to get away from this woman who spoke with ghosts.

"Daddy," Jess sobbed as she fell to her knees beside him and wrapped her arms around his neck. "Did you see her? Did you? They saved you, Daddy. Just like they saved Willy and Bobby."

Trent heard the wail of sirens in the distance, knew help would soon arrive. Struggling to raise his hand, he laid it on his daughter's head. "I love you, Jess," he whispered.

* * * *

Lina's stomach twisted painfully when she realized Trent wasn't looking at her. When she reached out to touch his brow, he flinched. Lina tucked her hand into her lap and looked away. She'd scared him. Just like so many others, she'd scared him. Only this time it was forever. He was the one. And now she was doomed to live her life missing a piece of her soul.

Slowly rising to her feet, she touched Jessica's shoulder in farewell, but she was clinging to her father and didn't even notice. She made her way to the front of the store. The robber was still lying on the floor inside the door, a lump forming on his forehead where the door had hit him. Merona's workings.

And now Merona was gone, too.

* * * *

Lina made her way back to her tiny one-bedroom apartment above Trent's office and began the packing process. It was a good thing she always traveled light and didn't have anything of value. She had no idea where she would go now. She supposed she'd just find another big city and try to lose herself in the throng of people that always inhabited such places.

Opening her closet, she pulled out her suitcase and laid it open on the bed. Next, she pulled out her clothes and dumped them in the suitcase, not caring that they'd get wrinkled. Who the hell cared? She surely didn't. In the space of one sunny afternoon, she'd lost everything important to her. Granna's company, the child she'd come to love and ... Trent. The One.

Stifling a sob, she zipped the suitcase shut and dragged it to the front door. She went to the linen closet and pulled out the big cardboard boxes she always kept nearby. She threw in her few towels and grabbed her toiletries, too. Then she went to the bookshelf and began loading in her books but then stopped. She glanced around the apartment she'd begun to think of as home. The first home she'd ever had. And she didn't care anymore. She didn't care about her books, her pretties, her things. None of it mattered.

As she dragged the box to the front door, she saw the crystal bud vase sitting on the coffee table in the living room. It was all she had left of the man she was meant to be with. How could everything have gone so wrong? Carefully she placed it in the box. If she had nothing else, at least she'd have memories of him. Of the short time she'd had with him.

Read the last page of your book, my child. You will learn the truth. I will be watching from afar from now on.

Lina had forgotten all about her diary. She went back into the bedroom and sank down on the edge of the bed. Pulling the leather-bound notebook from the nightstand, she opened it to the last page. There in Granna's fancy, scrawled writing she learned the truth.

I knew this day was coming, my darling child. I only wish there was something I could do to make it easier for you. You have made your decision, sweetling. He is the man of your heart, the man of your soul. Love him with every bit of yourself and you will know true happiness. I regret that I must leave you now, though I will never be far. I will always be watching over you, child of my heart.

Lina scrubbed her fist over her eyes to dispel the tears that blurred her vision.

This is the way it is done. When you've found your soul mate, your anchor must leave. Your life is now his, and his yours. There is no room for me. Remember me always, sweet Lina.

I will meet you again someday.

With all my love and hope for you,
 Granna Merona

Lina slammed the book shut and flung it across the room. It crashed into the wall and landed on the rug with a disappointing thud.

"Happiness? Is that what you think? Look at me now, Granna!" Lina cried, searching the room for her beloved grandmother. "Look at me! He hates me! There will never be happiness in my life!"

Great racking sobs rent from her heart. Granna was gone. She would never answer her again. Grabbing her pillow from the bed, Lina dashed for the front door.

Meow.

She'd almost forgotten Lucky. She cried all the harder as she picked up Lucky's bed, all four kittens included, and carried it out and settled it in the back seat of the car. She'd have to find a place for them. She'd have to let them go, too.

After quickly loading her few belongings into her car, she slipped the apartment key through the mail slot in the door of the sheriff's office. Lina ran to her car and climbed behind the wheel, ignoring the blazing heat inside. She sped out of town as fast as she could. She had to get away. Had to find some peace. Somewhere. Somewhere where she'd never see or hear or feel Trent again.

She was twenty miles out of Unegi when it came to her that she needed to try, just one last time, to see Trent. If she just gave up and ran away, she'd never know for sure. She needed to see him, just one last time.

Flipping a U-turn in the middle of the long, straight highway, she headed back to town. Even though hope surged through her heart, fear settled into the pit of her stomach.

* * * *

"Lina!"

As soon as Lina stepped through the doorway into the clinic's inner sanctum with the five private rooms, Jess bolted out of her chair near her father's bed and ran into Lina's arms.

"Hi, sweetheart," Lina said as she enfolded the sweet girl into her arms. "How's your dad doing?" Lina glanced toward the bed just in time to see Trent's eyes open. They trained on her. Icy blue. Hard. Angry.

"He's great! Doc said he can go home in the morning. He just wants to keep him for observation overnight." Jess gave Lina another squeeze. "I'll go get a soda so you can be alone," she added with a wink at Lina.

After Jess skipped out the door to the waiting room, Lina approached the bed. Trent's eyes never wavered. The harsh lines of his jaw never relaxed. "How you feeling?" she asked softly.

"What the hell are you doing here?" Trent demanded. His voice was every bit as harsh and unwelcoming as his eyes.

"I wanted to see how you were doing. If everything was all right with you." She was proud that her voice didn't falter, that the tears that she could feel didn't fall.

"I don't want you here. I don't want you around Jess. In fact," Trent said, his jaw flexing with agitation, "it would be best if you left town. It's just a damn good thing that I grew up with Stephen and he's agreed not to say a word about...."–he waved his hands almost frantically in the air--"any of this to anyone. My God, I even defended you to my mother!"

Lina swallowed the lump that rose in her throat. The sheriff had told her to leave town. That hadn't happened before. She'd never actually been run out of a town before.

"Trent." She stepped closer to the bed, thinking that if she could just touch him, just let him know what she was feeling, maybe things would be different. She reached for his hand. He snatched it back before she could make contact. Fear replaced the anger in the hard planes of his face. Dear God, he was terrified of her.

"Go. Now." There was no doubting his sincerity.

"Lina, I'm so glad you came in."

Lina swung around toward the voice. There stood Dr. Stephen Webb. Lina bit back the urge to cry. Squaring her shoulders, she forced a smile to her lips, though she wondered if it looked as tragic as it felt. "Dr. Webb," she said politely.

"Trent said you'd left town. I'm so happy you haven't." Stephen took her hand between his and smiled at her. "I can't believe it. I've heard of faith healers my entire life, but never in my wildest dreams thought that I'd get the chance to meet one."

Forcing a chuckle past her tight throat, Lina said, "We don't normally go around announcing ourselves. Causes a lot of...."--her gaze flicked toward Trent then back at the doctor--"discomfort."

The doctor's large, smooth hands gently squeezed her fingers in comfort. "Some people aren't as accepting of what they don't understand as others."

That darned lump in her throat was growing by leaps and bounds. She nodded.

"I'd really love to sit and talk to you, if you have the time," Doc added. "I'm intrigued. I'd love to hear some stories."

"She's leaving town. Today." This from Trent.

The tears were not going to be stemmed much longer. She gently pulled her hand from Stephen's and tucked it into her pocket. "He's right. I'm leaving. Goodbye." She dashed from the room before anyone could say anything else. It was over. All over. Trent hated her. She had to go.

"Hey, Lina," Jess called as Lina rushed through the waiting room. "Where you goin'?"

Lina stopped just long enough to pull Jessica into a tight hug. "I have to go, honey. I have to go." Tears freely ran down her cheeks now. "I love you. And your daddy. Take care of him."

Before Jess had a chance to respond, Lina pushed through the door into the hot desert sun. She rounded her car and got in, gunned the motor and sped out onto the road. She had to put as much distance as possible between herself and those she loved before she broke down completely.

Chapter Twenty-One

From the Journal of Lina Brennen:
"All good things must come to and end." I, for one, know that particular adage is always true.

* * * *

Jess ran into his room, her face stricken, her eyes tearing. "You sent her away?" she screeched. "How could you, Dad? She saved your life. She saved Willy's life. And...." A heart-wrenching sob tore from her. "And there were others I'm not supposed to tell you about."

Trent didn't know how to react. He could only watch in silence as Stephen wrapped his arms around Jess and hugged her. His daughter, his baby, leaned against another man and cried her eyes out.

His own heart was cold and empty. He'd trusted her. Trusted Lina, and she'd betrayed him. She'd exposed his daughter to the world he'd tried so hard to shield her from. From evil.

Jess pulled away from Stephen and turned on him. Tears ran down her face, but it was a face he didn't recognize. He'd never seen such anger in her eyes before. "Why'd you do it? Why'd you make her leave?"

His hands fisted in his lap. He didn't know how to answer.

"I can't believe you!" Jess yelled. "She ... she loved us." She turned back to Stephen and cried as he held her.

Abby came through the door just then, took one look at Jess, glanced briefly at Stephen, then glared at Trent. "What did you do?"

"I got shot, damn it!" Trent exploded. "I got shot and should have died! But she ... she ... she...."

"She saved your life," Stephen answered calmly.

"Lina?" Abby asked.

Jess sniffled and then went into her grandmother's arms. "He made her leave, Nana. He sent her away. He thinks she's evil but she's not. She's special. She helped me learn what was wrong with me. She taught me--"

"What did she teach you?" Trent demanded, his gut clenching.

Jess pulled away from Abby and stalked across the small room to his bed. She looked so much like him in that instant it almost brought him to tears. The lines of her face were hard, she was furious.

"She taught me about the spirit world. A world both of us have touched. But you got scared! She taught me to not be afraid of the things I don't understand, but to learn about them. And she taught me that not all women are like Mom. But you don't get it! You don't get any of it because you're so close-minded you can't see what's out there." She gripped the aluminum rail on the side of the hospital bed so hard her knuckles turned white. "You've been feeling and hearing Merona since the first day Lina arrived. I've seen you react to her. She touches you and you get a chill. You have a gift, too, but you're scared."

"That's enough," Trent said through gritted teeth.

"No! It's not enough, Dad. You sent away the best thing that's ever come into our lives. All because you can't accept what you are, who you are."

"Enough!" Trent shouted.

"Jess, sweetie," Abby said softly. "Why don't you go out to the lobby for a bit. I want to have a word with your father."

Jess glared at him for a long moment, then she turned on her heel and stalked from the room. Stephen followed her out, leaving Trent alone with his mother.

Abby sat down in the chair next to the bed, reached out, and took his hand in hers. Trent laid his head back on the pillow and closed his eyes. What a day, he thought. He'd been planning to propose to a woman this morning, shot at noon, sent the woman of his ... the woman of his dreams, he admitted, away, and possibly lost his daughter in the process. And now his daughter was talking about speaking with spirits. No, he couldn't allow that. He couldn't. No good could come from it.

"She's right, you know. You have a gift, too. We all do."

Trent's eyes snapped open and he turned his head toward his mother. "What?"

"Your grandfather was a great Apache shaman. Our people have always been very in tune with the spirit world."

"I don't want to hear this."

"You have to hear this, Trent. And you're going to, or I'll call Stephen in here to strap you to the bed until you hear what I have to say."

Trent pulled his hand from hers and folded his arms across his chest. Abby gave him an indulgent smile that made him feel like a petulant child.

"Your grandfather Dyami was a very powerful man, learned and well respected among all Apache. But he fell in love with a white woman. Some of his people turned against him, said he was turning his back on centuries of tradition by doing so. I don't remember my mother, but I've spoken to her."

Trent felt a little nauseous.

"Our people come from a long line of what is now called psychics. We can communicate with spirits, ghosts. I can, you can, Jess can.

Lina is a lot like us. Only she has another gift, too. She has the power to heal."

"How do you know this?" Trent demanded.

"Willy told me."

Trent frowned. "What's Old Willy got to do with this?"

"He was dying, having a heart attack, and Lina saved him. He said she knew he was in trouble and she came to him." Abby gave her sweet smile and shook her head. "He said it was magic. A miracle."

"It's evil."

Abby came out of her chair, leaned over him, and poked him in the chest. "So what are you? She saved your miserable hide today." She poked him again, her blue eyes flashing fire at him. "You'd be dead now if it weren't for her."

Trent swallowed. It'd been years and years since he'd seen his mother this angry with him. She made him feel like a misbehaving kid.

"I know what happened to you. I know. My father told me." He tried pulling away, but there was nowhere to go. "Yes, Trent, your mother talks to spirits, too. You're surrounded by us. Get used to it." And then her face softened and she cupped his cheeks in her hands, her eyes smiling at him. "My father told me what you experienced, and all I can say is, I'm so sorry you dealt with it alone. You should never be alone when you walk in the spirit world. Not ever. And not with the use of hallucinogens."

"But when I came to you, when I was young, you told me the old ways were not our ways. You told me it was all nonsense."

Abby sighed and laid her hand on his shoulder. "I was scared, too, Trent. I had to experience my own special connection to them. I hope you can forgive me."

Trent stared up into his mother's eyes. He'd never been so confused in his life.

* * * *

Trent lay in that bed for the next few hours contemplating his situation. It didn't do any good. The thought of Lina talking to her long dead grandmother, his mother speaking with her dead father, and Jess--dear God, his baby girl was talking to his own grandfather!

None of it made sense. It was all garbage. They were pulling his leg.

Yeah. Right. He'd seen proof of Lina's ... Jess called it a gift. It seemed more of a curse to him. She'd healed him. He should be dead right now, but she'd saved him. And Willy, and Willy's nephew. And ... "Holy shit," he whispered. The cat! That thing had been squished practically flat, and Lina had fixed it.

He had to talk to her. He had to see her. He needed her to explain everything. Because, damn it, he loved her. And he wanted her. He pushed himself up from the bed and looked down at himself. He wore the bottoms to a pair of scrubs. His clothes had been cut off him and thrown away. That was okay. He had a change at the office. He dug into the nightstand and pulled out his belongings. His wallet, keys, badge, and one diamond engagement ring. He pulled on his boots, the only thing that'd survived, and headed for the door.

"Just where do you think you're going?" Stephen demanded.

Trent turned toward his friend as he strode down the hall. "I have to talk to her." He held up the jeweler's box. "I need to understand."

Stephen glanced down at Trent's boots and grinned. "Might want to spruce yourself up a bit first."

Trent almost smiled.

Stephen's face went serious. "Take it easy on her, would ya? She was in pretty bad shape when she ran out of here earlier."

Trent nodded. Would she forgive him? Could he live with ... whatever the hell she was? Oh, God, he had to find out.

Trent walked out into the late evening and crossed the street toward the Sheriff's office. A car drove by and someone let out a wolf whistle. He glanced down at himself and groaned. He looked mighty ridiculous wearing nothing but mint green pants and cowboy boots. He unlocked the front door of the sheriff's office, flipped on the overhead lights, and stopped. On the floor was Lina's apartment key. He turned back toward the street. Her car was nowhere in sight. She'd gone already. His heart stuttered for a second. How would he find her?

He strode over to the police radio on the table behind his desk and picked up the mike. "This is Sheriff Trent Godfrey of Unegi. I need a statewide all points bulletin on a royal blue Ford Escort, Illinois license plate Alpha, Charlie, Peter, eight, three, five. That's Alpha, Charlie, Peter, eight, three, five. Over."

"Sheriff Godfrey, this is Phoenix dispatch. The plate on a royal blue Ford Escort is Alpha, Charlie, Peter, eight, three, five. Copy?"

"Affirmative. Please notify me if this car is spotted. Do not approach."

"Affirmative, Sheriff."

"Thank you. Out."

Trent unlocked his desk drawer and pulled out his handheld radio, turned it on, then went into the small bathroom and pulled down the jeans and denim shirt hanging on the back of the door. He found a pair of socks in his desk and got dressed. He picked up the radio, locked the office door, and headed upstairs to Lina's apartment to see if she left any indication of where she might be headed.

When he pushed open the door and flipped on the light, his stomach curled into a tight, painful knot. Most of her things were still there. Her crystals hung in the windows; books lined the shelves; herbs hung drying in the kitchen window. And the place still smelled like her. Verbena and incense. His Lina.

Guilt assailed him at the memory of the tears she'd been fighting when she came to see him in the clinic, the stricken look on her face, in her stormy gray eyes.

He slowly wandered around the tiny apartment, touching a crystal here, a book there. Then he came to that weird little mortar and pestle near the door. He took it down and rubbed his thumb over the smooth stone. The colors swirled in hues of pink, blue, and purple. They reminded him of the gauzy blouse she'd been wearing the day they met. The day she'd fallen into his arms and he'd been struck by such strong emotions, he didn't know what to do with them.

Still holding the stone bowl, he checked the bathroom. Her stuff was gone. Then into the bedroom. The closet was empty, one pillow missing from the bed. As he turned to leave the room, something in the corner caught his eye. He crossed the room, rounded the bed, and stared down at a book. Red leather cover, it laid open, pages down, as if it had been dropped. He picked it up and closed it. On the front, in gold embossed letters it simply read, "Journal." He sank down on the edge of the bed, his conscience warring with his curiosity. He'd thrown away the report Zach had sent him. Was it now time to learn the truth? Shouldn't he ask her first, instead of sneaking a peak?

The radio at his hip hadn't made a sound, yet. He had no idea where to find her. If he'd find her. He turned back the cover of the journal.

May 4, 1990

Well, it happened. What Granna has been warning me about for years. She told me I had to keep my gift a secret or everyone around would become suspicious and not like me anymore. She was right. Mom and I were at the grocery store. This little girl fell out of the shopping cart and hit her head really hard. She wasn't moving. I had to help her. Mom refused to. She always refused to help. She tried to pull me away. But this little girl was so beautiful, and her mother was so scared. So I touched her. Her skull was cracked. She would have died before the ambulance came.

And now we have to leave town. Mom is angry. She said she's lived here for over fifteen years and she finally had a place to call home. She told me she wishes she never had me. Granna says she's just upset, that she'll get over it, but I don't know. I think she hates me now.

Trent turned the page, and then another as he read on. Tears gathered in his eyes and he couldn't blink them back.

* * * *

Lina drove until she was too tired to go one mile farther. After the day she'd just survived, she'd been lucky to make it as far as she had.

She'd stopped in Phoenix and picked up a giant pizza, enough chocolate to sink a ship, and a six pack of Coca Cola--and not the diet stuff either. She was going to pig out tonight, and she didn't care if she gained a hundred pounds in the process. She'd also stopped and bought a can of gourmet cat food for Lucky and a small carton of milk. Lina didn't like eating alone.

Now, just on the northern outskirts of Phoenix, she pulled into the parking lot of a motel that looked affordable. The sign said No Pets, but she didn't care. Who needed to follow rules, anyway?

She went into the office and rented a room. It was still too expensive here. She should have gone on farther. She figured she'd head up to Seattle. She'd really liked Seattle when she lived there nearly eight years ago.

Her room was in the back, which was a good thing since she had to sneak in Lucky, the babies, and their bed. Once they were settled in a darkened corner under the desk, she went back out to the car for the food. She laid the pizza and bag of snack food on the scarred dresser, then dug out the can of cat food and container of milk. She rinsed out the soap dish from the bathroom to use for the milk, since she hadn't bothered to pack any of her dishes.

Jeez, was she stupid. She'd walked out of there with nothing. When she started over this time, she was really starting over.

Lina laid down on her side near the cat bed and opened the can of cat food. "Yummy," she said with a smile as Lucky extracted herself from her babies and stepped toward her. "Chicken and fish."

Lucky stuck her face in the can and began eating. Lina poured a bit of milk in the shallow soap dish. The four tiny kittens mewed miserably at having their momma leave. They tumbled off the bed and came toward her. Lina pulled them to her, to give Lucky some peace while she ate, and snuggled them against her chest. "You guys are so cute," she whispered as tears stung her eyes. "I don't know how I'm ever going to give you up." A choked sob slipped out of her. Lucky stopped eating, looked up at her, then licked her arm. Lina burst into tears.

* * * *

Trent paced back and forth in front of the sheriff's office, Lina's journal in one hand, her little mortar bowl in the other, waiting for a call. There was no telling where Lina had headed to, so there was no point in trying to go after her. She could have gone in any direction, and no one in town had seen her leave. It was almost midnight, and he thought he might go completely insane if he didn't hear something soon. He needed his Lina.

The phone inside rang. He slammed open the door and grabbed it off the hook. "Godfrey."

"Sheriff Godfrey, this is Captain Samuels with the Phoenix Police Department. We've found the car you're looking for. Would you like us to take the driver into custody?"

"No!" Trent shouted. "Just tell me where it is."

"It's parked behind the Sleepy Time Motel."

"Where is that?"

"Just north of the city, off route sixty."

"Thank you, Captain. Thank you so much."

"Will you be needing backup?"

"No. No. Everything's fine now. Thank you." Trent hung up the phone. Okay, he just broke a bunch of laws by having an APB put on his girlfriend, but who the hell cared? If he didn't find her....

He locked the office, got into the cruiser, and headed out to the highway. He figured he could be there in just over an hour. And then he'd have to get down on his knees and beg her for forgiveness. He could only pray that she loved him a fraction of what he felt for her.

* * * *

The pounding in her head woke Lina up. It took a few seconds for it to register that she was still lying on the floor. Her neck was stiff, and her eyes were scratchy from crying herself to sleep. Her head throbbed. She looked up to see Lucky staring at her with big green eyes. The kittens were all snuggled close against their mother, sound asleep.

The pounding wasn't only in her head. It was coming from the door. She sat up and glanced at the digital clock on the nightstand. It was just after two a.m. Had the manager found out she'd snuck the cats in?

Using the edge of the bed as a lever, she pushed herself to her feet and swayed slightly. She hadn't eaten in more hours than she could remember and her head felt fuzzy.

The pounding on the door was insistent, and wasn't helping her head any. She made her way to the door and looked out the peephole. Her chest tightened and her stomach began to ache.

Trent.

She dragged in a few deep breaths. "What do you want?" she called through the door.

"Let me in, Lina. I need to talk to you."

Her head fell forward and bumped the door. What more could he possibly have to say?

"Lina, please open the door."

He didn't sound angry. In fact, his voice had almost no inflection in it at all.

Meow.

She looked over her shoulder. Lucky was standing behind her, her fluffy little head cocked to one side, as if asking her why she didn't open the door.

"Lina."

She turned the deadbolt and pulled the door open. "What?"

He stepped toward her. She turned away and rounded the bed to put as much space between them as possible.

"Why are you here, Trent?" she asked as she leaned against the wall and folded her arms across her chest, proud that her voice was calm and steady when her insides were dancing a jig.

He held out his hands. She immediately recognized her journal and the pretty mortar she'd gotten at that little shop.

"You forgot your things."

"I don't want them." She straightened her shoulders, hugged herself, and met his gaze. That was nearly her undoing. He looked sad. Lost. The way she felt.

He stood there for what felt like hours just looking at her. His gaze roamed over her face, down her body. She glanced down. Her blouse was wrinkled, and her jeans had fared only slightly better. She looked a fright.

Then he set the items on the bed and came up to her. "Lina, I--"

"It's okay, Trent. I understand. You're not the first person to react to me this way. You won't be the last. I left Unegi. You didn't have to follow me to make sure. I don't stay where I'm not wan--"

His mouth landed on hers, cutting off her words. His hands came up to her face, and he held her so gently she nearly cried. Fisting her hands in the front of his shirt she shoved him back, breaking contact with him. "Don't!" She thumped his chest as she still clung to his shirt. "Don't do that. Not now. I can't--"

He kissed her again. Softly, tenderly. His hands came up and closed over hers. She slowly relaxed her grip on his shirt, and he lifted her hands to his shoulders. His lips caressed hers and she began to melt. He tasted so good. He smelled so good. She could easily lose herself in him.

Pulling back just a bit, she looked him in the eye. "I scared you," she whispered. "Why'd you come?"

Trent pulled her back against him and buried his face in her hair. He held her tight, but gently, his big hands splayed open on her back. His mouth brushed her neck when he spoke. "I love you, Lina Brennen."

She clung to him, her heart shattering. "But you hate what I am. And I can't change."

He shook his head and tightened his hold on her. "I didn't understand. Now I do. I read your journal, babe. I read it and I cried. I had...." His voice broke and he cleared his throat. "I had no idea.

None at all." He slowly pulled back and looked down at her with those beautiful blue eyes. "I am so sorry."

Never had a man looked more sincere or guiltier than he did at that moment.

"Jess is kind of like me."

He slowly nodded. "I know. So is my mother."

Lina's eyes widened. "Your mother?"

A tiny smile quirked his lips. "Yeah." He kissed her again, this time with more urgency. Lina opened her mouth to him and his tongue swooped in to mate with hers. She shivered and gripped his shoulders, unsure if her legs would support her much longer. When he came up, he was grinning. "Seems like I'm surrounded by you guys."

Lina's laugh felt a little strained. "What now?"

Trent glanced behind him, then spun her around and backed her to the bed. "Now...." He lowered her to the bed and came down over her. "I'm going to hold you prisoner until you accept my apology and come back to Unegi with me."

Lina's heart soared. He wanted her. And he wanted her as she was. Trent, her Trent, whose soul hers was a part of, accepted her. She threw her arms around his neck and squeezed him tight. "Are you sure?"

Nuzzling her ear, he whispered, "I've never been more sure of anything in my life. I need you, baby. For now and for always."

"Forever?" She speared her hands through his hair and lifted his head so she could see his face. He'd said forever?

That slow, sexy grin spread over his lips, making his eyes sparkle like the bluest ocean. "Forever." He leaned down and kissed her then, and this time he held nothing back. His tongue swept into her mouth. His teeth nibbled and nipped, and his hands tugged at her clothing.

The man had an uncanny way of stripping her naked without so much as breaking contact. His mouth roamed over her neck, down to her breasts, then further. Lina threw her hands over her head and sighed with happiness as her body accepted his touch as if she'd been made just for him. Her skin heated and tingled everywhere his lips touched. She felt the welcome ache grow between her thighs. And when his mouth closed over her heated, damp center, she cried out in surprise and excitement, lifting her hips, spreading her legs wide for him.

Trent brought her to a mind-blowing climax with nothing more than his lips and tongue. As Lina tried to catch her breath, still feeling as if her body were attached to small electrodes that kept sending shocks through her system, she heard Trent's deep chuckle. Before she could form a snappy retort in her mind, he was over her, in her, and all she could do was gasp in surprise.

When he didn't move, she slowly opened her eyes. He held himself over her, propped up on his elbows so he didn't squish her, and smiled at her. In that smile, she could see his love. Feel it. Tears stung her eyes and she tried to blink them back.

His smile faded. "Don't cry, baby. Please." He placed a soft kiss on her jaw. "I'm so sorry. I...." A kiss on her cheek. "I hate that I hurt you."

Shaking her head, she said, "It's not that. I accept your apology."

"Then why are you crying, babe?"

"Because I love you so much, and I'm so happy you came after me."

He brushed the tears from her cheeks with his thumbs and smiled again. "My daughter was going to disown me if I didn't. Possibly even my mother." He kissed her temple. "And I wasn't sure how I was going to live without you in my life."

"So...." Lina wrapped her legs around his waist, pulling him deeper inside her. She grinned with wicked delight at his quick intake of breath. "Is my apartment still available or have you already rented it out to someone else?"

"Nu-uh. If you come back, you're not going to live there."

Her smile faded. A chill began to settle in her bones. "Why?"

He traced her bottom lip with his tongue. "You're going to be right where you belong. In my house. In my bed. Every single night. When I get home from work, I want to kiss you hello. When I leave in the morning, I want to kiss you goodbye."

Lina wasn't sure if she was hearing right. She wanted to believe so badly, but just hours earlier he was running her out of town. Telling her to stay away from his daughter. "What about Jess?"

Trent wrapped his arms around her, pressed into her until she moaned. He chuckled and the vibrations of it went through her like fireworks. "How would you feel about being Mom to an almost teenager? I've already gotten her approval of you. Now the decision is yours."

Lina's mind warred with her body. He knew all the right buttons to push. "What about more children? I want babies." She squeezed her eyes shut, waiting for his answer. Her heart thudded erratically against her ribs with excitement and fear.

His teeth closed lightly over her earlobe, sending another shot of fire through her veins. "Maybe sooner than you'd expected. I didn't bring any condoms."

Lina gasped and thumped his shoulder with her fist. "You what?"

He laughed this time. Low and sexy. "Well, I had to figure out a way to get you to come home with me--ouch!" He jerked back when she pinched his biceps. "You little minx."

She wasn't sure she'd survive this. She wanted to laugh, she wanted to cry. She wanted Trent to make wild love to her, but he still wasn't moving. "So, you get a mom for Jess, a woman in your bed morning and night, and I get babies. Is that the deal?"

He leaned up on his elbows again, then reached over to his jeans near the edge of the bed, and drew out a small black box from the pocket. "No, baby." He opened the box and pulled out a sparkling diamond ring. "You get this."

His eyes were dark now, serious. His strong, square jaw looked tense. She had a feeling he was about to ask her to marry him. Her heart set up such a rapid-fire rate, she thought she might just keel over dead. Good thing she was already lying down.

"You get a man who won't always be easy to live with." That sweet half-grin made her heart melt. "I have a little bit of a temper sometimes." Tears gathered in her eyes again even as she laughed. "But you'll have my love forever. My undying devotion." He glanced at the ring, then back to her eyes. "I love you, Lina. I never want you to feel like you don't belong. I want to spend the rest of my days with you, protecting you from ... from small-minded jerks like I was. You are the most amazing, special, wonderful woman I've ever known. Your grandmother said we're a part of each other. I believe her. I'm begging you now, Lina Brennen, to stay with me. Forever." He took a deep breath and through her own tears, she could see his. "Will you marry me? Put up with me? Love me, for the rest of my life?"

Lina shook her head.

Trent's mouth fell open. The stricken look on his face would have melted her heart if his beautiful speech hadn't.

"No, Trent. I won't love you for the rest of your life. I'll love you for the rest of eternity. It's the Brennen way."

His mouth crushed hers in a bruising kiss that made the rest of the world disappear. And then he began to move within her and she knew, she knew without any doubt, that she was home.

Epilogue

From the Journal of Lina Brennen:
Happy endings do exist. I've found mine. Or maybe this is just one more beginning. A beginning sure to be filled with joy and happiness, love and laughter, and the man of my dreams. The man of my heart. The man who holds half of my soul. Thank you Granna. You were right. Unegi is the place I belong.

* * * *

Trent stood between Jess and Abby at the opening of the little cave on Devil's Peak, and watched his gorgeous bride slowly make her way toward him on Willy's arm as the sun slowly set behind them. A smile spread over his lips. Stephen Webb, who'd be performing the ceremonies, standing just behind him, clapped a hand on his shoulder.

"You've done good, Trent," Stephen whispered.

Trent could only nod. His throat had become suspiciously thick with emotion, and his eyes misted a bit. He'd been blessed. He knew that now. Lina had helped open his mind and heart to the world around him, to the Maker, and to all the wonders of the spirits that surrounded them. It hadn't been an easy road to travel. At times he'd been absolutely terrified, but he'd done it for the love of his life, his Lina.

Four months ago today, he'd talked her into coming back to Unegi. She'd insisted on waiting to get married until Willy got up the nerve to propose to Abby.

He cast a quick glance at his mother. Her smile was tender as she watched Willy approach. Her blue eyes glistened with tears.

Jess's hand slipped into his and gave him a squeeze. He turned to look down at her and her smile took his breath away. His baby girl, now a teenager, had a mother she could be proud of. She'd even begun calling Lina, Mom.

"I love you, Daddy," she whispered.

"I love you, too, baby."

She grinned, then leaned her cheek against his shoulder.

Yeah, Stephen was right. He'd done good.

* * * *

Lina took Trent's hand as Willy released her to move next to Abby. Her heart thudded too hard, and her stomach felt just a little sick. She never thought this day would come.

Trent leaned down and softly kissed her cheek. She wanted to throw her arms around him, needed the anchor, but she held herself back. She could get through this. She had to. Because she had a surprise to give him. She smiled as she gazed into his indigo eyes.

Stephen started reading an old Apache prayer Trent had chosen. Her heart did a little flop. She was so proud of him, of the progress he'd made. He was embracing his heritage, even the parts he'd once been so terrified of. He'd made contact with his spirit guide for the first time just two weeks ago. And Dyami had shown himself to Trent. He sat for hours upon end talking with Jess now, discussing all the things she'd never thought he'd talk about.

She squeezed his hand and was snared by his gaze. His gaze held so much emotion she felt tears prick behind her eyes. She'd found The One. And together they'd have a lifetime together.

Stephen finished the prayer and bowed his head respectfully. Willy began reciting his vows to Abby.

Trent took both her hands in his. He rubbed his thumb over her knuckles and never broke eye contact with her. His lips curled into a smile as he raised her right hand and kissed the back of it. "I love you," he mouthed silently.

She repeated his gesture, bringing his hand to her lips and kissed his knuckles. "I love you," she whispered.

Abby began her vows.

Lina wondered how long this would go on. She wanted to get it over with, even as she knew that thought wasn't proper.

Abby fell silent and Trent began, in a low tone, his voice choked. Lina felt the tears try to come again.

"My love, my life. The first time you stumbled into my arms and looked up at me with those bright stormy eyes, I was snared. From that moment on, I was drawn to you like nothing else in this world. I will spend each day of my life living for you, loving you, learning from you, and keeping you safe. With all my heart and soul, Lina, I am yours."

Lina blinked rapidly, trying to stop her tears. He was so ... perfect. He reached up and brushed away her tears, even as he smiled at her. "Don't cry, sweetheart," he whispered.

A little giggle slipped out. He did hate it when she cried.

"Well, let's get a move on, sweetling. You've got some news to share."

Lina swung around at Merona's voice, but saw nothing. Trent chuckled. Jess giggled. Abby laughed. Willy and poor Stephen looked completely lost as they glanced around to find out what everyone was laughing at.

Licking her lips, Lina took a deep breath. "My love, my life, the only man meant for me." She blinked back more tears, turned, and glanced at Jess. Jess nodded and pointed to her side. Dyami was there. Lina couldn't see him, but she sensed his presence. And so was

Merona. She turned back to Trent. "I love you with all my heart and soul. I promise to be a...." She bit the inside of her cheek to hold back her grin. "Well, I'll try to be a good wife."

Trent chuckled and took a tiny step closer to her, still holding her hands in his.

"I promise to love you each and every day of my life, and beyond. With you, I've found the love I didn't think was open to me, the safety of your arms, the tenderness of your heart. With all my heart and soul, Trent, I am yours."

Stephen fumbled with his little piece of notebook paper.

"The rings," Jess whispered.

Lina stifled a laugh.

"Right," Stephen said. "Please exchange your rings."

Trent reached into his pocket and withdrew a sparkling gold band. "Take this as a symbol of my eternal love." He slipped the ring onto her finger, then brought her hand to his lips and kissed the ring.

Jess handed Lina a band, wider and larger than her own, to slip onto Trent's finger as she repeated the words he'd just given to her. Willy and Abby did the same.

"Well then," Stephen said as he chuckled. "I guess there's just one thing to do. Kiss your brides, gentlemen."

Jess laughed and clapped her hands as Trent pulled her into his arms and laid a kiss on her so hot and filled with love, it would go down in history.

"What's your news?" Trent whispered against her lips.

"You heard that?" Lina asked.

He nodded and pulled her snug against him. "I've been hearing that old bat since before I knew what it was."

Lina laughed and threw her arms around his neck. "I love you."

"I love you, too. News, please."

"Tell him!" Jess all but shouted.

Trent raised one raven brow at her. "She knows?"

Lina shrugged, grinned. "She knows lots of things."

Trent squeezed her a little tighter. "Tell me," he growled playfully.

Her heart near to bursting with happiness, she whispered, "We're gonna have a baby in about six months."

Trent's face went completely blank. His smile fell, his eyes widened. He glanced down at her stomach, then back at her eyes. "No," he whispered.

Lina threw her head back and laughed. "The man is speechless!"

Trent swooped her up in his arms and swung her in a circle as he laughed, too.

* * * *

Jess sat at a corner booth in the Tumbleweed Diner and watched her father dance with Lina, her new mother. The whole town had shown up for the reception, though they'd wanted the ceremony to be private and special, which it had been.

"So, what do you think?" Merona asked.

"I think it's wonderful," she answered. Jess had yet to tell Lina that Merona hadn't really left, she'd simply moved on to take over Jess's spiritual raising until Lina's baby girl was old enough to need her. She didn't want to hurt Lina's feelings, but Merona swore that Lina would be happy about it.

"I think they make a lovely couple," Dyami said in his gentle accent. "And I could not be happier for my beautiful daughter. She deserves this happiness, even if it did come so late in her life."

"You talk like she's old," Merona chastised. "She's still so young and vibrant."

Dyami chuckled. "To you, perhaps she is. But I remember when she was in nappies. She'll always be my little girl."

"You sound like Dad," Jess said as she rolled her eyes. "Do you ever let us grow up?"

Merona patted her arm, sending a wave of chilling gooseflesh up her arm. "Now, sweetling, your father only wants what's best for you. You know that."

Jess nodded. "I know."

Abby and Willy huddled in another corner booth, heads together, giggling like children. Jess smiled. All the people she loved had found what they needed. Her gaze shifted back to Lina and Trent. And Lina had brought her dad so much happiness.

"Wanna dance?"

Jess looked up to see Levi Ringstad, a boy she went to school with, standing next to her.

She smiled and stood up. "Sure." She headed for the center of the diner near her parents.

Levi carefully placed his hands on her waist and she laid her palms on his shoulders. A wave of dizziness washed through her and her chest tightened.

A picture of Levi, a few years older than he was now, seated on a hay bailer, flashed in her mind. A wire snapped and lashed back toward him....

The End

Printed in the United States
58599LVS00001B/142-159